EMPEROR'S NEW QUILT

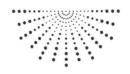

D1738926

EMPEROR'S NEW QUILT

A TAYLOR QUINN QUILT SHOP MYSTERY

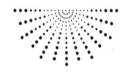

TESS ROTHERY

CHAPTER ONE

$\mathcal{T}$he trusty little Comfort, Oregon Town Hall with its western façade and wooden sidewalk stood proudly between the library and the defunct Timber and Loan like the set of a Hallmark movie. Storm clouds had hung over it all day long, and the street in front, pitted and in desperate need of repaving, glistened with gathered rain. Just beyond the Town Hall, a rainbow arched its thin watery hope. The cold November rain had stopped, and things were going to be okay.

Tucked a few blocks behind Main Street, the original heart of the cozy town had been built on Center Street. But the promise of being the center of Comfort had gone unfulfilled, like so many half-formed plans do.

Today the Town Hall building seemed to steam its guests in that just a wee-bit-too-warm way as its radiators burbled and bubbled. The Comfort Quilt Shop Owners Guild had gathered, once again, at their three round tables. Off to the side sat a card table full of snacks such as the famous bean-brownies Carly, who ran Bible Creek Quilt and Gift, favored, and several airline branded snack trays from June, who ran Comfort Cozies. Her husband was a flight attendant.

1

Taylor Quinn, owner of Flour Sax Quilt Shop, had recently come across a great deal on lemon almonds. After filling the little freezer of her fridge and also the snacks bin at work, she realized she may have overdone it, so she brought half a dozen bags for the potluck.

She hadn't yet discussed her shopping with the counselor who was helping her through the grief process. She'd lost her mother to murder two years earlier, and her dad to a tragic accident, as a kid. Taylor wasn't slow-witted. She knew her issues with shopping would need to come up in counseling, but for now, walking out of a store laden with too much of whatever she had gone in after, felt good.

Maybe freedom from compulsion would feel even better.

Maybe not.

The Comfort Quilt Shop Owner's Guild meeting was full today. The owners, their seconds in command, two husbands, and a couple of kids who didn't have babysitters filled up the tables.

Carly, the unofficial leader, was having a hard time getting everyone's attention.

"Ladies and gentlemen, please!" The emphasis on please was both exhausted and exasperated. "We've had a long month, I know."

The bustle in the room only increased. From behind Taylor, a small voice cried out, "But I don't want a bean-fart-brownie!" A quieter, grown-up man's voice responded, "Just eat it!"

Carly sighed, pressed both hands on the table, and tried again. "As much as none of us want to discuss the tragic events at the Cascadia Quilt Expo last month, we can't..."

"I don't want it!" The small voice was a desperate wail now.

"Eat the crackers, then." The adult male tried a soothing tone.

Taylor glanced back. She didn't know the child, but she recognized the man as the flight attendant.

"Listen, we have one item on the agenda, folks. One," Carly seethed.

"Just do it." Shara Schonely, owner of Dutch Hex, the quilt shop that focused on an atmospheric collection of goth and Amish themed fabric, spoke sharply. "None of us are in the mood for Robert's Rules of Order."

"Oh, Shara..." Carly exhaled slowly. Shara had always been the stickler for rules before. "Fine, ignore the kids and guests. June, Shara, Taylor. This quilt was left behind, and it's pretty amazing."

She held up the quilt in question.

Shara gasped.

June whistled softly.

Taylor narrowed her eyes and tilted her head as she examined it.

The quilt was folded into a thick square, and they could only see a few feet of it. The creamy field fabric had yellowed with age, but the small portion showing was also covered in dark appliqué that had been delicately embroidered in light, silvery-gray thread. Time and age had done its dirty work, but the charm and quality of the tiny stitches couldn't be denied. Though the object wasn't large, it seemed heavy as Carly shifted it in her arms.

Carly cleared her throat. "This was part of the Cascadia Quilt Expo quilt show. It was displayed with the historic quilts, and it's attribution says it was made in Oregon Territory, 1820-1840."

"Verified?" Shara challenged.

"I don't know. The rest of the file is missing. It just had the title and age card attached. The rest of the info was with the organizers, and you know it's not been easy..."

Sue Friese, the head of the annual Cascadia Quilt Expo, was busy organizing her defense on a murder charge.

"What do you want us to do about it?" Taylor posed the only

important question and then nibbled her bean-brownie. She disagreed entirely with the child. These healthy-ish treats were her jam.

"Thank you, Taylor," Carly said. "We just need to agree on what to do with it until we find out who it belongs to."

"We've all got plenty of storage," Taylor suggested.

June clucked in disapproval. "But Taylor, a quilt like this is historic."

"Possibly, but it's not like we run a quilt museum."

Carly nodded warmly. "The Comfort Flour Mill Museum has asked permission to display the quilt."

"I don't know..." June's voice was soft and wistful, she reached out to touch the quilt but stopped herself.

"I would be glad to display it in my shop." Shara sat up stiff and prim. Today's Amish adjacent outfit was a baggy maxi-dress in navy-blue cotton, similar to the comfortable looking dresses the ladies on the covers of Amish novels were always wearing. She paired her dress with Doc Marten boots and a silky kerchief around her head, instead of a *kapp*, but she never wavered from her aesthetic.

"It's not an Amish quilt," Taylor couldn't help pointing out.

"I suppose you want it." Shara's tone was acid.

"I vote museum," Taylor said.

"Seconded." Carly looked relieved to have a motion on the table. "All in favor?"

June, Taylor, and Carly all voted in favor. After a moment, Shara agreed.

"Thank you. It's a relief to get that off my back. If this turns out to be as old as the ticket says, it's quite a coup."

"If it can be verified." Shara's voice was solemn. "I hope the museum knows how to take care of vintage fabric." Shara stood, nabbed two airline snack trays, and left.

"Meeting adjourned," Carly called out as the door shut behind Shara.

For the sake of the kids and spouses, Taylor was glad the meeting was over, but her curiosity was piqued. She hadn't thought about the Oregon Quilt Project in years, but the index of quilts and their history was a big deal. It was an important piece of archival work both for the history of the country and for the history of women. Being able to contribute something special to the index would be terribly gratifying.

She tried to catch Carly's eye, but the owner of Bible Creek Quilt and Gift yawned deeply as she wrapped up her tray of brownies. She wasn't sure how to start out, but she'd be happy to help figure out where the quilt had come from. A healthy little mystery to solve sounded just about right.

Taylor would text Carly later and ask her out for coffee. It was time she invested a little more in her relationship with the quilt guild anyway. Her counselor had encouraged it, at least, and why not start now?

"Hey, Taylor! Hold up!" The woman who stopped her was vaguely familiar.

"I'm Shawna Cross, from the museum. I came as a guest of Carly. Thanks for your vote of confidence."

"No problem. It only makes sense." Taylor wrapped her arms around herself. She'd walked the few blocks to the town hall, but even though the rain had stopped, it was bitterly cold out.

"Have you had a chance to really look at it?" Shawna glanced at a Volvo down the block but didn't move toward it.

"No, this is the first I've heard of it."

"It's a remarkable piece. I've never seen anything like it. I'm a historian and blogger, not a quilt expert. I'm sure the quilt can tell us more about itself if some experts look at it, but if the tag was right and this was from Oregon, then there's been nothing else like it."

Taylor shivered. It was cold, but this was exciting. "Do you mean like tourism money exciting? As a shop owner, that's pretty important to me."

Shawna shook her head. "I don't know about that, but I know if we can convince whoever owns it to let us keep it at our museum on a long loan, we won't turn it down. A historic piece with strong, interesting provenance can lend so much credence to a museum."

"Have you been in the industry long?"

"No, I was a hobbyist until very recently." She looked away. "But I'm going back for a degree. I knew as soon as I started volunteering that this was the right thing for me." She paused, tracing the damp ground with the toe of her shoe. "If this is legit, if this quilt was really stitched in this region before the Oregon Trail settlers arrived, I could have something cool to write about for a thesis. Something truly new in the overstudied field."

"And if it's not?" Taylor's heart was heavy for Shawna. There just hadn't been European women in Oregon before the wagon trains arrived. And quilting hadn't been taken up by the local tribes before that time, either.

Shawna's eyes were round and full of hope. "Even if it's not as old as the tag claims, it's a wonderful research project. And a potential thesis. And blog fodder. And the podcast. I haven't started yet, because I've been waiting for the right thing to launch, and I think this is it."

"Then no matter what the truth is, it's something to write about?"

"Exactly. Finding the truth is what's important. Learning what it is and why, is the heart of history. It took me a long time to really grasp that. I hate to say it, but my ex was right." She rolled her eyes.

"Best of luck." Taylor turned toward home. It felt like Shawna was in the mood for a long heart-to-heart, but Taylor wasn't interested in her man troubles.

"Thanks. It's the first thing I've been excited about in a while.

Real mysteries don't come up very often." She waved and turned toward her car.

Taylor shivered.

Real mysteries had come up far too often in her life.

TAYLOR STROLLED to her little house on Love Street tangled up in tantalizing thoughts about mystery quilts. She hoped to make herself a cup of tea and have a quiet evening Googling Oregon history, but when she popped open the back door and stepped into her kitchen, her pleasant evening blew away in the wind.

"Hey." The chagrinned face of her pretty blonde sister stared at her from her seat at the old, pine table.

Belle held a chipped coffee mug that said "Baker Tailoring" in faded letters. Grandpa Ernie, the tailor of the mug's fame, sat across from her, glowering from under his bushy eyebrows. And to the side, his head in the fridge, was young Jonah Lang: famous on the internet, newly minted millionaire, and teen husband of Taylor's sister Belle.

It was a lot to take in.

She hadn't seen them since getting the call about their impromptu wedding.

Belle was eleven years younger than Taylor, and though they were sisters in every sense but the biological and legal, they hadn't lived in the same house for very much of their lives.

Taylor's mom had been given legal guardianship when Belle was a baby. It was a long story, and for some reason, staring at the unexpected face of her sister brought it back, in all its knotty details. Though Taylor had intended to mother her sister through the last of her teen years, it had turned out to be unnecessary, as Belle had scampered off to college early, without looking back.

Quite like Taylor had done about ten years earlier. At least the not looking back part. Taylor was smart enough, but very few people in the world were Belle-smart.

Taylor turned her gaze to Jonah.

Jonah was definitely not Belle-smart.

Belle had claimed Nike was going to get Jonah through his last year of high school—some tutoring and testing kind of thing that kid-stars did. But Jonah was hardly a kid-star. He was an eighteen-year-old boy who had dropped out of high school because he was making a mint on YouTube, TikTok, and Snapchat, not to mention the Nike sponsorship deal. Taylor scrunched her mouth up. Nike? As much as Jonah claimed Nike was using him to target the "soft" and "pretty boy" market, she still found it confusing. She'd Googled him just the day before. He was trending as "White Boy of the Month," but she wasn't sure if that was good or bad.

"Don't stand there with your mouth open like a fish." Grandpa Ernie banged a knuckle on the old cookie tin that still held Grandma Delma's salvaged buttons. Taylor had plans to incorporate the buttons into a wall hanging but hadn't started yet.

Taylor closed her mouth.

"These two kids are fools." He harrumphed into his salt and pepper mustache. Grandpa Ernie's dementia was usually more pronounced in the evening, but he had his oxygen in and seemed to be fairly with it. At least Taylor agreed that Belle and Jonah were fools.

Who got married at their age?

Fools.

Children.

But as Belle had so carefully explained: teen marriages were only bad when there was no financial means for survival or when it interrupted your education. She already had her BA, and he was a millionaire. Plus, she had her trust fund—the half-a-million-dollar life insurance policy their mother had left behind. There wasn't any reason for them not to get married.

But that conversation had been two weeks ago. At least the first one had, and the rest of their chats had taken place via unsatisfying text messages.

"Finished up in Beaverton, then?" Taylor asked.

They had been at the Nike headquarters last Taylor had heard. And next, Nike was supposed to send them to New York for something or other.

"We decided not to go with the Nike thing." Belle shrugged lightly. Her face glowed with youth and happiness. It didn't seem to bother her at all, this switch up in plans.

"So back to the fashion thing or back to grad school?" Taylor sat at an empty chair. Her sister had lacked focus over the last year. There had been interesting starts and stops, though. From museum work in Hungary, to a random twist to fashion. There had been talks of writing books and going to grad school. But who knew what it was now? After all, it had been weeks....

"No. Not yet." Belle looked up at her young and adorable husband.

Jonah was leaning on the counter with one of Taylor's seltzer's in his hand. "Nike's been really cool. I liked working with them, but they want to have more control of my image than I like."

"Not enough money, eh?" Grandpa Ernie challenged.

"Nope. Not for what they were asking. They wanted me to cut the quilting stuff entirely." Jonah had gone viral posting outtakes from the Flour Sax Quilt Show. "I can't do that to the Juvies."

Taylor caught Belle's eye. Jonah's Juvie's were his fan base, mostly teens and young adults who couldn't get enough of his big brown eyes and curly hair. Taylor had a feeling they couldn't care less about the quilting.

"You should have heard the outcry." Belle didn't look upset

about the fans directing her family's financial future. "Besides it wouldn't be fair to Flour Sax. We owe all of this," she glanced at the huge diamond on her all-important finger, "to the family quilt store. If we can keep this up for any length of time it will be great for your business, and for the town."

Grandpa Ernie grumbled under his breath.

"What's that, Gramps?" Belle asked.

"Can't fault you for that." He looked like he wanted to. "Only right to take care of your sister after all she's done for you."

"Exactly. As soon as we find a place here in town, we'll settle in."

"But what about grad school?" Taylor asked.

"Plenty of online options. I'm not going to drop my dreams for the Juvies, don't worry."

"But which dream aren't you dropping?" Taylor couldn't help but needle this sister who had left her on tenterhooks for so many days.

Belle laughed. "I know what it must look like, but you have to admit, I'm pretty young to have to decide for sure, one-hundred percent, what I want to do with my life. Did you know what you wanted to do when you were nineteen?"

Taylor shook her head. At twenty she'd been halfway through her four years at Comfort College of Art and Craft, just down the street from her house, and she'd been at war with herself. She'd realized around that time that the last thing she wanted to do with her life was be a professional artist. She liked art, but she didn't live, eat, and breathe it.

"I won't let her fail." Jonah's impish smirk was hard to trust.

Taylor had been taken in by an imp in her youth too.

"It's not just any online college. She's working with Lewis and Clark on the project about your grandma and the shop and all of that. It'll be amazing. And when it's done, then fashion school, if she wants to. Or anything at all." Jonah gazed in wonder at Belle.

Taylor threw her hands up in surrender. "At least you won't go hungry while you figure it out."

"Nope. But you don't mind if we crash here for a minute, do you? We'll buy our own place, but we just got home. It might take a few days."

Taylor thought it should take more than a few days—you can go broke fast doing things like buying houses with cash. "Take your time. My home is your home, always."

"You're the best." Belle stood, kissed Taylor on top of the head, took Jonah by the hand, and led him out.

"They're too young to get married." Grandpa Ernie's big eyes looked sad.

"I wish we had been invited to the wedding," Taylor said softly.

"Selfish. Those kids are selfish."

"Probably so." Taylor kissed him gently on top of the head. "How about you and I watch a little Barney Fife?"

He stood slowly and reached for his walker. "That Quinn woman sent over one of her kids today. Don't want her here. I think she's going to steal from us."

Taylor followed Grandpa Ernie all the way to his room. His previous nurse, Ellery, had been one of Taylor's many cousins on the Quinn side. "That Quinn Woman" was Taylor's paternal grandmother, and the new nurse was a young cousin named Coco who was staying in town with the Quinns indefinitely. She was a shoe-string cousin and little more than a babysitter for Grandpa Ernie. "Then we'll fire her," Taylor said as Grandpa settled into the recliner in his room. She'd meant them to watch his favorite show together, but apparently, he wasn't in the mood.

"I don't need a nurse or a babysitter." He pulled the plastic breathing tube from his nose. "But I don't mind this oxygen. It's not great, but it's not so bad as I thought it was gonna be."

She looked at him with love, so much more himself, despite

the degenerative nature of his dementia. It wasn't going to get better, but with oxygen it seemed like it wasn't getting bad as quickly as it might otherwise have.

That was something, at least.

The rest of it, the young couple, the cousin Coco foisted on her by her lovable but meddling Grandma Quinny, and the abandoned quilt that needed a new home all paled in comparison to more happy years with Grandpa Ernie.

CHAPTER TWO

*M*aking coffee the next morning at 6:00 AM, the current issues made themselves important in the form of a skinny, half clad, mop-headed, teen boy sitting importantly at the kitchen table staring at his phone.

After a few moments of awkward silence, he turned to Taylor with a grim look on his face. "You've got to do something about Clay."

Taylor sighed. She had a feeling this was true but there was a layer of guilt to her break-up with Clay Seldon that she couldn't move past. If she hadn't sold her condo out from under him, hadn't run home without even a conversation, then maybe?

But her counselor told her to forget the maybes.

Her counselor was kind and wise. She'd shone a revealing light on Clay's narcissism. The good counselor had helped Taylor explore the misgivings she'd had over their four-year relationship and see clearly that her running home, like she had done, was not only her running to her sister's rescue, but also her subconscious rescuing herself from an unequal relationship.

"Have you talked to your mom yet?" Not so very long ago,

Taylor had discovered her friend Roxy was having a clandestine affair with Clay.

"I don't talk to her about men anymore."

Taylor couldn't blame him. Her own mother had been widowed for a long time, and she had avoided any hint of dating talk. There was nothing pleasant about picturing your mom on the hunt for a man. "Clay has a way of sticking around."

"I've noticed." Jonah frowned at his screen. "The Juvies are interested in helping."

A snort of laughter escaped Taylor. "But what can your fandom do about your mom's boyfriend?"

"Anything I want, probably. But I'm not sure what I want yet."

"Him drummed out of town on a pole?"

Jonah shook his head. "Nothing so dramatic."

"Can I be very honest?" Taylor took her fresh cup of coffee to the table. "I'm a little scared to bring this up with her."

"My mom has terrible taste in men. Clay is a terrible man. I ought to have seen this coming." He grimaced and shoved his phone away. "I really could make the Juvies do whatever I want them to. It's insane, isn't it?" He looked up at Taylor with big, puppy eyes. Almost scared.

Taylor tilted her head and considered the boy. She hadn't known him well before he got famous. Just another face in the crowd. He'd done a good job editing their YouTube show, but other than that, the only things she knew of him were the kinds of things a doting single mom with one kid would say. You know, the good stuff. "It's a bit scary," she agreed.

"I don't like it." He stood and stretched, then headed out, pausing in the kitchen door. "Let me know how it goes with Mom."

"Sure."

Jonah had left his phone on the table and Taylor contemplated it. Sometimes going to counseling can make a person feel like they know a lot about psychology. Taylor was that kind of person, and she wanted to apply all her new knowledge to Jonah.

He'd grown up alone with his mom. No dad in the house, no siblings.

His desire for an early marriage could have easily stemmed from his childhood longing for a more traditional homelife.

And he'd looked scared of the power that came with fame.

Maybe his rush into wedlock had been to give him someone to share the troubles with. A burden shared is halved? Wasn't that the saying? The dark isn't as scary if you're not alone? Maybe. But didn't most people just live together these days? She and Clay had, and probably would have indefinitely, considering the way he never had proposed.

She'd see Roxy this morning at the shop. It was their first Flour Sax Quilt Show planning meeting in what felt like forever. They were going to decide on all sorts of things, starting with, "Do we even keep doing this or not?"

They had a long day of work ahead of them. Roxy and Taylor in the shop, Clay at the desk in the back doing his book-keeping thing. If she was brave, she'd bring up the Clay situation this morning, while it was just the two of them.

She wasn't sure she was brave.

TAYLOR AND ROXY stood across from each other separated only by the reliable old worktable they used to cut fabric in Flour Sax Quilt Shop. The table was a nicked and scarred second-hand find Laura had brought home. It performed its current task of giving each woman some much-needed personal space very well.

"So..." Taylor looked across the table at her friend.

Roxy was several inches shorter than Taylor, and slim to the point where one wanted to call her "elfin." Her abundant short, dark curls, and her large, dark eyes contributed to this. You'd have called her a brownie, if you were pushed. The mischievous little elves the Girl Scouts had named one of their age groups after.

But she didn't look mischievous today, though she did look like she had something up her sleeve.

Taylor plumped her oversized purse on the worktable and dug around in it for her phone. She ought to be saying something about the Clay situation but found herself tongue-tied. The footsteps in the apartment upstairs—Clay's footsteps—were part of the problem. She'd brought Clay here, with his disarming manner and insinuating ways. Technically he'd brought himself, but she'd offered him the apartment and the job. Even if she could convince Roxy to dump him, it would create something less than a peaceful work environment.

Finding her phone, she checked her messages. A short one from Bible Creek Quilt and Gift shop owner, Carly, was the most recent—asking her about lunch to discuss the abandoned quilt.

"Hmmm…" Taylor looked up again. "Roxy, have you ever heard of the 'dump' quilt?" The dump quilt was an abandoned quilt, found literally dumped on the side of the road. An intriguing crazy quilt of no origin, it had come to mind as she contemplated the new mystery quilt.

"Dump quilt?" Roxy rolled her eyes. "That's not very subtle."

"No! I'm sorry. I didn't mean you or Clay or anything. It's a real quilt."

"Me and Clay?" Roxy's brows drew together. "Me and Clay?" She laughed. "I thought you meant Belle and Jonah."

Taylor swallowed. Belle and Jonah was another issue she didn't want to discuss. She didn't understand why, but she felt guilty about it. As though, if she'd been a better sister, she could have prevented it. Isn't that what sisters do?

Roxy, as the parent involved, would never have been able to prevent the wedding. Any interfering on her part would have just made things worse. But big sisters were supposed to be the cool person you turned to when things were messed up.

Cool.

Huh. Taylor shifted in her sensible New Balance shoes.

She hadn't been cool in at least five years. And despite her new and perfectly fitting high-waisted "mom" jeans, she was far from it now.

"Yeah, um. Sorry. It's a found quilt that caused a stir in the quilt community a while back. We've got another one, but we're hoping we can uncover its origins this time." Taylor tapped the screen of her phone. A few weeks back, Jonah would have sent her a Snap of her mom saying something apropos, but he didn't. Maybe Belle had made him see sense. Taylor had mostly hated the Snaps. Each one had been a reminder that her mom ought to have been alive.

But now she missed them.

She smiled in spite of herself. Her counselor had thoughts about that too. She'd encouraged Taylor to take that magic second look at a Snap, that one last view, and try to enjoy all the clips she had saved, but Taylor couldn't. That second view was the last view. If she watched them again, they'd disappear.

"I see." Roxy watched her cautiously.

"You don't think I want Belle to dump him, do you?" Taylor pushed the purse aside and leaned on her elbows. "I like Jonah."

Roxy lifted her eyebrows. "Even after all those messages from your mom?"

"That was hard. Still is, sort of, but I've been working through it. I can't keep letting grief take over like that. I have to be okay with feeling pain and then move forward."

"That's good advice."

"I have a good counselor."

"I wish the kids had gotten some counseling. Even now, it

would be nice. I know that lady over at the Methodist church does premarital counseling. Do you think she'd help?"

"Would they go to a church for help?" Taylor didn't know too much about what life had been like at her house after she'd left for college, but she did know that after her dad had died, she and her mom hadn't ever gone to church. Not even for Christmas or Easter.

"Heck if I know," Roxy said. "But I wish he would. Clay's been taking me, and it's nice."

"Clay's been taking you to church?" Taylor scrunched her face. "That might be the funniest thing I've ever heard."

Roxy laughed. "Just twice. It's not like we've been seeing each other long."

"Are you, seeing-each-other, seeing-each-other? Or is this just...um...a fling?"

"Don't know." Roxy shrugged. "I do know my son is staying at your place. Did he tell you to talk to me?"

Taylor nodded, as though she'd gotten caught doing something wrong.

"He's hated every man I've ever dated. You remember Hector Reuben? Sweetest man ever. No relation to the Comfort Reubens though." Roxy waved her hand an inch or so above her own head as though indicating Hector was short, like her.

"I think so. I remember a cute guy, kind of stocky."

"Short. He was short; five-foot-four at the most. Tall enough for me, of course." She looked up, as though the ceiling was far, far above her head, which it kind of was. "But so sweet. I think I loved him. Jonah pitched such a fit every time I went out with him, so we had to break up."

"How long did you date?"

"Only about a year, but a year goes fast when you have to fit dates around a working life and a kid. It was over before it started, or so it felt."

"I'm sorry."

"Me too. I wanted to marry him." A far-away look crossed Roxy's face.

"Whatever happened with you and Jonah's dad?" Taylor had wondered forever, and it felt a little impertinent to ask, but she plunged ahead anyway.

"He's military. He was gone a lot. A whole lot. He's an amazing man too. A good man." Roxy sighed but wrinkled her nose. "I got lonely. And I was really young…" Her face flushed a vivid red.

"Ah."

"Life is complicated." Roxy looked away.

"Sure, but Clay?" Taylor pressed.

"Do you know how many people live in Comfort, Oregon?" Roxy lifted an eyebrow.

"A few thousand?"

"If that." Roxy glanced at the ceiling again, where her current squeeze was thumping about like he was moving furniture.

"What about online dating?" Taylor nudged.

"Sure. That's always fun. But you have to admit, Clay Seldon is adorable in his own way."

Taylor did admit it but didn't feel like she'd accomplished her task from Jonah. "I don't think he's serious about relationships."

"It's early days. I'm far from serious, too." Roxy chuckled softly.

"But eventually…"

Roxy shook her head. "At my age, you have to accept that you can't always get what you want."

"But Roxy, you're what, forty?"

"Just over."

"Didn't you know forty was the new twenty-nine? Don't settle just yet." Taylor tried to play it off like she was just having fun.

Roxy smirked.

It was the kind of smirk that told you, you'd put a foot in your mouth.

Taylor had a feeling there was someone standing behind her.

"Hey Clay," Roxy said.

"Hey, Babe." He came around the table and kissed the top of her head. "Don't let Taylor talk you out of our plans tonight, okay? One girl's trash is another girl's treasure." He offered his lopsided grin to both ladies.

Roxy laughed.

"Tell me about your new filming plan. You're YouTube views are in the toilet." Clay changed the subject.

On that sour note, they shifted their conversation to work, but Taylor was unsettled for the rest of the morning. Lunch with Carly from Bible Creek Quilt and Gift would be a great distraction from the troubles at her home base.

lour Sax Quilt Shop was open from eleven to six on weekdays, but since Taylor started much earlier than that, she didn't mind skipping out for lunch mere moments after opening. Roxy didn't seem to mind either, and from the googly-eyes Roxy and Clay were exchanging, she didn't have to guess why.

Carly and Taylor met at the Tillamook Cheese Factory Outlet next door to Taylor's shop. Much to the chagrin of the town's favorite lunch spot, Reuben's Diner, the cheese outlet had started serving something resembling a lunch.

The two small town business owners both ordered Ploughman's Lunches—a meal stacked with thick slices of vintage extra sharp white cheddar, smoked black pepper white cheddar, and Farmstyle Baby Swiss, as well as crusty slices of bread that must have come from some out-of-town bakery, thin slices of yellow onion, a small crock of whipped butter, a fat juicy pickle, and a mug of strong Stump Town Coffee. Taylor didn't hate that she could get this within feet of her own shop's door. Especially not in late November in Oregon. Despite the rainy evening they'd just had, most of November had been worryingly dry. It would be a drought year, for sure, and skiers would be crushed.

Carly's shop was named for the creek that was nestled along the edge of their town—and the creek had been named for a salesman who claimed his last name was Bible. Maybe that was true, maybe it wasn't, but it worked in Carly's favor with her church themed merchandise. Her shop was usually hopping. Carly was a motherly woman, soft, round, large bosomed, but not overweight, or at least not much. Her auburn hair had a shining white streak in it, but it looked elegant and her Bible Creek Quilt and Gift uniform of crisp white blouse with a subtle logo on the pocket came across like something you'd buy at Nordstrom's. Taylor shifted in the pastel polo she'd bought at a huge discount, in bulk. Flour Sax employees would be wearing those discount polo shirts for years to come. There were just so many of them shoved in the second bedroom of Clay's apartment.

Taylor was at least ten years younger than Carly, but she felt dowdy in comparison.

A cross with small pink stones in it sparkled on a chain around Carly's neck. On anyone else, it would have seemed tacky to Taylor, but on Carly, it just struck one as nice. Quality. Reverent even? Grandma Quinny was a fan of Carly's shop. Carly gave off Grandma Quinny vibes.

"Did you deliver the mystery quilt to the Flour Mill Museum?" Taylor asked as she layered butter, onion, and peppered cheddar on her fresh baked bread.

"I did, and I had a long talk with Lorraine Love while I was there. She doesn't just run the museum because she's family. She has a degree and experience. She recently moved back from a year in Atlanta where she had been a historian in residence at a small museum. Before that, she worked for the Oregon Historical Society."

"I wonder if Belle knows about that."

"Your sister's interested in history?" Carly asked.

"Yes, I think so. It's hard to tell."

"I remember my girls at her age. Doesn't feel like so long ago, but two of them have well established careers now. I never thought it would happen."

Taylor appreciated the sympathy and gave Carly an affectionate smile. "What did Lorraine have to say about the quilt?"

"She was interested. She has a friend who is a textile expert. She'd like to have her look it over."

"Does this expert know quilts?" Taylor was already spreading another piece of bread with butter.

"It's Erika from the college. You know Erika, right? She works in the fiber arts department and has a specialty in historic quilts for her own work. A bit controversial as she unpicks them and makes new things, but that's art isn't it?" Carly lifted one shoulder as though art were incomprehensible.

"Good that we've found someone with the right qualifications." Taylor sipped her coffee as she contemplated how to phrase the next question. She didn't want to sound unappreciative—to dismiss this old quilt the way Carly had just dismissed art. "Is there some kind of, um, financial reward for being the oldest quilt made in Oregon Territory?"

Carly shook her head slowly. "The insurance value of a quilt is in direct relationship to who owns it. Take the dump quilt, for instance. Found on the side of the road, literally dumped. The owner must have thought it was just rags. Praise the Lord the women of the Oregon Quilt Project knew better. If our mystery quilt was shelved up in an attic somewhere, it wouldn't be worth much. If it was on display in the Smithsonian, it would be invaluable."

"And no word from anyone related to Cascadia about it?"

"No. We've torn the school apart looking for more information, but to no avail. We've posted in all the Facebook groups, but no one has claimed it."

"If they're going to display it at the Comfort Flour Mill Museum, it would be kind of neat to pull together a few more and have a real show. Something we could advertise."

Carly's eyes twinkled. "That's why I called you. I've already talked to Lorraine about it, but I knew you'd be the best person to help plan it. You always think like a businessperson first. Let's brainstorm ways we can work this to the good, shall we? The murder of the young author put a real damper on business."

They brainstormed types of exhibitions they could create with the quilt as their inspiration. By the time they'd had more cheese than was healthy for an American, they had a plan. "I'll talk to Lorraine this evening," Taylor said as they bussed their little table. "And you keep on Erika. If the school will lend the museum some antique sewing tools, and we can press our elderly friends and neighbors to unpack their old favorites, we might have something."

"You're a darling. Thank you. And say hi to your grandmother for me, will you? I haven't seen her on Sunday in a while. Hope all is well."

"Will do." Taylor hadn't thought of her grandparents Quinn as church going people, but she supposed it would explain her penchant for Carly's shop over Taylor's.

THINGS WEREN'T any more comfortable at Flour Sax the rest of the day. Clay made sure of it, from winking at Roxy when Taylor was looking his direction, to stealing kisses when customers were around. She began to feel bad for her friend, wondering if Clay was only dating Roxy to get under her own skin.

She left for the day, agitated, and not ready to deal with anyone she'd find in her house.

Instead, she went to the museum, hoping it was still open at seven in the evening.

The old flour mill building—a looming board edifice white-washed and in good repair—stood on the far edge of town. It wasn't the original location for the mill, not being anywhere near the Nestucca River that used to turn the wheel, but by dint of hard effort, it had been carefully moved for preservation. A light shone through the little window of a side door, so Taylor knocked.

The door creaked open. It was on a chain, and a small, pale face peeked through. For just a second, Taylor thought it was a child, but the face looking up at her had long ago lost the full-ness of youth.

"Can I help you?" As she spoke the little lady straightened up. She was short, but not as short as she had seemed. But she was also thin, to the point of frail, and so fair you could see the blue lines of veins in her forehead.

"Evening. I noticed the light on and wondered if anyone was in. I'm Taylor Quinn from Flour Sax. I was wondering if you were free to chat about the mystery quilt."

The lady behind the door slid the chain lock open. "Come on in out of the cold, please."

Taylor came in gladly.

"Can I fix you a cup of tea? Or maybe an instant cappucci-no?" The side door to the mill museum led straight to a cozy little office. A large, steel desk with mostly intact avocado-green enamel stood at the far side. The lady had likely been working there, from the seat of the wooden, rolling desk chair, as the desk was covered in papers and a laptop was open to a Google search.

A charming hutch, painted black, stood across the room

from the desk and was set up as a makeshift kitchenette with an electric kettle, hot plate, and a large selection of things to drink and munch. The glass-doored upper cupboards were stocked with books. A quilt, made from real flour sacks the mill had once used for their product, hung by the door.

Taylor was mesmerized by the full collection of sacks in one quilt. She knew quilts like this existed, several did in Comfort, but this one was the "real" one. The one the matriarch of the Love family had made when she was in her nineties. Taylor hadn't seen it in years.

"I can always tell when a quilter stops by." The lady filled the electric kettle at the water cooler. "I'm Lorraine Love. Nice to meet you."

"Lorraine Love?" Taylor asked with an emphasis on the last name.

"Yes, another prodigal daughter returned." She spoke with the soft, quivery voice of a much older woman.

"This is a semi-retirement for me," Lorraine continued. "Previously I curated for the Oregon Historical Society and worked with Fort Vancouver as well."

"This quilt…" Taylor wasn't trying to ignore Lorraine, but the heirloom flour sack quilt kept calling her name. "It's so full of color after all these years."

"Yes, Grandmother Love made it. It's always hung, never been used or washed. We keep it out of light. Quite remarkable, I think."

"It is…" Taylor knew better than to touch it, but she longed to feel the fabric that had so rarely been handled and never washed. A rare specimen in her own experience. Even the oldest quilts in her own family had been made for use, to keep warm, to protect and comfort.

"But that is not the quilt you came for. Please, make yourself comfortable, or as comfortable as can be here."

She gestured to an old wooden chair, similar in era to the wooden desk chair, but of a humbler background.

Taylor sat. "Thank you, and I'd love a cappuccino. I'm excited you're going to put on an exhibit for our mystery quilt."

"I'm pleased." Lorraine sifted the powdered drink into a mug printed with "Love's Mills Loves Millers," which must have been a company gift to employees at one time. Lorraine's hands were smooth and fair, much younger than her voice, but they trembled as she poured hot water from her kettle onto the powder.

Taylor glanced at the water cooler again. It was simple and old, like the rest of the room. A ceramic base, though the water was in a plastic barrel. No hot water tap.

"Thanks."

"The tours, especially the miller's daughter tour, are very popular field trips for the school, and often we draw little crowds in the summer. I'm hoping a gallery with feature exhibits will attract more people. Though our town isn't old by some standards, there are many good stories here."

Taylor nodded and tried to think of a good story about Comfort. Grandma Quinny could rattle them off by the dozen, but the really juicy ones weren't coming to Taylor's mind.

Lorraine twinkled mischievously. "I'm considering asking The Oregon Historical Society for a loan of the Willamina Murder Quilt. It just feels like it belongs here in Comfort, don't you think?"

Taylor tilted her head in assent. Willamina was their nearest neighbor, and all things considered, Comfort was a better place for the local murder quilt than Portland was. The city didn't deserve everything, after all.

"But as it currently stands, they don't owe me any favors, so I hesitate to ask." She looked away for a flicker—Taylor almost missed the moment of hesitation. "Do you think the college would loan us your Grandmother Delma's suiting quilt?"

On display at the Comfort College of Art and Craft was a

quilt Delma Baker had made from scraps of the bespoke suits Ernie Baker had tailored.

"We can always ask." A little giddy love bubbled in Taylor's heart. She missed her Grandmother Delma. A classic, white-haired, cookie-baking grandmother on one hand, and a hard-nosed businesswoman on the other. Sneakily transforming the family business to a quilt store by slowly adding little things for quilters until, one day, the books told the story—the quilt store made more money than Grandpa's suits did. Grandpa Ernie had been a sport, but he'd long reserved his right to grumble about the good old days when men knew how to dress.

Taylor mused on the collection at the Comfort College of Art and Craft. "They have a couple other quilts not on display that could be great in the exhibition. One of Reynette Wood's quilts would be a lovely addition." Reynette had been hired to work in the fiber arts department but was tragically poisoned by her son-in-law before she could begin. "It would be nice to have an important modern piece. There are some other, older ones, as well. I think your family has donated a couple through the years."

Lorraine was writing notes, her small white hand flying smoothly across the page. "These are strong ideas. Thank you." She looked up, a smile in her eyes. "It's funny the things you forget about when you have been gone a while." She laid her pencil down. "But since you mention it, I do remember when Grandma Love donated several family quilts. One in particular comes to mind. It came over on the wagon train. Old in itself, though not made in Oregon. I think the idea that this particular quilt was made in Oregon at such an early date is what is so tantalizing about it."

"But could a quilt as old as they claim really have been made here? If so...where?" Taylor chewed her lip and tried to remember her state history. The first big wagon train push had come through in the 1840s. The Astoria Company had brought colonizers in 1812, and earlier still, was Fort Vancouver. The French and Canadian fur trappers hadn't brought European women with them, instead partnering with native women, who they later abandoned. Native American women had a rich quilting history. "Would the Chachalu Museum be willing to lend something to the exhibit?"

Lorraine looked up and away, a longing in her eyes. "I will ask. That would be an act of generosity on their part. This is their land, after all."

Comfort bordered the Confederated Tribes of the Grande Ronde Reservation, but Lorraine was right. The border was false, and Comfort was land that the tribes had lived on for centuries.

"Have you had a chance to really look at the quilt?" Taylor asked. Her own glimpse of it had been unsatisfying. Old? Sure. But remarkably old? She hadn't been close enough to tell.

"Carly brought it over, but I haven't researched it thoroughly yet. I'm not an expert in textiles, but I do feel competent to date the item. Are you interested in being there for the examination tomorrow? Having more experts on hand can often help."

"I'd love to, thank you." Taylor accepted the offer with pleasure. Having Belle and Jonah at home meant she didn't have to figure out how to convince a young day nurse to stay late with Grandpa Ernie. And she didn't hate being considered an expert, either. In the meantime, she'd have to pull out a few history textbooks to do some reading this evening. She stood and offered her hand. "Thank you so much for the invitation. I'll let you get back to your work and see you tomorrow."

Lorraine took Taylor's hand in both of hers. Taylor had expected a cool, or even chilly, handshake, but it was warm and loving. "Thank you. It's a nice feeling to be welcomed home, isn't it?"

A loud knock on the door prevented Taylor from answering.

Lorraine hadn't locked it when Taylor came in, and the door popped open to reveal Sissy Dorney.

"Lorraine." Sissy never faded into the background and had a personality that seemed to extend several feet around her at any given time. But at this moment, she seemed even larger than life, with the billowy black smock she wore at her salon and her hair in exceptionally tall curls. "I've been trying to reach Tansy all evening."

"Would you like to sit? May I make you a cup of tea?" Lorraine was nonplussed by Sissy's bursting in on the quiet, comfortable office. "Kids can be so difficult when you most need them, can't they?"

Tansy was Sissy's stepdaughter.

Taylor tilted her head and gave Lorraine another long look.

"She's not my kid, but she owes Pyper an apology, and we're going to get it." Sissy crossed her arms and leaned forward, hovering over the much smaller woman.

Lorraine sighed softly, then clucked a little. She went to her electric kettle, tested it against her hand, then poured water into a mug that said "Comfort and Style"—Sissy's salon.

Taylor longed to slip out and start her research, but Sissy stood firm, not moving from the doorway.

"I haven't spoken to her this week." Lorraine put a bag of Good Earth Tea in the water and passed it to Sissy.

Sissy accepted it with almost a snarl. "I don't like to fight with you, Lorraine. You know I don't."

"As you've said in the past. Please, sit." Lorraine pushed the wooden desk chair out for Sissy.

Sissy didn't sit. "I'd make Phil deal with this, but you know how he is."

Lorraine shook her head. "Indeed. It would be terrible for him to have to take sides between his girls, wouldn't it?"

"I should probably sneak out." Taylor locked eyes with Sissy and nodded toward the door.

Sissy frowned at her. "Oh, fine," she stepped into the office. "But after what Tansy wrote on her blog," she pronounced the word blog as though it tasted bad, "about her own sister!"

Taylor escaped but was torn. Part of her itched to Google Tansy Dorney's blog, but another, more logical part of her brain, wanted to steer as clear from that little family drama as possible.

CHAPTER FOUR

$\mathcal{T}$he building that housed Flour Sax was approaching one-hundred-years old, and though it had been "modernized" in the 1970s, it still felt close, damp, and stuffy in the winter.

The public displays of affection Clay had been engaging in all the next day also felt suffocating.

But it had rained a little, and outside, the air smelled of fresh earth, the healthy decay of fallen leaves, and had just a hint of future snow. Taylor breathed deeply on her walk to the museum that evening. Even if it rained on her walk back home, it would be worth it. The fresh night air was a balm to her soul.

Though Comfort was in those rolling foothills of Oregon's Coast Range Mountains, Taylor was a walker by nature, and only drove her mom's old Audi when she absolutely had to.

Taylor called Hudson on her way to the museum, at least in part, to push the memories of her ex hovering around Roxy like a bee, out of her mind.

"Love." Hudson's deep voice growled over the word as he answered. "It's been too long. Come over tonight."

"I'm all yours after this little quilt consult." She inhaled deeply, letting her lungs and heart fill with things that made her happy.

"Are you ready for Thanksgiving?" Hudson asked.

The happiness deflated, a bit.

She'd tried, again, to host the holiday, but there was too much competition. Roxy claimed Jonah and Belle, and though Roxy had invited Taylor, Hudson, and Grandpa Ernie, Taylor wasn't up for spending the holiday with Clay.

Hudson's mom had claimed him and his Grandpa Boggy, and though Hudson hinted Taylor could come along, there hadn't been an invite from his mom, not an official one.

She'd probably be with her Quinn relations on the strawberry farm instead, which would be lovely, and overwhelming. She was thankful for her family, and not just for being a port in the storm. She really did love those crazy folks. But her heart longed to have Hudson, Belle, Jonah, and Grandpa Ernie all to herself, around the table in their rarely used formal dining room. She didn't hold out hope for Christmas as Colleen, Belle's bio-mother, had elicited promises from Belle and Jonah to come, and to bring Taylor and Grandpa Ernie with them.

Maybe Easter?

She sighed.

"Something bothering you?" Hudson asked.

"Not exactly, but you know the holiday season and sales..."

"I do now, that much is true. Let me take you out for lunch sometime this week. Any time, you pick. Text me and I'm yours. I've finished up the Blueland Farms job and have some free time."

The Comfort Flour Mill Museum loomed ahead. "I'd like nothing better. In the meantime, I'm here, so I'd better start thinking like an expert."

"You are an expert, and my love. See you tonight."

"Absolutely."

She pocketed her phone and tried to hold on to the happy feeling going to Hudson's gave her. Happiness unclouded by guilt or worry. Belle and Jonah had vowed they'd be home with Grandpa Ernie all night. Knowing he was safe at home with family was half the pleasure.

Taylor met Lorraine in a shiny, new, metal outbuilding a few yards past The Miller's Daughter, the little museum café.

The building seemed to be a combination staging and storage space. It was delightfully temperate. Not too hot, and not too cold. Rare for a metal structure. Taylor supposed it would have to be if it was where they kept historical...stuff.

"Taylor, lovely of you to come." Lorraine held out both hands in welcome. The small woman looked younger tonight. Her fair hair was clearly streaked with white, but also, naturally quite blonde. Her eyes were soft, and she wore a crisp white lab coat over a flowing skirt of dark turquoise with gold embroidery similar to fabric you'd see in a sari. "You've met Shawna, I hope?"

Taylor greeted the earnest blogger who had dreams of podcast success. "Good to see you."

"Thanks." Shawna rubbed her hands together.

Though Taylor didn't have anything concrete to gain from this, her spine prickled in anticipation.

"And Erika, have you met Taylor Quinn? She runs Flour Sax."

"Taylor." From the thin, steely hair slicked back into a low bun, to the almost communist khaki pants and shirt she was wearing, Erika exuded no-nonsense. "I arrived early and had a look at the blanket."

Taylor cringed. Blanket. Again. A fiber arts expert should know better than that.

"In my opinion, we need to be cautious when dating this." Erika gave Taylor an apologetic look.

"Hmmm." Taylor nodded.

The quilt in question was spread across a stainless-steel table, ready for its autopsy. Laid out in its entirety you could see it was just a partial quilt. Though it almost reached from end to end on the table it was far from touching the ground on the sides. The once-dark appliqué glowed charcoal under the bluish fluorescent lights. The same lights gave a sickly hue to the yellowed field fabric. But Taylor knew enough from her years in the fiber arts world to know these were good signs. Signs of age and life had to exist if this were to be a proper piece of history.

"What date were we starting with?" Taylor asked.

Lorraine passed Taylor a pair of thin white cotton gloves. She put them on and stepped closer to the piece. She wanted to run her fingers over the surface, feeling for thickness of thread, and steadiness of stitches, the texture of the fabrics.

Though the fabrics were drab, the overall piece was lovely and unlike anything Taylor had seen in person. If it had been whole it would have been a double bed sized quilt. A primitive tree of life medallion held pride of place in what ought to have been the center but was just off now. Taylor ducked for a better look at the edges to see if it had been cut, but they had frayed to a soft fuzz that wouldn't answer any questions.

The field fabric was textured like linen, but perhaps was a cotton blend. A common fabric through the years. The appliquéd pieces were a mix of leaves and fish, both similar to Pacific Northwest Native American designs. The work reminded her of *Broderie Perse* quilts, though that actually referred to fussy cut bits of brocade, where this looked like wool from suiting that had been embroidered by hand and then applied. Most of the fish were in perfect condition, covered in tiny, silvery scales. *Broderie Perse* had been popular in the very early nineteenth century, right about the time the ID card had said.

The four women hovered over the quilt, circling it silently as they contemplated what they saw. Erika made notes on a small notepad. Shawna took photos, no flash, with her phone.

Taylor wanted to ask questions but didn't want to interrupt what had grown to feel almost sacred.

The confused style didn't help them get closer to their goal of proving the claims on the data card. There had only been one European woman in the whole Oregon territory between 1810 and 1820, the infamous Jane Barnes of Astoria. If the stories were true, though she was hired as a seamstress for the boat trip over, she wouldn't have had time to create something like this blanket.

Surely the person who submitted this luscious piece of needlework to the expo hadn't thought Barnes was the seamstress behind the work.

Taylor peered at the stitching as though it were fine print on a contract. Each of the four women did, examining the minute details. In the section Taylor had at hand, little bits of thread stuck out around the border of the appliqué, as though something had been unpicked. She looked up to see if anyone else seemed to notice. She wanted to ask about it, but her ego didn't want her to. She ran a quilt shop. Shouldn't she know exactly what she was looking at?

Shawna let out a low whistle, breaking the studious silence of the group. "Sailcloth."

Erika nodded.

Taylor rubbed her cotton clad fingertip over rough, age-yellowed fabric and nodded. "Or wagon canvas. Cotton duck…"

"Pooh." Shawna brushed it aside. "That would make it ages too new. At least three decades. Ladies weren't quilting like this on the trail. They were making piece work with their cotton muslin, like we do."

Taylor shrugged lightly, not willing to place money on her idea, but not willing to dismiss it, either. There were a few very old quilts in Oregon, back to the 1700s even, but they hadn't been made here. The oldest known blankets made by Europeans dated after the first wagon train.

She tilted her head. The fish appliqué, despite the embroidery on the fabric, had the look of a native Pacific Northwest artist, though she figured it could be a copy. "Did women make quilts from the canvas tops of their covered wagons?" she posed the question to Lorraine.

Lorraine shook her head slowly. "I hesitate to say a thing was never done, but canvas was a sturdy and useful fabric for the pioneers who would need tents, lean-tos for animals, roofs for cabins, maybe even mattresses. A woman who could afford to use her wagon cover for something like a quilt would likely have had the means to find softer, gentler fabric. Quilting to pioneer women could be what we now consider a meditative act. A soothing action to do in hard times. Making a quilt was an act of creating both comfort and beauty. It was a luxury. They would want it to be as soft and attractive as they could make it. The cover of their wagon...." She shook her head solemnly. "I think this would not have been a common act."

"This has the feel of a flax linen, like an English sail, not an American cotton duck canvas you'd find on a wagon." Erika spoke with authority.

Shawna was bouncing on her toes, excited about the idea she was brewing. "I think the appliqué fabric might be from a British sailor's rig, his uniform. How could this be anything but a quilt made in Astoria? And if so...." Shawna caught Erika's eye.

"Jane Barnes." Erika said the name with reverence.

"Surely not." Lorraine's voice was hushed. "When would she have? How could she have in the limited time she lived here?"

Taylor flicked the loose strings on the appliqué of the fish she stood over. She agreed it looked like wool on linen, but how likely was it to be from a nineteenth century sailor suit? But these little thread bits had surely held something more on here, like beads or buttons.

And bead work or button work paired with the fish imagery implied that no English woman, the famous Jane Barnes or not, had made this quilt.

She moved to the end of the table and stood next to Erika. She hadn't given the medallion image in the middle much attention.

Tribal fish, the tree of life medallion, the loose threads that might have held beadwork in place. These needed consideration. Her expertise was definitely not historic needlework—and what she did know about textile history was limited to feed sacks and learned at her family store, rather than the classroom. But after all that, there was no shame in asking. She stood straight, stretching out her back. "Are we sure it's European in origin?"

"Yes."

"No."

Shawna and Lorraine answered at the same time.

"Linen field fabric," Shawna defended her point.

Lorraine held out a cotton gloved hand and hovered it over one of the fish. "This figure does not seem English, though the embroidery does. I'm very glad we have Erika with us."

Erika was still bent over the quilt, a magnifying glass in hand. She grunted softly. "We're not going to answer all of our questions today. And we may never have enough information to verify the claim that it is the oldest quilt made in Oregon. But I see no reason not to display it and discuss it as an old and meaningful object." She straightened up and frowned at the group. "I'll need to take a sample, something from the frayed edge will be sufficient. And many pictures. The wi-fi here isn't strong, so I'll be doing further research from my own office. You'll be able to reach me there. Email is always best."

Lorraine glowed. "Thank you for your commitment to this

research. Ladies, I haven't had dinner yet. Would anyone like to travel down to Reuben's Diner with me?"

"I've got plans, I'm sorry." Taylor took her gloves off. She might have liked to discuss this quilt at length and get to know Lorraine better, but she didn't want it as much as she wanted to spend her night with Hudson.

CHAPTER FIVE

$\mathcal{H}$udson East was the first person to acknowledge that he had initially fallen for Taylor because she was a sort of damsel in distress. Maybe it was a weakness in himself, but he'd always been drawn to people he could help, whether romantically or just as friends.

And anyone could see that Taylor's hard-to-get thing was what had hooked him completely. Not that she'd been *playing* hard to get, but it had taken a long time for her to decide he was the one.

When you looked at it like that, you might even call him a sucker. But he didn't mind. As long as he had Taylor, you could call him whatever you wanted.

Taylor was warm-hearted. Like him, she was drawn to helping others. She was smart, but not a show-off. Funny, but not in an attention seeking kind of way. She loved family but didn't seem to be in any hurry to have one of her own. She was pretty as anything. Beautiful, even, in that healthy, sun kissed small town way he loved. And she was coming over tonight.

He whistled as he set the table. Steaks were ready for the grill. He had a bag of Caesar salad in the fridge and a bottle of local *pinot noir*. He contemplated turning some music on... maybe jazz? He didn't like jazz, but she had lived in Portland for quite a while and might like it. Country was always good, but he wasn't sure Taylor was a fan. She never switched stations in his truck or anything, but she never sang along, either.

The view from his A-frame cabin on the hill was hidden by the dark of the late fall evening, but his patio was framed in small, white Christmas lights that he turned on for the sake of atmosphere. What he was after, tonight, was romance. Seduction. Showing Taylor how much he loved her.

Blues maybe? He clicked through his phone and found a good playlist. His speakers, tucked into the home he'd built almost entirely by himself, played it low and deep, thrumming through the house. He nodded, satisfied.

Though they'd gone out to dinner three nights earlier, it still felt like it had been too long, and he wished he could convince her to just move here. He hadn't invited her. He knew how she felt about being able to keep her grandpa in his own house.

And he didn't blame her.

He looked up at the trusty, reclaimed barn-wood beams that crossed the expanse of his house. But he wasn't interested in moving into her crowded little house in town.

None of that mattered tonight. All that mattered was Taylor was coming over and they had the night to themselves.

The doorbell rang and his heart seemed to skip. He laughed out loud. It really did feel like that first overwhelming crush he'd had. He'd been a freshman in high school, and she'd been a senior. Glorious with her honey blonde hair and gray-blue eyes and a saucy smile that seemed to know things. Taylor Quinn had been amazing in high school. Still was.

He popped his neck as he walked to the door, hoping to relax just a little. Not that he minded if she knew how excited he was to see her, but he liked the idea that she could lay down her day's stress when she came over, and him being relaxed would only help.

He pulled open the heavy, walnut slab door he'd rescued from a tear-down in McMinnville. "Hey babe," he drawled.

"Ha!" his mother stared him in the face and laughed. Not once, not twice, but four solid "ha's" in a row. "Don't you look a treat!" She strode into his house, shedding layers of winter clothes as she went: rain jacket on the back of his leather sofa, scarf on the side table, gloves on the dining room table, hat on the counter in the kitchen. "Hmmm. This looks good." She picked up the bottle of wine he'd pulled out and contemplated the label. She set it down and began to pull open drawers.

"Mom, what are you doing here?" His heart was in his throat and his face was hot with an anger that almost felt childish.

"Getting in out of the rain. It's miserable."

It wasn't raining.

"Why aren't you home?"

"It's a long story and you will need to ask your step-father about it."

He sucked in a breath to prevent him from saying something he'd regret. "It's late."

"Yes. You really ought to have built a spare bedroom on this crazy cabin. I hate thinking of you sleeping on that old couch every time I come to stay."

"You..." Words failed. His heart was slamming into his ribs, like it wanted to break out. He clenched his fists to keep himself from turning her by the shoulders and leading her back out the door she'd come in by.

His mother hid her age well, her hair was still thick, and any white was carefully covered in deep chocolate brown. Her face had been "done" when he was in high school, but he suspected she'd gone back for more work. She, like him, was built on broad lines, wide shouldered, and athletic. Her hands, glittering with large, showy rings hinted at her age, despite her heavy investment in good creams. She'd become a mom for the first time in her forties and spent the rest of her life trying to fit in with the other moms of kids in Hudson's grade.

He shook his head to clear his mind.

He hadn't seen his mom recently, and she always made a big impression. "I have plans this evening. You can't just show up like this."

"Your own mother can't just drop by?" She held up the wine bottle opener with a look of triumph. "Ah-ha!"

"I've got a date. Can't you tell?"

"Aren't you just seeing that Quinn girl?" She poked the tip of the corkscrew into the top of the bottle.

"Taylor. Yes."

"Then what's the big deal?" She stared at the bottle in confusion and tried again.

He scratched his forehead and glanced at the clock. His mom liked Taylor, in theory. Always said she did. But she hadn't actually seen his girlfriend since Laura Quinn's death.

"Have a glass of wine. Cook yourself a steak. I'll take Taylor out, but you've got to get yourself a room somewhere else by ten. Call Aunty Brenda."

"Her house doesn't have a view like yours."

"It's November. There's nothing to look at."

Cheryl stared at the wine. "A bottle cap? Really, Hudson." She clucked but unscrewed the lid. "You want me gone by ten so you can bring a girl home. Oh, how times have changed."

He ignored her and texted Taylor. *Will pick you up at your place. Dinner out, then mine, sound good?*

She responded fast enough with a heart. So that was good. Not that she'd ever been mad about a change of plans or anything like that at all. She was easy going.

He exhaled sharply and grabbed his coat. "Ten, Mom. Call Aunt Brenda now."

His mom waved her phone at him. "You don't have to tell me twice. I know when I'm not wanted."

As she followed that by filling one of the wine glasses almost to the rim, he doubted she meant it.

⁂

THERE HAD BEEN no sign of his mom, his bottle of wine, or any of the rest of the abandoned romantic dinner when he and Taylor had come home, so the rest of the evening had been nothing but perfect.

The next morning Hudson woke up calm and content. The sun had risen on another cold, but sunny November day. The farmers in the area hated it. The few hints of rain hadn't been nearly enough yet. Crops would suffer for this early fall drought, even the grapes. Though he was sorry for them, he couldn't help being glad. Sun was good. So good, his plan B for life was based on it. A good builder could find work anywhere, even somewhere perfect like Montana, where the sun was always shining. He lay back, arms crossed under his head. A ranch. A bigger truck. A better cabin with two or three bedrooms. A river in the distance he could fish. Plan B was pretty good. He didn't hate it. But this sunny November morning meant plan A wasn't so bad either.

Next to him Taylor murmured, half asleep. She was curled up on her side, her forehead resting next to his chest. Taylor also made plan A good. He ran his hand through her hair, and asked in a quiet voice, "Want coffee?"

"Hmm." She closed her eyes lightly, her face relaxing. "Coffee."

He ambled into his kitchen, knowing his face was a goofy grin. It had been a good night with a good woman. The refrain played again and again in his head. If this was the best life had in store for him, he was satisfied.

He was pulling a half empty can of coffee from the cupboard, when the front door creaked open.

"Hudsy, oh Hudsy!" the not-mellifluous voice of his mother rang through the open beamed house. He stared at her, his heart sinking.

She held out a pink bakery box.

"Got us some breaky. You don't mind my bringing Aunty Brenda with me, do you?"

Aunty Brenda could have been his mom's twin but wasn't even her real sister.

"Mom, what are you doing here?"

"Thanking you for dinner. Those were good steaks." Cheryl and Brenda strode into the room and took seats at his dining table like they were in a bar. "You should have stayed and had some."

Before Hudson could think up a way to send his mom and her friend away again, Taylor pattered softly into the kitchen. In her little, thin-strapped, cotton camisole and a pair of even smaller panties, she was just what he wanted to see in the morning.

But not while his mom and Brenda were in the kitchen.

He did a shuffle-step so he stood in front of her. "Hey Babe, we, um, have company."

"Oh!" Taylor's voice was small, surprised, and not very awake.

They walked backwards, in tandem, to the bedroom. "Have my bathrobe, and my apologies."

She chuckled. "No, it's fine. You look as surprised as I am. Is this why the plans changed last night?"

"Yup." He kissed her, thankful, again, for her unflappable personality. The way she rolled with life no matter how awkward it could get. When you had gone through as much hard stuff as Taylor had, being seen in your underpants by two strangers wasn't all that big a deal. Apparently.

"They brought breakfast, at least."

"Great. I'm starving." She gave him a squeeze around the waist.

He considered locking his bedroom door and staying in for about half an hour, but his mom's laughter from the other room killed the mood.

"I think it's donuts, at least," he said.

"I love donuts." She kissed his cheek. The touch of her lips warming him from head to toe.

"TAYLOR, it's been a while. You're all grown up now." Brenda managed to say, "grown up," in a way that sounded "old." Brenda herself was easily in her sixties.

Taylor ran her hand through her hair. "It has been a few years. Good to see you."

Cheryl passed the box of donuts to Taylor. "You're busy with your little shop, I see."

"True. Always busy, but you understand the life. If I remember, don't you have a flower shop?"

Cheryl tipped her head back and laughed. "I remember the days, but I sold it. Got a wonderful deal. Money down and a percentage going forward. The only way to own a business, in my opinion."

"Don't listen to her, dear," Brenda said. "She's been insufferable since the sale. No one believed she could get seven figures for a flower shop."

"Location, location, location. It was next door to a funeral home."

"It was the web address, more than anything." Brenda smirked. "What was it, Flowershop.com? Something absurdly basic she picked up in the 1990s and just held on to."

"Sounds wise." Taylor poured herself a cup of coffee.

47

"At least she owns the place. Or do you?" Brenda lifted an eyebrow.

"We even own the building." Taylor spoke with pride that warmed Hudson's heart.

"You're just about there, aren't you, Hudsy?" Cheryl asked her son, but then turned immediately back to Taylor before he could answer. "His dream was to own a firm—custom dream homes. You know, the street of dreams style. He won't be building for other people forever." Cheryl looked up at the vaulted ceiling of his dramatic cabin. "This place is just a taste of what he can do."

Hudson popped some bread in the toaster but didn't respond. He and Taylor hadn't talked much about his dreams, or hers, for that matter. It was enough to handle the day to day of working as a contractor and doing his one-off handyman jobs. Between the two of them, they had plenty. Sure, he had wanted to build custom dream homes when he was younger. But it had been a long time since seeing his name "in lights" had been a motivation to him. In fact, as his mom droned on about his taste and style and what he was going to do someday, a ranch in Montana sounded even better than ever.

People in Montana quilted, didn't they?

Taylor could always sell out and open a new shop somewhere far from his mom.

"We don't want to bother you kids," Brenda said, standing. "Just dropping off goodies and saying hello. Since she's in town on a spree, I thought I'd take your mom to spend the day at Spirit Mountain."

Hudson didn't love the idea of his mom spending the day at the casino, but it was definitely better than her spending the day at his house.

"Win big, Mom." His smile was sincere. He really was glad she was leaving.

Taylor glanced at the clock on the microwave. "I'm off too.

YouTube doesn't film itself." She padded off toward the bedroom, a donut in one hand and coffee in the other.

Montana. A big truck, and Taylor. Plan B...or maybe not? He could see their life so clearly with the sun shining down on her golden head, warm and breezy in the summer, framed by heaps of white snow in the winter.

He wasn't sure where the love of Montana had come from. He'd been a couple of times for family vacations as a kid, but not recently.

Nonetheless, it stood out, especially this morning, as the ideal place to live. Forever.

ROXY AND TAYLOR managed to film a segment of the YouTube show dedicated to re-dying out-of-style fabrics. It was fun, messy, and made both of them laugh. She was relaxed and content. She'd been repeating it to herself over and over the last few days. But having Belle home made everything better. Want to investigate a mystery quilt? Belle will take care of Grandpa Ernie. Want to stay a little late at your boyfriend's house? Belle is there!

She had a feeling that Cheryl had been trying to put her in her place back at Hudson's. That she wanted Taylor to feel less than because she wasn't rich. But running a legacy business, three generations in the same family, made the idea of selling sound ridiculous to Taylor. She wouldn't let Hudson's mom get her down. Not now that Belle was home and everything was so much easier.

Hudson was great. Really good, through and through. But it had been fun being on the arm of a different man every weekend, too. And it would have been even more fun if she hadn't been worried about Grandpa Ernie and who was taking care of him most of the time.

But that was all silly. Her heart was giddy with feeling loved and secure. That was all. She didn't even mind the way Clay kept photobombing her shoot, or that she had splattered navy dye on her pink work polo. None of it mattered because Flour Sax, Belle, and Comfort, Oregon were the three most perfect things in the world.

Around eleven, when the shop opened, Sissy Dorney strode in.

"You're working with Lorraine over at the museum, aren't you?"

"I wouldn't call it working." Taylor was on her hands and knees scrubbing dye spots from the dusty rose indoor-outdoor carpet. She had only just noticed them and hoped to avoid stains.

"But you were consulted, correct?"

"Sort of, I guess. I'm not an expert, but we did talk about the mystery quilt and other ideas for the exhibition. What's wrong?" Taylor stood carefully, her knees wobbling a little after so long in a crouched position, and trying not spill her bowl of soapy water.

"I was reading Tansy's blog last night and she was making some absurd claims."

"About the quilt or something else?"

"The quilt," Sissy spit it out like Taylor was slow to understand.

Taylor flinched.

She took her bowl of soapy water to the back door. If Sissy wanted to snap at her, she could follow. She opened the door and dumped the water into her potted bamboo.

Sissy followed. "There's no way that thing's really two hundred years old, is there?"

"Could be. If so, it wasn't made in Oregon Territory. But even if Tansy claimed it was, what's so absurd about that?"

"She didn't claim it was. She claimed it was a case of insurance fraud. She thinks someone established the existence of this historic quilt by having it in your show, then attempted to lose it to claim insurance money."

"Why didn't they just keep it or destroy it? Is Tansy usually a conspiracy nut?"

"Who knows with Tansy. It's always something."

Taylor sat on the little camp chair that was always on her stoop. "What's the big deal?"

"There's no love lost between me and Tansy, or me and Lorraine, but I don't want to see you looking like a fool."

"That's sweet of you." Despite the accusatory tone of Sissy's concern, Taylor was touched. It was nice to have someone like Sissy looking out for you, even if it wasn't necessary.

Sissy walked down the steps and began to pace the back alley where all of the dumpsters were hidden. "I guess she's just mad at her mom and wants to make her mom look bad. Can't blame her, but that kind of advertising will be bad for your business, won't it?"

"I don't know. I guess it depends on what kind of audience Tansy has."

"Pfft," Sissy said. "Piddly. But that Shawna from the museum shared the link with her Twitter, and she has a million Twitter followers. They seem to share each other's stuff."

"What? How?"

"Don't know exactly, but Shawna blogs too. For a lot of different places, I guess, like online magazine's or something. Her biggest credit is The Atlantic."

"Impressive."

"That's what I'm afraid of. Who's going to take your shop seriously if you're tied up in a fraud case?" Sissy stopped in front of Taylor and crossed her arms.

"I guess it depends on if her audience quilts. People come here for the fabric and patterns more than anything else."

Sissy looked up at the back of the shop, a little disbelief in her eyes.

"It's not the season right now...."

Business was slower than it should have been, and the murder last month was probably to blame. Sissy was right. Fraud wouldn't help. Quilters were well-read people, and intelligent. Taylor stood. "I guess I should go talk to Lorraine. Want to come?"

"To talk to Lorraine?" Her lip curled in disgust. "No thanks."

They went back into the shop. Roxy and Clay were watching the old Laura Quinn Flour Sax YouTube shows on the little laptop where Taylor kept them running all day.

"It's about integrity." Laura smiled at the internet audience. "If the fibers are weak, the whole thing falls apart. But you can save it if you carefully unpick it and rebuild it from the inside out."

Sissy didn't seem to notice the sage life advice couched in sewing terms, but Taylor did.

It was about the internal strength of fabric, of course, but if you lost your good reputation—your integrity in business—was there really any way to rebuild it?

She sighed as she gathered up a jacket and her bag. A bad reputation would ruin any business, especially one that served a tight knit and discerning community.

CLAY WATCHED the scene between Sissy and Taylor with interest. Sissy was a no-nonsense woman who got things done, but she'd be a nightmare to live with. Taylor had been great to live with. The kind of woman who'd take care of you and not mind it. Never bossed him or nagged him. They'd been friends for ages before he'd become the unlucky victim of a heartless landlord. She'd rescued him the day he found himself homeless, but he knew he'd lucked into something good long before that night had turned their friendship to love.

He missed her a lot, sometimes. But mostly he was just glad they were friends now. She still had a way of taking care of him. Keeping him from homelessness. Introducing him to Roxy.

He prickled with pleasure at the thought. Roxy was up on the little pseudo hall in front of his apartment door, reviewing what they'd filmed.

She was something else.

He'd actually been shocked when she had taken him up on a cheeky proposition. He'd been bored and kidding around with her. She was wildly attractive, and he'd imagined taking her home with him plenty of times, but he had never expected her to take him up on it.

Talk about getting lucky.

It had started late summer when his upstairs apartment was far too hot to be thinking about sex. Taylor had been tied up planning for the Cascadia Quilt Expo. She didn't know her right from her left at the time, so it had been easy to sneak around unnoticed.

Apparently, Roxy's son Jonah and Taylor's sister Belle also thought so.

Which was the main flaw in his current situation.

It was one thing for his lover to be the young mom of a teenager, even if that teen was an internet star. It was an entirely different thing to be dating a grandma.

That was the risk, as he saw it. Two kids dumb enough to get hitched on a whim like those two were probably just dumb enough to get pregnant too. And if he was dating a grandma, that was as good as him being a grandpa.

He was not ready to be a grandpa.

He found he was doodling as his mind wandered and began to make a list. The best way to avoid early grandparenthood would be to make sure Jonah didn't become a dad. And the easiest way to do that, would be to....It was ugly, the idea forming in his mind, but good. If he could get Jonah to leave Belle, he'd have years before this was an issue again.

Having been an eighteen-year-old boy, himself, once, Clay thought it should be easy as anything to get Jonah to leave Belle. All he had to do was distract him with more pretty girls. And since Jonah had an actual fan club of young, pretty women, that should be simple.

Clay's list consisted entirely of ways to get Jonah's Juvie's to come to town. Online, Jonah might flirt, sure. But in person, a teenage boy was almost guaranteed to fall for temptation.

Black Friday, the biggest retail shopping day of the year, was just around the corner. If he could think of some way to bring the Juvies to town for Black Friday...

The light, limping steps of Roxy sounded on the stairs, and her curly mop of hair peeked around the corner. "Hey, you."

He slid the paper into the drawer, sure that Roxy wouldn't approve.

"Hey."

"You're blushing." Roxy dimpled at him. "I swear, you get cuter every day." She tousled his hair, then went around to the front of the shop to take over for Taylor.

Roxy. She was outstanding. Literally the cutest woman he'd ever been with.

If he could get Jonah to run off with one of his fans, this little fling he was having could easily become the great love of his life.

THE COMFORT FLOUR Mill Museum was closed, but the front doors were open, and Taylor found Lorraine at the desk that sold tour tickets.

"Good morning." Lorraine's voice was warm, but her eyes

were glued to a large reference type book spread open on the desk.

"Do you have a minute?" Taylor had that shy feeling kids get when they're interrupting grown-ups at work.

Lorraine looked up. She wore round, wire-rimmed reading glasses with an elegant, gold safety chain. She removed her glasses and let them fall gently against the downy white sweater she was wearing. "Was there something I could help you with?"

"I feel sort of silly bothering you with this."

Lorraine smiled with a closed mouth. She didn't offer platitudes about it being no bother.

"There's been some gossip about this quilt, and I'm concerned it might be bad for business."

"About the undocumented quilt's origins?"

"Tansy's been blogging about it. Could you possibly talk to her?"

"Are you requesting that I censor critical scholarship?"

Taylor flinched. She wasn't used to being spoken to in that tone. "I'm asking you to talk to your daughter about her libel."

Lorraine folded her hands. "What has she published that is libelous?"

"All of it. She's making it sound like we're stupid."

"Science thrives on rigorous peer review."

"What science?" Taylor knew this wasn't her best response, but she had that spinning feeling you get when someone is talking around a point and over your head at the same time. She understood Lorraine just fine, but she didn't trust she could pin her down. "Tansy's just a blogger making stuff up. Click bait."

"It is my personal policy not to interfere in Tansy's work."

Taylor hadn't talked to Sissy much about Tansy or about Lorraine, in fact, Lorraine hadn't come up once in the few years she and Sissy had been friends. It occurred to Taylor that Lorraine's policy might more broadly be not getting involved in her daughter's life at all.

"You know," Taylor's mood had shifted, instead of confusion or anger, she felt pity. "Not all of us have our mothers anymore. You ought to spend more time with Tansy while you still can."

"Ah. I see." Lorraine nodded. "It is easy to project your own situation onto ours, but there are no parallels. I'm sorry you are displeased with Tansy's writing. I personally found it very provocative and am even now doing further research on our piece so that our exhibit can provide the most information possible to guests."

Taylor leaned forward to look at the book. "Have you learned anything in our favor?"

"The truth is in everyone's favor, Taylor. If this quilt is, as Tansy reported, a fraud created for someone's personal gain, that too is a story. And if you consider the materials, a rather interesting story. Who had access to fabrics of that age? What would they have had to destroy in the creation of this piece? What had inspired this artist to create a tree of life? No, there's never any harm in knowledge." She set her glasses back on the end of her nose.

Taylor took a deep breath, readying herself to launch a defense of good business, just as soon as she could think of one.

Lorraine looked up again. "Shawna is currently out in the workroom preparing a few pieces that are on loan for the exhibit. Why don't you join her and give yourself a few moments to look over the quilt again?"

Taylor nodded. Even though she knew she was being passed off, it sounded like a good idea. "Thanks."

"Indeed."

THE DOOR TO THE METAL, shed-like outbuilding back behind the café was open. Taylor gave it a light knock, then let herself in.

The florescent lights seemed to buzz, and a cold wind circled through the space as though it had come in with Taylor and wanted out fast.

In the middle of the room, on the same table the quilt had been spread out on, lay Shawna Cross, the museum's faithful helper, with a pair of sharp silver Gingher sheers in her back.

THE CALL to the police and their arrival and the questions...it was all a blur. Familiar in a way it shouldn't have been for someone who ran a local quilt shop for a living.

It shouldn't have been so normal—seeing Maria and Serge, looking around for Reg. Having to be brave as she faced the sheriff himself.

The questions.

The statements.

Signing things.

Shawna, on the table, with a slick, dark red stain soaking through her winter fleece had shocked Taylor.

Her heart had leapt to her throat.

She had screamed, even.

But the racing adrenaline and the sore throat from screaming and the rest of it had been done before. There was a word for what she was feeling, and she searched her memory for it as she stood to the side, letting the professionals do their jobs.

She exhaled slowly, using the round breathing technique her counselor had taught her and contemplated the words that could describe this moment.

In control. That was one set of words. She didn't feel like the world was collapsing around her.

Secure. Another good one. As the familiar faces of the local sheriff's department did their job, Taylor felt safe. She'd known them to work their tails off in the past, not giving up till the killer was caught, arrested, and even convicted. From investigations to testimonies in court, these folks were good at what they did.

Confident.

Yes, that was the word that summed it up. She felt confident that they—she included herself in this—would get their killer.

And that was why her blood was pumping so fast.

She was ready to hunt for this killer. For the person who had done this to a young woman who had so much to look forward to.

When the coroner had seen Shawna's body taken away, Taylor led Lorraine back to that cozy little office with the makeshift tea station.

"We need the security of normal right now." Lorraine had allowed herself to be led, but back in her office, in her territory, she did the ritual of filling her kettle, letting it boil, and pouring the cups. She put a dash of something in hers, likely alcohol to calm her nerves, but Taylor didn't ask for any. Her mind felt sharp, her senses keen. She didn't want to lose any of that.

"Did you see anyone come onto the property?" Taylor asked from her seat in the hard, wooden chair.

Lorraine adjusted the tea bags, sorting them by color, or brand maybe. "I was fully engrossed in my studies. I hadn't seen anyone since Shawna arrived for her shift."

Lorraine's words were wispy, perhaps even slightly slurred. It made Taylor think of Grandpa Ernie after a recent, and particularly difficult stroke. Lorraine's hands trembled, but her face was calm. Maybe it was shock. Or maybe she'd had a tipple of something earlier in the day. But that wasn't fair. Lorraine was in shock, surely, and as she was a new acquaintance, Taylor had no idea what that looked like in her.

"Had Shawna mentioned anyone coming by to see her?"

"No, she had her work to do and I had mine. Ships passing and all of that. I'll have to call Tansy." Lorraine patted her pockets, then looked around the room. "I believe I left my mobile on the front desk. Will you excuse me?" She glanced from wall to wall. "It's midday now, isn't it? I ought to call my daughter. No, the officers said this is a crime scene, we should vacate."

Taylor stood. "Of course."

Lorraine took a sip of her tea and then put it on the counter. She opened the exit door and shut it as soon as Taylor had walked out.

Lorraine was in shock. It would be good for her to spend some time with her daughter, but it would be a shock for Tansy as well, since she and Shawna were friends.

Taylor needed to get back to her store, but on the way, she called Sissy. "What?" Sissy sounded like she didn't have time to mess around.

"Thought you'd want to know, there's been a murder."

The words that poured out of Sissy on the other end of the call weren't the kind Taylor would have said to her Grandma Quinny, that was for sure. The breathless stream of invective was both creative and loud. Taylor thought she spotted some lines from Hamilton but couldn't be sure. "Feel better?" she asked when Sissy went quiet.

"No." Sissy was panting.

"Do you want the details?" Taylor tried to sound serious. This was murder after all.

"Yes."

"It was Tansy's friend Shawna. Scissors in the back. She was flung over the table in her workshop." Taylor felt remarkably distant from this one, possibly because murder was so common place in her town now.

"Sheers?"

"Yeah, fabric sheers, Ginghers. I saw them myself."

"Good. They won't think it was me or one of my stylists." Sissy sounded relieved.

"Should they?"

Sissy started in again, but Taylor stopped her. "I guess you don't have any clients in the salon right now?"

"I'm at the gym."

Comfort didn't have a gym.

"I'm glad you're taking care of yourself. But I think you need to try something more...I don't know...maybe...kickboxing? Have you tried that?" Taylor was on blue tooth as she drove a sedate twenty-five miles an hour down to her shop. She would have much rather been walking. "But really, why such a strong reaction? Tell me more about what you're feeling, if you can put it into um...different words." Sissy's tantrum had tickled Taylor. She wanted to get to the root of it but had to tease her just a little."

"How many murders, Taylor, does it take to kill a small town? Two? Three? We're on five in just a couple of years. No one's going to come out here for a little getaway."

"No, but they might stop by for quilt fabric and discount cheese and to get their hair done." Taylor tried to sound cheerful.

"That won't help the new hotel, will it?"

Taylor pulled into her parking spot behind the shop and turned off her car. "The what?"

"Hudson hasn't told you?"

"What new hotel?" Taylor pressed.

"Just a little something some of us local business owners have invested in. I cannot believe you aren't in on it, or that Hudson hasn't..."

"Is he building it?" Taylor had a hard time getting the question out.

"Yes."

"Is he going to, um, run it?" Taylor's gut was in a knot. She'd just found a murder victim. It made sense to feel a little sick. She couldn't be feeling like this just because Hudson hadn't told her his big plans.

"You'd better call your boyfriend. It sounds like he has some things to explain to you. In the meantime, I have some calls to make."

Taylor was certain these calls weren't calls of sympathy to Shawna's family.

CHAPTER SIX

aylor went to the shop first and confirmed that Roxy and Clay were still alive. Not that she thought they were at risk, but it felt good to see them, even if they were sneaking a kiss when she found them.

The store was empty, but they were technically engaged with moving some seasonal fabrics around to make a fresh display. Action was good. Kept a staff feeling productive and hopeful. New displays created content for Instagram and Facebook, which was basically free advertising. She caught Roxy's eye, gave a quick thumbs up, and left.

She needed to check Grandpa Ernie. Sure, she had no reason to think whoever had killed Shawna Cross, blogger, museum volunteer, and would be podcaster, would even know about her grandfather, but like a mother-hen, she wanted to make sure everyone who lived in her nest was safe. She ran the few blocks, because she could and because she needed it and because the burning in her chest felt right. She was beginning to think this calm, in-control feeling, plus the desire to make sure everyone she loved was still alive, was her own shock at play, and she didn't want to be in shock.

She panted as she stepped out of the cold, hard air into her home—cozier than she had expected. A faux electric fireplace sat in the real, unused fireplace, letting off a warm glow as well as soft, warm air; a concession to Grandpa Ernie's oxygen tank.

Jonah and Grandpa Ernie sat at a card table in front of it, with a chess board. She glanced under the card table, to see that the coffee table was where it was supposed to be, just tucked under and at a funny angle to accommodate the legs of the chess players.

"You ought to be at work, young lady." Grandpa Ernie didn't look up from his chess board. He wore his oxygen, and though concentrating intensely on his activity, he seemed alert, cheeks a healthy pink, hands hardly shaking.

"Just coming by to say hi." She chewed her lip. She didn't want to say the word murder in this safe, cozy place.

Jonah made a silent move with a pawn.

She'd never learned to play chess but had fuzzy memories of Grandpa Ernie and her dad playing together, in front of a real fire. But in a different house. In another life.

She felt out of place in the homely scene, the chess players registering her presence but returning immediately to their duel. "Is Belle around?" Taylor broke the silence again.

"She's off with the Realtor looking at a place."

"You didn't want to see it?"

Grandpa Ernie moved his knight but didn't look happy.

Jonah stared at the board. "I don't really care, you know?"

She did not know. Well, she did know that Jonah was young, only eighteen. Married in a rush during a crisis, and playing chess instead of say, finishing high school, but she could not understand buying a home without seeing it.

"But you're going to live there." Though she was relieved to see they were alive, she was confounded by the boy's disinterest in his future.

"I'll live a lot of places in life, I hope." He stared at the board with eyes narrowed in concentration. "Plus, this is a business, not a home."

"Excuse me?"

"Google content house." He moved another pawn. "Ha!"

Grandpa stared at the boy, then made a move that captured the pawn.

Jonah slouched back into his chair with his arms crossed. "I used to be good at this."

TAYLOR DIDN'T Google content house, but later that evening when the whole family was home, Jonah was in the mood to explain his plans for a house full of young, rich social-media influencers.

"Can't trust a house full of teenagers." Grandpa Ernie frowned over his reading glasses at his new grandson.

"It's not going to be a house full of teenagers." Jonah smiled with his whole body, like his mom. His curly hair stood out around his head as he raked his hands through, frequently. He paced the room, a bundle of nervous, excited energy spilling out of him as he spoke.

It seemed like Grandpa Ernie was trying to wind the kid up. Something about the twinkle in Grandpa's eyes. "You're a teenager."

Jonah laughed, loudly. "Yes, yes I'm a teenager. But Belle's almost twenty, and I couldn't have anyone living in the house that's not eighteen. We don't want that kind of liability. Besides there's plenty of creative energy left in people who are twenty. Twenty-one, even."

Taylor choked on her coffee. If Jonah thought twenty-one was on the outside end of potential creative enthusiasm, he must have thought she was ready for the retirement home.

Belle's eyes had a twinkle just like Grandpa Ernie's. She seemed to know he was just teasing Jonah up, but didn't mind.

"It's not all that different from a dorm or a boarding school. Which is why," she lifted one eyebrow, "it's a good business idea. We charge for more than mere rent, and the people qualified to live in the house will have a steady stream of high-income. Jonah's far from the only influencer millionaire out there."

Grandpa's frown deepened and the sparkle almost died out of his eyes. A millionaire to a man old enough to have served in Korea was a big deal.

Belle continued, "To be honest, we won't require a million a year in influencer revenue or anything like that. If someone is really creative, we'll absolutely let them in, even if they only make half a million."

This time Grandpa choked on his tea.

"What do the Juvies think of your idea?" Taylor asked.

Jonah's brow darkened.

Belle coughed softly.

"Did I just step in something?" Taylor asked.

Jonah shook his head fairly violently and responded with enthusiasm. "You didn't step in anything. We're still trying to figure out what kind of role the Juvies will play in this. Obviously, we can't invite them to live with us unless they're influencers themselves." He looked over at his new, young wife, his eyes pleading with her for permission, maybe. "And you know that some of them are qualified."

Belle's smile lost a little of its sparkle. "Yes, dear."

"I told you this was a terrible idea. If I were you, Belle, I wouldn't let any teenage girls live in the house with my husband."

Taylor stifled a laugh. There was something about the way her deep-voiced, shaggy-dog of a grandfather said "my husband" that was hilarious.

"We won't do anything foolish, Gramps." Belle's face crumpled in suppressed laughter. "We just have details to work out, not problems."

"Easy details, Gramps. Easy details," Jonah agreed. "It'll come together so fast, and it'll totally be worth it, and we won't regret turning down the Nike money." His jaw twitched. Taylor had a strong feeling that he already regretted turning it down.

Taylor's phone rang in a very timely manner—after only about fifteen seconds of awkward silence between the newly-weds. She apologized and took her call up to her bedroom. After all, it was Hudson and she would much rather talk to him alone.

"Hey babe." Hudson's voice was warm and sexy. "What do you think of Montana?"

"It's got a big sky?" Taylor flopped onto her bed, happy to escape reality for a moment.

Hudson responded with a hearty chuckle. "That it does. We're about ready for a vacation, aren't we? Maybe not right now. It's pretty snowy and not going to get less snow anytime soon, but how about we head up to Montana this spring?"

"Mmmm. Mountains." Taylor savored the idea of a sunny vacation under the Big Sky in the snowy mountains of Montana. Nothing wrong with a vacation like that.

"Fantastic. I have a friend out there who has a business proposition for me. If you don't mind a working vacation."

"I don't mind a working vacation." Taylor found herself saying something she didn't mean. What kind of working vacation can a contractor have? His work was physical—long, hard days. He'd hardly be up for a hike in the woods or skiing or whatever else it was you did on vacation in Montana.

"I've got another business prospect going." He sounded less sure of himself now. "I've been waiting for some details to sort themselves out before I brought it up, but we've got a lot of green lights."

She braced herself. She didn't like this idea of him having big business secrets from her. It wasn't that she felt like she needed to know all of the details of his work life, but this thing where everyone else in town knew about his life and she didn't felt wrong.

"Bible Creek Care Home isn't reopening," Hudson said after a moment. "And a few of us in town don't like the idea of it being empty."

She still didn't respond.

"Do you know Simon Reuben?"

"Sure." Simon was the eldest of the Reubens in a town that had always had a lot of Reubens.

"He worked out a seller contract with SecureCare, you know the company that owned the property. He wants to redevelop it. It'll be a pretty big job for me. I'll be working on it all winter."

"That's pretty cool." Taylor felt a little better. Him redeveloping a property wasn't the same kind of secret as him owning a hotel. Gossip had a way of making things sound much worse than reality.

"Simon Reuben is buying the property, and a few of us guys are redeveloping it and planning to run it. Just got a finance guy to run the business side. In fact, it's your old buddy John Hancock."

Did she sense a little teasing in his tone? John Hancock was her buddy in that they used to casually date. She'd really liked John but hadn't seen much of him since he had started dating Tatiana, the math genius.

"Anyway, I'm going to be the construction manager on the building project. We've got some hospitality people involved. When it's up and running some of our roles will change, but we're all investing equally, or as equally as we can make it work." He was sounding flustered, perhaps because of the dead silence on the other end of the phone.

It wasn't just a hotel he was building. This was something

bigger. Something complicated. And she had been in the dark while he had been dreaming and planning the project. She wasn't rewarding his confidences with soft murmurs of interest. She was just listening in silence and feeling a little sick.

"Most of the residents of Bible Creek Care Home found housing elsewhere after the troubles well, you know, the murder and the explosion and the fire and all of that. But there are enough people in temporary living situations like Grandpa Boggy that we know the senior apartments will be welcomed back. That will be half the building. No nursing care this time. No memory wing. Those are great and all, but we decided we were too far from emergency care. The other, perhaps, half is going to be a hotel."

"What does Comfort need a hotel for?" Taylor's voice was brittle. She regretted the tone, but on the other hand, it was a good question. It wasn't like there was more to do here then you could accomplish in an afternoon.

"You're in luck." He sounded relieved. "We had to answer that one in our business plan. The first group of people we figure will stay in a hotel are friends and family of our residents. All of these apartments will be one bedroom and one bath. The hotel side of the campus gives guests a place to stay. And there will be enough rent built in, that guests of residents can have a hotel discount."

"Giving discounts before it's even built?" Again, she sounded snide. She sat up in hopes that better body posture would help her hide her attitude problem.

"Just listen for a second. I'm almost done." Hudson's voice wasn't sexy anymore. "There are things to do here. We're not far from the casino. You quilters have been working your tails off for years to turn this into a destination town. Then there's the vineyards and wineries. And it's not like we're building a three-hundred room hotel or anything."

"Once you build it, you're done?"

"Not exactly, but we don't have to talk about those details now." He sounded frustrated and disappointed.

She couldn't blame him. That's how she felt too. She wouldn't push him for the details now. She'd wait until she felt less of whatever the horrible word was that described how she felt. Left out? Yeah that was probably it. She felt terribly left out. "Sorry." She slumped back down into her pillows again. Good posture wasn't enough to make her sound happy right now. "Someone mentioned this to me earlier and I guess I was, well... okay..." she took a deep breath. "I'm feeling petty because you didn't tell me sooner. Other people already knew about it. I don't understand why this isn't the kind of thing you'd have wanted to talk to me about just because. Sissy even seemed annoyed I hadn't invested. Why wasn't I asked to invest? Never mind." She took a deep breath. "We should probably talk about this some other time."

He sighed, possibly in relief. "Okay. We'll talk about it later. But the only reason you don't know about it was because you were completely tied up in getting that quilt expo to town. You know you didn't have a minute for anything else while you were planning that, right?"

She blushed, even though she couldn't see him. The expo had been huge. Or was supposed to have been. It was supposed to have been the thing that turned their little town into a destination.

The kind that might need a hotel.

Crap.

He probably had some kind of point.

"Montana sounds fun." She tried to say it with a smile.

"It sure does."

They ended the call, neither of them satisfied. But as Taylor began to Google Shawna Cross so that she could turn her mind to murder instead of the more troubling relationship problems, she tried to remind herself that in good, even great, relationships, not every conversation will be a perfect conversation.

※

BACK AT THE shop the next day, Taylor found things were under control. The newest stock had been put out. The newest sale had been advertised. But the customers were probably not coming.

The cold, hard day outside looked like a perfect day for shopping to Taylor, but she had to admit that any day seemed perfect for a day of shopping. Wishing the rest of her town felt the same, she paced the store, fronting shelves, straightening things on hooks that didn't need straightening, bustling about tidying things that didn't need to be tidied. She was in the way, and she felt it.

She started to pull open the drawers of the desk in her makeshift office under the stairs, ready to empty it all out and straighten it, when Clay hollered at her from the cash register. "Taylor what on Earth? Didn't someone just die in this town?"

"What? I'm sorry, what do you mean?" Taylor, though mentally invested in the case, wasn't ready to admit that to her ex.

"You are a brilliant and wonderful woman and you own this store." His words were as sweet and sincere as saccharine. "I appreciate and value the kind of hands-on leadership you offer us. But this place is empty. There is nothing to clean. I've got the cash register, and Roxy has the sit-on-a-chair and wait-for-someone-to-come spot. Why don't you go out and solve that murder?"

Taylor laughed nervously and flipped through the papers in the top drawer. "I can't just interfere in a random murder investigation."

Clay narrowed his eyes and tilted his head. "You can't make me believe you aren't already working on this case."

"I mean, I plan to help as much as I can. Anybody would, I'm sure." Taylor crumbled the edge of a piece of notebook paper covered in pencil.

"Head up to my apartment," Clay directed, "and do some of that online research you like so much. Hasn't that been hugely helpful in the past?"

Clay's words needled her. She knew she fully intended on nosing her way into the crime, but she didn't want the whole town to know about it.

She looked around her store, so beautiful, tidy, and empty.

Roxy was sitting on the stool at the worktable reading a quilter's magazine. Clay was at the register playing on his phone, probably a little electronic billiards.

"Okay. I will. You don't mind me hanging out in your place?"

"If it gets you out of my hair, I don't mind at all."

She rolled her eyes and decided not to go upstairs. Instead she headed to the classroom space where their little coffee station and Grandpa Ernie's old threadbare corduroy recliner reigned supreme. She helped herself to a stick of soft caramel and settled into the worn and comfortably familiar chair with her laptop.

Shawna had been killed at the museum. If the murder was quilt related, maybe it had something to do with her blog. She opened it up and dug right in, reading everything she could find by both Shawna Cross and her friend Tansy Dorney.

When Taylor found the post where Tansy mentioned her little sister Pyper—Sissy Dorney's daughter—she knew she was almost there. Though she agreed that Tansy hadn't painted Pyper as the sharpest crayon in the box, she thought the story of the two of them at a pub quiz night was both charming and well-written. She didn't see any reason for Sissy to go screaming at Lorraine about it. But it shouldn't have come as a surprise that the mother and stepmother had contention between them.

The next few blogs were a different story, and after reading, Taylor had some questions for Tansy.

❀

TANSY WAS willing to meet Taylor, but only at her mom's office at the museum.

Taylor wasn't excited about having Lorraine there as a witness. She suspected it would be difficult to get Tansy to be truly open while her mom was listening.

With all three women in Lorraine's small office, the room seemed to close in around Taylor. The hard, wooden chairs looked harder and the comforting antiques felt shabby.

Taylor stood at the hutch hoping that her casual posture would put everyone at ease, but Lorraine and Tansy sat stiffly across from each other with the large desk between them, their straight spines and lifted chins a mirror of each other.

"I'm so glad you could get together this afternoon," Taylor said. "Things are really slow at Flour Sax, so I spent some time reading your blog." She smiled big, hoping it reflected in her eyes. She wanted to take a sip of her tea, but her hand was shaking. Loraine was so intelligent that it was hard for Taylor not to suspect she thought everyone else was a fool. "I thought about texting, but it seemed like this could use a real conversation, you know?" Taylor invited them to engage with her by making eye contact and nodding.

Tansy tilted her head to the side. Her face was softer than Lorraine's and not just because she was younger. She had the same snub nose and round cheeks of her half-sisters and brother. A Dorney trait. And her eyes were kind.

"Like I said, I was reading your blog. I noticed you were very supportive of Shawna's work. Lots of comments back and forth on each other's posts, lots of ping backs, and pins and things." Though a decade ago blogging had made many writers famous, Taylor wasn't that familiar with it. It had sort of gone out of style.

Tansy sniffled. "I'm sorry." She dabbed at her nose with a tissue. "I just...I can't believe she's gone."

Taylor inhaled slowly, held her breath for a second and then let it out. Grief was rough, and she was just now to a place where she could sit with someone in their loss without being overwhelmed, herself. "I understand your pain. You know I lost my mom not long ago."

Tansy nodded. "But you wanted to ask about our blogging."

"There's no rush. I appreciate that you are willing to even try to talk right now." A hint of guilt twisted at Taylor's heart. She hadn't come here to sympathize and didn't feel like a nice person for where she wanted to take the conversation. "You and Shawna had a couple of blogs that got a lot of attention last year. You had tons of comments, but not all good, if you know what I mean."

"Oh, I know what you mean. We had some trolls. And then it seemed like there was a whole troll farm attacking us." Tansy folded her tissue in her hand. Her face was pulled with sadness, but she was speaking clearly and working to keep herself in control.

"That's what it looked like to me too. The blog that got you the most negative feedback was about plagiarism, specifically against a children's book author."

"Not exactly," Tansy said. "The book we wrote about had stolen art, therefore a copyright issue, but not plagiarism. It was a self-published book, and I'm not sure the author knew the law regarding the rights to the artwork."

"Yes, that's right. Thank you for reminding me. I noticed that a lot of the comments talked about how you guys were picking on someone too little to fight back."

Tansy's eyes fluttered as though holding back tears. "As though we would ever do that."

"And then Shawna's blog had comments from some of the same negative..."

"The same trolls, yes," Tansy interrupted. "Her blog was about designs that had been stolen from an artist and used on t-shirts and a few other of those kinds of products. But the company that stole them was a pretty big fabric company, and so it wasn't a case of the little man getting picked on."

"But the trolls were still awful, weren't they?" Taylor asked.

"It was pretty rough." Tansy glanced at her mom, who gave her a small nod of concern.

"Shawna wrote her artist copyright blog first, right?"

"Yes, that post was a few months before the children's book."

"But even with all the negative feedback, her blog about the art theft was what got Shawna in the eye of Huffington Post, which was the first of her publishing credits, right?"

"Yes, but what does that have to do with me?" Tansy's chin quivered. Her mom reached a hand toward her, and though it should have been a reassuring type of motion, it looked stiff.

Taylor paused. She knew what she wanted to ask, but she was having a hard time working up to it. In the comfort of Grandpa Ernie's recliner, it seemed the work of a moment to ask Tansy if she was envious of Shawna's success. But staring at the sad woman before her in the tiny, shabby office, it wasn't coming out. "I'm not sure if you knew that I've been kind of helpful recently at solving other murders."

Tansy merely nodded.

"Those internet trolls were so angry about the posts that made Shawna famous. I just wondered if something one of you wrote about this mystery quilt might have sent a troll over the edge."

Tansy closed her eyes.

"Taylor, I understand how finding the body must have

affected you deeply," Lorraine's quivery voice interrupted. "But I think what you're doing right now is only going to harm you and my daughter in the long run." She glanced down at her arm, and clenched and unclenched her small, pale hand. "Think carefully before you do anything that could end with either of you getting hurt."

The already stiff form of Tansy seemed to tighten. Her chin lifted and the lines of her mouth firmed. "I'd be happy to look into these trolls with you. I would do anything to help catch the person who did this to my friend."

"Thank you. I don't want to rush you but let me just ask this one thing. On your recent blog about the mystery quilt, several of the comments read as though they could have been written by some of the trolls from last year. Do you think that's true?"

"They've been hounding us for ages. Which comments were you most concerned about?"

This was Taylor's best chance to carefully make her point. Not that Tansy would admit to professional jealousy, but she was hungry to see the blogger's reaction to the idea. "Give me just a moment..." She took out her phone, found the blog, and scrolled to the comments. "This one read like so many of the others. Let me know what you think." Taylor read aloud the three-paragraph missive that ended with, "You're just doing this because you're jealous. You can't make anything great yourself, so you have to take everyone else down." Though it didn't accuse Tansy of being jealous of Shawna, it got to the heart of that as a motive.

"Oh, that one. I hate it so much. How dare he say I can't create anything myself on a blog I created from scratch? You know I've been blogging since 2009?"

Taylor did some quick math. Tansy would have still been in Middle School back then.

"I just hate it when people try to destroy original work..." Tansy's face shifted from one of anger to that light that shines when you've had a brilliant idea. "I think that troll was doing exactly what he accused me of. He's envious of what I've created with my blog. Sure, I'm not getting book deals, or influencer famous for my writing. But I have a steady audience, a steady back list of posts, and enough traffic every day that the blog pays for itself. I bet that troll is a failed writer."

"I wonder how hard it would be to figure out exactly which failed writer he is..." Taylor mused. She didn't think an internet jerk had really murdered Shawna, but she wanted to keep an open channel of communication between herself and Tansy. Envy had caused people to kill before. Even people who had seemed like friends.

"Someone who has more knowledge of how things work behind the screen might be able to, but that's not me." Tansy stared at the ceiling. "Shawna's Owen would have been good for that."

"A friend of hers?" Taylor asked.

"Her boyfriend. It was always a little rocky, but the saddest part is they were off just now. I knew they'd get back together, they always did. They'd been on and off together longer than me and Logan. I wonder if Logan would call Owen for me and ask?"

"Has anyone spoken to Owen about Shawna's death?" Taylor's pulse quickened. She'd love to talk to the on-and-off-again boyfriend. Murder was usually someone close, after all. If not professional jealousy from Tansy, then an ex was a great bet.

"I'm sure the sheriff has, but that's so cold. Someone who cares should talk to him, make sure he's okay. He was really upset about the new guy she was seeing."

Taylor nodded assent. "I'd be happy to talk to him, if you'd like."

Tansy pulled her phone out. "Let me text you his number. Someone should talk to him, and maybe..." She swallowed her emotions. "Maybe speaking to him would help you both." She cast a glance at the upright form of her mother.

"Thanks. I should probably let you all go. I appreciate you speaking with me."

"Be careful. Murder isn't a game." Lorraine stood and went to the door. The interview was over.

TAYLOR WAS JUST WISHING she had parked closer to the office when Tansy hailed her. She paused till the girl reached her.

"Thank you for meeting me at the office with Mom," Tansy said panting for breath. "I got away as quickly as I could. You might know Mom and I haven't been close lately."

"I don't know much of anything."

They stood in the shade of a bare oak tree and the cold winter wind whipped through Taylor's jacket. Tansy stamped her feet a few times as though trying to stay warm, so they began to walk again. Taylor's car was around the corner, by the front gate. She couldn't have told you why she'd parked so far, but it probably had to do with wanting to be near an exit. She still had troubles with the idea of being trapped.

"I wanted to talk to you with my mom there so I could see how she reacted to the conversation." Tansy blew onto her fingers. "It's not that I think she's capable of murder. At least not when she's sober."

"Go on." Taylor unlocked the car, but didn't rush getting in. This was already going in an unexpected direction.

"But I don't think she's been sober. And I think she's the only one who had both access and motive."

"Let's get in the car." Taylor glanced over at the museum. "It's warmer and private."

They both got in, and Taylor started it hoping it would warm up fast.

Tansy buckled up, but she sat as stiffly as she had in the

office, almost not touching the back of the seat. "It seems absurd to me to kill over an old blanket."

Taylor cringed. If anything deserved the honor of being called the quilt it was that historic piece, even if it didn't turn out to be as old as everyone hoped it was.

"But my mom's level of investment in this quilt being old is absurd. Just absurd enough that I think she might have been willing to kill for it."

"Let's go somewhere we can talk and not freeze to death." Taylor crossed her own house off the list as Grandpa Ernie, Jonah, and Belle would all be there. Flour Sax would obviously be public, as would any place they could eat. She'd have to take Clay up on his offer of his digs after all.

"Okay." It was a quick drive down Main Street and Taylor was almost too excited about getting Tansy alone to notice the line of cars near her shop. Almost.

Thankful the sunny day had brought out the shoppers despite the cold, she pulled her car around the corner of Love Street and parked about a block away.

Tansy was thin-lipped and nervous as they walked to the back door of Flour Sax. "It's not that I want Mom to be guilty," she began to apologize for her fears, but Clay was waiting for them at the back step and interrupted.

"Go. Go anywhere but here." His voice was low, but he waved his hands dramatically. "The place is full of press and they all have questions for you."

CHAPTER SEVEN

*T*he look on Clay's face froze Taylor.

Her heart leapt to her throat and her instinct said "run!"

She grabbed Tansy's hand and dragged her back to the car, but when she got there, two men stood at the driver's side door.

A tall lanky man in khakis holding his phone out offered a friendly half-smile. The other, a shorter, older man looked irritated, and maybe a little dyspeptic.

Tansy squeezed her hand and they kept going.

The men at her car didn't look like scary people, but at the pace her heart was going, she couldn't stop. When they arrived at Taylor's little house, she glanced back once and saw the men conferring with each other.

She suspected they were going to follow, but they could still see her, and didn't hustle. At her front door she hesitated. There were too many cars. Jonah's, Belle's, and one she didn't recognize.

"Come on," she dragged Tansy around to her back shed.

The small lawn needed to be mowed and the bushes were

overgrown. She didn't want to notice it, but at the same time, it all seemed so glaringly unkempt, and she was ashamed.

She wrenched open the door to the shed and shoved Tansy inside, pulling the door shut with a click behind her. It was a great big shed that some previous owner had electrified to use as a workshop. She flipped the switch and leaned against the closed door. There was very little room to stand as it held almost all of the things that had furnished her life in Portland.

Cardboard boxes were stacked on her old couch, the armchairs that matched, a couple of dressers, and the vintage aluminum dining set she had been so excited to find at the antique mall. Tansy sat nervously on the arm of the sofa and leaned her head back on the Ikea dresser Taylor used to share with Clay.

"Who was that?" she asked.

"Reporters, I guess." Taylor was surprised to find she needed to catch her breath. "I feel ridiculous. I'm so sorry for making you run and for dragging you in here."

Tansy laughed softly. "I ran too," she said. "When a friend's been murdered the way Shawna was, everything is shaded with danger."

"You wanted to tell me something about your mom, and I didn't want to take you in the house. There were too many cars out front. But we're alone in here." She looked around the space that barely held the two of them. The only other people in the shed were the painting of two dancers in the rain, but they weren't paying attention.

"Mom hasn't been well for a lot of years," Tansy said. "Her drinking is what broke her marriage up, even though she blames Sissy." Tansy rolled her eyes, as though the idea were absurd.

Taylor cringed inside. Sissy was her friend, but she kind of knew what Tansy was implying. Sissy, with her brash, bossy manner wasn't the kind of woman men left their wives for.

"But murder...it takes a pretty strong motive to kill some-one, don't you think?" Taylor rubbed her thumbs together, trying to find a self-soothing action to lower her heart rate.

"It would, but I was thinking about...and I'm sorry to bring it up...but the situation with your mom. I read a lot about it. Didn't the murderer do it because she was envious of your mom, on behalf of her daughter? Something like that?"

Taylor sucked in her breath. It was true, the woman who had killed her mom had done it because she was jealous for her daughter's sake. "How common could that be? Aren't most murders about sex or money?"

"This quilt, though it seems so insignificant to people like us, could be really important to someone like my mom. It wouldn't be about money. Not the kind of money you'd kill for. And it certainly wouldn't be something even I would recognize as fame, but it would equal her name in history books. Publishing credits. An opportunity to rehabilitate her professional reputa-tion, which isn't very good right now. She tried moving across the country for work, but she couldn't keep it together in that job, either."

"Knowing how much it meant to your mom, why did you write that it was a fraud?" Taylor asked.

"This is going to sound awful and I'm sorry for it in a lot of ways, but when there's an alcoholic in your family, or really anyone with an addiction, you set boundaries around yourself. Draw a line between things they can and can't interfere with. Would I drive my mom to the hospital if she'd been in an acci-dent? Absolutely. But will I let her dictate my career or my rela-tionships? No. It's too easy for someone with issues like that to drag everything else around them down. When I saw what Shawna was writing, I shared it. I have some notes of my own I was going to pursue along the same lines, but Shawna didn't mind. She didn't think I was stealing her ideas. We were almost working together on it." Tansy grew wistful. "We probably would have, eventually. She's been my best friend for a long time, and she always offers to launch my career." She paused. "It's so hard to talk about her in past tense. She'd been offering to launch my career for ages, and maybe she could have. I know she's not famous yet, but she was on her way. And I could have maybe been the Gail to her Oprah." She sighed and closed her eyes. The pause was long enough for Taylor to take a turn, but she didn't. "I just didn't want to ride anyone's coattails. Even my best friend's. Would you?"

"No, I wouldn't." The only parallel Taylor could think of was how her YouTube videos were nowhere near as popular as her mom's had been. And how her use of her mom's platform had done so much less for her than it had done for her new brother-in-law.

Like Tansy, she wanted to get by with her own skills. To make it on her own knowledge and expertise. She had never wanted to ride someone else's success. "No," she repeated. "I wouldn't have wanted that. I completely understand."

"She and I were both working the quilt story, but we had our own angles. As soon as Carly started posting in quilters groups, we were on it. There just seemed to be something special about this quilt. But after speaking to my mom, I began to worry."

"And the worry was that your mother might have killed Shawna because of the blog—possibly for her own academic interests, or possibly to further your career." Mother as a killer was a painful image, and Taylor hated that Tansy was wrestling with this fear.

"When you say it out loud, it doesn't seem right." Tansy's eyes narrowed and her mouth scrunched in frustration. "But when I think of my mom, and I think of the other damage she has done, and I think of how she is when she's been drinking, it also doesn't seem wrong." Her shoulders slumped.

"I'm sorry for making you run. I'm sorry for dragging you all the way back here," Taylor said. "Let me drive you back to the

museum so you can grab your car. And let's keep in touch."
Taylor pushed the door open and it bounced off of something.
She looked down and saw a pair of black Chuck Taylor high-
tops. She looked up and saw the smiling face of the tall reporter
who had been waiting at her car.

"Taylor Quinn." His voice was lower than it ought to have
been.

Taylor found herself looking up from under her eyelids at
him, but shook herself out of it. "Who's asking?"

"Graham Dawson. *Oregonlive.com.*"

He handed her a card—a funny analog introduction to a
digital news site. And it was odd to hear him say he worked for
Oregonlive.com and not *The Oregonian*, the aged and respected
state newspaper that ran the website.

"Can I buy you a coffee?" Graham's casual body language
and friendly smile shouldn't have made her shiver, but they did.
Behind that crooked half-smile and floppy hair was something
that pulled at her. Something that made her want to invite him
in and tell him everything.

"Sorry," Taylor said. "I was just on my way out."

He peered into the shed and nodded at Tansy. "Nice to meet
you."

Tansy said a small hello in response.

He walked with them all the way back to the car. The silence
was palpable. Or maybe it was Graham and the vibes he was
giving off. He loped along beside them with long strides, hands
in his pockets, not pressing them for anything.

And yet Taylor felt in her bones he was going to change her
life.

She didn't want it to change.

At her car, he stopped just to the side of the driver's door.

"I'm not in town for long. I'd really like a chance to talk to
you for the newspaper. You've got to know you're a pretty
newsworthy name in our little state right now."

She shook her head, only half wishing he'd go away. "I don't know what you're talking about."

"Amateur detectives aren't as common as the bookshelves would make you think, and this little town has a pretty good one." He lifted one eyebrow, and her heart seemed to stop.

Panic. What she was feeling must be panic. Nothing else made sense.

The short, round man that had been at the car earlier came sneaking around the corner. "Hi there."

"Come on," Graham said under his breath. "Help me out here."

A woman in a boxy red blazer and jeans with stylish holes in the knees bounded towards them from the other side of Love Street. "Taylor Quinn, do you have a minute?" she asked.

"Move," Taylor hissed to Graham.

"Not till you promise to only talk to me." He had leaned close, and she could feel his breath and smell the mint of his toothpaste.

"Get out of my way or I'll call the police."

He crossed his arms and leaned on the door to the backseat.

"I'm not kidding." Taylor's jaw hurt from suppressing the smile that kept trying to erupt. This wasn't funny. Or it shouldn't have been.

"You don't have a phone on you."

"I do too." Taylor pressed the pockets of her jeans looking for her phone.

"I'm already calling." Tansy was on the other side of the car but held her phone out.

"Please?" Graham shifted to the side.

Taylor hit the alarm button on her car fob, sending the electronic wail through the air.

The short reporter slumped away.

The woman skidded to a stop on the sidewalk.

Graham didn't touch her, but he seemed so close. He wasn't

technically in her way, but she found she couldn't move, either nearer or farther from him. "I'm going to be at Loggers tonight; I'll have a booth to myself, and I'd really like to talk to you." He invited her with that crooked, half smile she was finding so hard to ignore.

Taylor inched the door open and squeezed herself in. Then she leaned her head out. "Physically blocking my access to escape is assault, and next time you do it, I'll file charges." Her heart was racing, but not from panic. She hadn't meant a word of that threat.

Tansy was waiting for her in the passenger seat.

Taylor backed out carefully knowing that if she hit a reporter with her car, she'd be in serious trouble. But once they were on the road, she drove east, away from the museum, to give themselves some distance. And yet, she glanced in her rearview mirror, looking for this Graham with the crooked smile. When she spotted him watching them drive away, her heart quickened.

"Holy crap." Tansy exhaled like she had been holding her breath for hours.

"That's exactly what I was thinking." Taylor drove with white knuckles while Tansy called her mom letting her know she'd come pick up her car later. She dropped Tansy off at her place in the nearby town Willamina.

She didn't dare go home or to the shop, so she drove out to Hudson's house. She belonged at his house anyway. He'd given her a key a long time ago and she kissed it before letting herself in. It's not that she wasn't willing to talk to reporters. She didn't have anything to hide, but she'd never been ambushed before. Not like that. It triggered that fight or flight instinct that had gone into overdrive when she'd had to fight off her mother's killer. She repeated it again, liking the sound of that better than the alternative. She'd panicked, and that explained her flush and her racing heart and all of the other strong, strange reactions to the man she'd never seen before in her life.

She slumped into the leather loveseat and stared out at the rolling hills of Yamhill County, thankful for the amazing escape that was Hudson's handcrafted A-frame cabin. She was ready to call Owen, the boyfriend-of-the-deceased, to see if he could account for his time during the murder. But the officials would have thought of that. She sighed and didn't call. The sheriff didn't need her help.

"Fancy you coming by." The reverberating voice of Hudson's mom came from behind her. "Didn't expect to see you so soon." There was that hint of disapproval in Cheryl's tone, as though Taylor had come by for a dirty afternoon.

Taylor turned in her seat, leaning on the back of the sofa so she could see Cheryl in the kitchen. "To be honest," she began, figuring honesty was the best option, "I had to run away from work. A bunch of reporters are there today. I guess they want to make a meal out of our murder."

"Murder is news," Cheryl said in a correcting tone. "Have you had lunch yet?" She began to spread mayonnaise on bread before Taylor could answer. "Speaking of news, my boy is the talk of the town."

"Can you blame the town?" Taylor wasn't surprised Hudson's mom would turn the conversation to her son. She didn't seem like the kind of lady who likes other people to have the spotlight.

"His plans for that old folks' home are just delightful. Can you imagine the people who live in those tiny little apartments having a hotel right on site where their family can stay?" She smashed both sandwiches, smushing the tuna salad, lettuce, and tomatoes together.

"Sounds like a nice idea." Taylor's mind didn't have room to freak out with jealousy or insecurity about this right now. She was too busy formulating questions for Owen. She'd call him, even though she knew there was no point.

"After the mess you made of it, I mean, I can't believe you got it bombed." She walked around the kitchen island and set the smashed sandwiches on the dining table.

Taylor didn't rush to join her.

"Hudsy told me all about how you wouldn't quit meddling in the death of the chaplain, and the killer set off a bomb that destroyed everyone's homes. You'd think that would teach you to mind your own business."

She took a big, messy bite of her sandwich. Taylor expected it to fall apart, but it didn't.

Hunger got the better of her, and she joined Cheryl at the table.

"I never could have imagined someone would set a fire in the old folks' home." Taylor took a bite of her sandwich. A blob of tuna and half a tomato slice fell out.

Cheryl tsk'd. "You certainly didn't seem to be able to anticipate that one. It makes me wonder."

"It makes you wonder if I've learned my lesson? I would like to think I have." Taylor tried again on her sandwich with a little more success, though now her mouth was too full to chew discretely.

"Which is why you've run from the reporters, right? You'll be leaving this murder alone?" There was a shifty look in Cheryl's eyes.

Taylor tilted her head. Why had Cheryl come to town just now? And had she known Shawna before the murder? "Did you know Shawna?" Taylor wasn't in the mood to beat around the bush.

"Sure, it's a small town. We all know each other. I just feel so much sadness for everyone who knew her well. I'd only met her a couple of times, but she seemed lovely."

There seemed to be a war going on inside Cheryl as her eyes

narrowed and her mouth twisted. Cheryl was also not the kind of woman to admit not knowing someone.

"You could say I know the family."

"Oh!" Taylor didn't have to feign enthusiasm. Apart from the ex-boyfriend and her blogging bestie, Taylor hadn't heard one word about Shawna's family. "That's fantastic. Can I ask you a few questions?"

"You haven't learned anything, have you?" Cheryl laughed, but it was so superior.

"Just a quick question. I can't go back to work because of the reporters. I can't go back home for the same reason. We might as well talk about the thing that everyone else in town is talking about, right?"

Cheryl pursed her lips. The appeal to gossip worked. "Shawna's family was new. Her mom moved to town when I was in eighth grade."

That meant Shawna's family must have been in town for the last fifty years. This tracked with Comfort, Oregon's idea of new in town.

"Good people?" Taylor asked. Good people was relative to who you were asking and could depend on if they went to the right church, shopped at the right quilt shop, or had the same vices you had. But most people could pass based on how well they kept their yard and if their kids stayed out of trouble.

"Yes, good people. Shawna's father wasn't from around here, either, but he was a hard worker. Her mother was a good house-keeper. Methodists. Shawna herself, I don't know. I don't remember her winning any awards or championships or anything like that, but I don't remember her getting in trouble either."

"She was a bit younger than me. Around Hudson's age, I guess," Taylor mused. She couldn't picture Shawna. Those younger kids all blurred into a generic crowd. "Sissy's stepdaughter Tansy is her best friend—was her best friend," Taylor added.

Cheryl clucked in a motherly way.

"Poor child. I always liked Tansy. Such a pity she married so young. And Logan...now there's a family that's not good people."

"Were Tansy and Shawna friends of Hudson's?" Taylor ignored the rabbit trail that might be Tansy's in-laws.

"Much, much too young. I think he graduated when they were still freshman."

Since that was exactly the age difference between Hudson and Taylor, and Hudson was the younger one, this felt like a pointed dig. Taylor braced herself for further attacks but kept at it with her questions. "Are Shawna's folks still in town?"

"No, they moved away a long time ago. I think over to Bend. Don't know if they're still there. I do feel for Tansy, though. A dear friend of mine died a few years back as well, and it's not been the same."

"I'm sorry." Taylor meant it. Untimely death was the worst. "Would I have known your friend?"

Cheryl shook her head. "She wasn't from around here, and it was just an accident. Not a murder."

The word accident made Taylor wonder. So many murders hid under that innocent word.

There was a knock at Hudson's door. Cheryl glowered at it. "Hide in the bedroom and shut the door behind you. I'll get rid of them."

Taylor did as she was told but leaned her head against the door so she could listen. The door was solid. Probably hand-made by Hudson or someone he knew. It fit like a glove in its frame. All in all, it was gorgeous, but really hard to hear through. Or would have been if the person on the other side of the door had been anyone but Sissy Dorney.

"Your ears must have been burning," Cheryl said.

Taylor joined the two women in the front room.

"It's been too long." Sissy laughed and gave the stiff, older woman a big hug.

Cheryl disengaged quickly, but her face didn't look as irritated as Taylor had expected.

"Tansy called," Sissy told Taylor. "God bless that girl, but if you wanted your hideaway to actually be hidden you should not have told her where you were heading. If those vultures are looking for you, they'll find you in a heartbeat. I can only imagine the number of people that little gabster has already told."

"Coffee? Water? Something stronger?" Cheryl offered.

"Got any tea?" Sissy asked.

"Coming right up." Cheryl moved to the safety of the other side of the granite slab counter and put the water on to boil.

"Taylor, this town is crawling with reporters, and we all know what happened last time." Sissy's warning came from love. You could tell by the way her big, warm eyes were glued to Taylor.

"What do you mean?" Taylor sunk back into the leather sofa, not wanting to be read the riot act from her friend.

"What do you mean what happened last time? That poor girl was murdered at the quilt expo, a tragedy that cost Comfort businesses quite a lot of money."

Taylor closed her eyes for a moment and wished she hadn't left the safety of that big heavy door to the bedroom.

"All of the businesses that were looking forward to tourist money. The cafés, the antiques. Even the market and me. Free afternoons at a big event like that should have packed my salon out for facials and nails." Sissy rummaged through a box of tea bags Cheryl held out.

"It was worse for the deceased and her sister," Taylor murmured.

"I'm not an idiot. But it was bad for all of us too. And it's not even been a month. Another murder about another quilt."

"Is that what people are saying?" Cheryl asked.

"It is, untill someone comes up with a hotter story."

"Has it even been twenty-four hours? Give me a little time. You know murders don't get solved overnight." Taylor took her plate to the kitchen and dumped the remains of her lunch in the food scraps bin.

"They ought to. We've got a lot riding on this new business." Sissy settled onto a bar stool with a sigh.

"How much have you invested?" The kettle whistled and Cheryl poured hot water over the tea bags.

"Enough, that's how much." Sissy turned to Taylor. "You need to talk to those reporters. Make one statement, make it consistent, and never stray from it."

"What good would that do for your old-folks-hotel?" Taylor was used to Sissy bossing her around, but that didn't mean she liked it. She took out a mug and held it like a beggar toward Cheryl, hoping for her own cup of tea.

"We've got to get ahead of the murder story. We can't let it grow into something bigger than it really is. We can't let the news create a serial killer in this town." Sissy blew on the hot drink that she cradled in two hands.

"You're saying you've come to help me frame my statement?" Though Sissy was a gifted hair stylist and a loving mother, Taylor suspected her own education in marketing was more useful for coming up with a press release. Nonetheless, she dug up some paper and pens and went to the dining table where she could spread out.

Cheryl joined her, ready to give her two cents.

Before they had barely burned their tongues on the first sips of hot tea, Sissy jumped from her seat and pointed at the big picture windows. "Who's that lurking out there?"

"Tansy did spread the word fast." Taylor hid her face behind her large mug.

"I'll get rid of them." Sissy stormed to the front door.

"You both get in the bedroom," Cheryl argued. "And I'll take care of them."

Taylor watched the shadowy figures move in and out of the bushes and groaned in dismay. It wasn't journalists begging for a quote. It was Belle, Jonah, and some lady who was probably their real estate agent. "Hold on I'll take care of this one." She went out the side door. "Hey there! No trespassing."

The Realtor was unmoved, but Jonah stopped. "Sorry! I'm sorry!" He stared. "Oh, hey, Taylor."

"What are you doing here? This place isn't for sale." Taylor leaned on the rail of the patio.

The real estate agent tilted her head knowingly. "A one-bedroom cabin? On all this land? The owner's fortunes are only increasing. He's been in a serious relationship for an awfully long time." She laughed but sounded like a bad actress. "It's only a matter of time."

"The owner's not home. You all need to move along." Taylor could see the lady's point. On paper, it looked like Hudson would be moving on to something bigger and better any minute. But that wasn't something either of them had talked about yet. She had her place and he had his. Period.

"But you live here, don't you?" the agent asked. "You could let us have a little look around."

"I don't live here. It's not my house, and you need to leave." Taylor's sense of humor was failing her.

"Calm down." The agent stepped over a young azalea to join Taylor.

"I'm perfectly calm. If you'd like to see me not calm so you can compare, then tell me to calm down one more time." Taylor wrinkled her nose at the woman.

"Honestly, it's okay. Hudson's place is too small. We're going to need lots of bedrooms for lots of people. Not a little cabin like this." Jonah was blushing, but Belle was staring into the distance at the glorious view.

The Realtor stretched her arms out. "All of this land," she said. "Think of all the cabins you could build. It wouldn't be Hype House," she over-pronounced the name of a popular house full of influencers. "It would be a Content Compound."

"Jonah, I told you she doesn't get it." Belle sounded annoyed.

The Realtor, whose name tag said "Bonnie," scrunched her lips as a truck drove up the driveway with tires crunching in the gravel. Hudson was home.

Taylor wasn't sure if this was better or worse. She went back inside to meet him at his front door.

The first thing he did was greet her with a sweaty hug and a big kiss.

"Hey Baby. Having a party without me?"

"Not exactly," Taylor glanced around at the driveway full of cars.

"It's cold out here, should we invite everyone in?" Hudson lifted one of his thick eyebrows. A light drizzle had begun to fall. It wasn't enough to make anyone really wet, but when he stepped inside, everyone followed him. Despite the imposing personalities he had to compete with, Hudson took natural control of the situation. "I'm not sure what brought you here but *mi casa es su casa.*" He narrowed his eyes at the real estate agent. "Bonnie, right? It's not literally your house, though."

She laughed that fake laugh again. "I wanted to show the kids a type of home they might not have considered..." her voice trailed off.

Hudson had turned to Belle. "Hey Sis. Good to see you. Jonah." He offered Jonah his hand. "Pardon me if I'm a little rough. I've been excavating some land up in the mountains. Friend of mine wanted a well before the ground froze." He leaned over and kissed his mom's cheek. "Thanks for playing hostess for me." And finally, he turned back to Taylor. "Glad to see you're here and not holding a press conference at your shop. I stopped there first. Jonah and Belle, my place isn't for sale, but I could always build you something similar if you're interested."

"Well," Bonnie the agent sounded like she wanted to discuss the idea further.

"If you're off," he strode to his door and opened it, "I'm sure Taylor can give the kids a ride home."

Bonnie pulled some business cards out of her pocket and set them on the coffee table. "I'll just leave these then."

"Don't worry about us, Taylor." Belle put her hand on her sister's arm. "We've got two more properties to see before we're done today.

Bonnie tilted her chin up in victory, and the three left together.

"That woman did not tell them my house was for sale, did she?" Hudson asked Taylor as soon as they were gone.

Taylor blushed. She didn't want to repeat what Bonnie had said about their relationship.

"Bonnie just said what the rest of us are all thinking." Sissy wasn't shy. "You all won't be wanting a one bedroom forever. But forget her, we've got to get a statement figured out for the press."

Hudson caught Taylor's eye, his own twinkling with laughter.

Taylor's blush deepened. Why was she so uncomfortable with what Hudson clearly considered a joke? A night at his place here and there was lovely. But the whole town thinking they were ready to lock this thing down was wildly uncomfortable.

Cheryl interjected, "This is what I hate about this town. The gossip. You are far too young to be thinking about a family, Hudson. Your father was almost fifty when we had you. You've got plenty of time."

Sissy snorted. "You think Taylor can wait another twenty-five years to have kids? You're crazy. She's pushing it as it is."

"Sissy!" Taylor shouted.

"It's true. In what, three more years it would be a geriatric pregnancy."

"What's wrong with that?" Cheryl challenged. I was over forty when I had Hudsy."

"Ladies." Hudson cleared his throat.

Taylor sidled up to Hudson. "I'm going to slip away. Should I take Sissy with me?"

"I'd say take me, but I need a shower. Come over later. We'll put on a movie and have some pizza. I'll take care of these two."

"You're the greatest." Taylor kissed his cheek.

Sissy was deep into the story of how her surprise pregnancy with Breadyn had been so much harder than her first with Pyper, so many years earlier.

Once she was safe in her car, Taylor made a sympathy call to Shawna's recent boyfriend Owen. She told him she was a new friend of hers, which was only a small stretch, and that she just wanted to see how he was.

He suggested they meet for coffee, now, if she was free. Because he wasn't doing okay.

SHAWNA'S EX WAS AVERAGE, but handsome. If you could be both at the same time. He was of average height, and maybe a little on the heavy side, but he looked like a good snuggle. His hair was mere stubble, clearly shaved to hide a receding hairline, but it worked. The thing was, he had lovely, big, green eyes, and a friendly face. It seemed odd, as Taylor sat across from him in a back booth at Reuben's Diner over a cup of coffee and slice of pie. Should he be smiling right now?

"You say you were a new friend of Shawna's." Owen's voice

was soft and sad and his smile fell, though he had one of those mouths that always seemed to curl up, just a little.

"Yes, we haven't known each other for long. I'm sort of new back in town."

"She grew up here. Did you?"

"Yes, but she's quite a bit younger. Around seven years or so. I think I didn't babysit enough. Maybe if I'd been more of a go-getter, I'd know folks her age better." Taylor cut a small bite from her pumpkin pie. She wasn't really a fan, but that's what you get this close to Thanksgiving.

"Thanks for getting in touch. I was devastated when her parents called to tell me what happened."

"Have they come to town yet?"

"No, they're snowed in up in Alaska. Her boss at the museum had to give the positive ID. I hear you found her." He fidgeted with his fork but didn't eat anything.

"I did. It was pretty bad."

"She was a really great girl, you know? We met online when we were practically kids. Dated on and off since high school."

"Had you kept in touch since you broke up?"

"It was right before that big thing at the college. Early October." He picked up his mug and looked down at the inky coffee. "We were fighting over which Halloween party we should go to, a Zoom party with her online blog friends, or the block party with actual people. I really wanted to get to know some people in real life. I get tired of being online all the time."

"That wasn't very long ago."

"Hardly any time at all. I believed we'd make up. We always did. Here, look." He slowly took his phone out of the inside pocket of his vintage Member's Only jacket. "She was already texting me a few days before Halloween. She was so excited about that mystery quilt."

Taylor read the texts with interest. One had pictures. Most were just a few words. But they seemed friendly. Loving, even.

She tried to remember what Shawna had mentioned about her ex when they spoke the night of the guild meeting, but it hadn't seemed important at the time. "Tansy mentioned something about a new man. Someone Shawna might be seeing."

He shook his head. "Online dating app. Maybe one date? I don't know. I said she and I met online, and Shawna was always happier with those kind of friendships. Distant. Less commitment. I wasn't worried about this guy."

"Did she usually jump into online dating when you guys were fighting?"

"Only once before. I think to try and make me jealous." His mouth was still turned up at the corners, but his eyes were pleading for sympathy. "It worked."

"A fight over which party to go to doesn't seem like enough to break a long-term relationship. Even if it was usually a bit rocky." Taylor and Hudson rarely fought. She couldn't imagine him doing something that would make her mad enough to run to online dating just to make him jealous. It ought to have been comforting, but it was rather passionless.

"The party was more than just a social thing to her. It was about networking and the future. Everything was. Even that quilt. She thought it was going to make her career. And I was too stubborn to support her the way I should have. I should have been here. She shouldn't have died." He wiped his eyes with the back of his hand.

"Sudden loss like this is so hard."

"Have you been through something like this?"

Taylor nodded.

He had a look of almost hope in his eyes.

That idea that a burden shared is lessened came to mind again, and she found herself offering him a long look of sympathy. Maybe he thought if she could make it through, he could. "Yes," she said simply. "Both of my parents, though years apart."

His face fell momentarily, but he shook his head and tried to look appreciative. "My folks have been gone for a while too. Somehow, though, this is different. Because we were supposed to be together, and now I can never make up for not supporting her."

Taylor thought she deserved more time with her mom and had made mistakes in not visiting enough but decided against arguing over it. Grief should not be a competition. "You wouldn't have any idea who would have wanted to do something like this to her, do you?"

"Maybe I watch too much TV. That's what her parents said. But a stab wound sounds like some kind of lunatic, don't you think?"

"Sure," Taylor agreed.

"All I can think of is how I hope he doesn't try again."

Taylor suspected he had a lot more on his mind than just that, but he was in shock right now, and probably not entirely sure what he was saying. "Have her folks said anything about a future funeral?"

"She's already at the funeral home, going to be cremated. Then, I don't know. Maybe when they're freed from the ice, they'll come down and have one, or maybe she'll be mailed to them. I wasn't their favorite person."

"Because the relationship was so on and off?"

"And because I don't have the same kind of education they do. They think I held her back. I probably did." He took a long breath through his nose. "Some people are snobs about school. I didn't have the chance to go. But my work never stopped Shawna. She just didn't want to go to college before now."

"I'm just really sorry about your loss. Do you live nearby?"

"No, not really. But I drove up as soon as I got the news. I've tried to get in touch with Tansy, but she won't get back to me."

"I think she's still in shock. She gave me your number."

"I figured." He drained his mug. "I think I want to drive around. Go see some of our favorite places. Might even go to the beach. Stare at the ocean. Thanks for texting. No one ever thinks to call the ex." He left a ten on the table as he stood. "See you around."

She let him go, though she felt like she'd barely touched the surface. He hadn't even tasted his pie, and she'd barely started hers.

As soon as the little bells on the diner door jingled his departure, Graham slid into her booth. "You could use a little practice in interview techniques." He picked up the fork and helped himself to Owen's pie.

"They didn't cover investigative journalism at Comfort College of Art and Craft." Taylor did her best to maintain her cool. She wasn't going to let this man rattle her.

"Life's funny that way, isn't it? Everything points you in one direction. You diligently prepare for it, but somehow, you end up hunting down murderers anyway."

"You on the *Oregonlive.com* murder beat?" Taylor attempted to eat a bite of pie, but her mouth was dry. Nerves. This man made her incredibly nervous. That was why her palms were sweaty and her face was so warm.

"Usually." He didn't seem to sense the sarcasm in her comment. "I got the feeling, listening in, that you didn't go into that conversation with questions in mind."

"True." She scraped the top of her pie with her fork. She should send him away.

"Looking back, what do you wish you'd learned?" He leaned on his elbows, genuinely interested in what she had to say.

"Where he lives."

"You mean proximity to the murder, don't you?"

"Yeah, I guess I do." She glanced out the window to Main Street and prayed no one would see her with Graham.

"What else?"

"Where he was the day she was killed."

"Ha." His big brown eyes crinkled, and he shook his head in

laughter. "We all want to know that. What did you want to learn that he might have actually told you, if he was guilty?"

"Maybe what their usual fights were about." She pressed her fork into the pumpkin custard a little harder. Her rookie answer to his question embarrassed her.

"Okay, I dig it. You had him talking about their past ups and downs, and the family not liking him for not being educated. He mentioned on his own that he wished he'd supported her more. But you wanted to know what else, exactly?"

"Maybe what kinds of things annoyed him about her."

"Maybe?"

"Definitely?" She put her fork down and made eye contact, then laughed. He was so pleasant and relaxed, like he really wanted her to feel comfortable and to get better at this. "I do wonder what might have made him mad enough to kill. But then, did you see him? Did he strike you as a murderer?"

"White man in his late twenties to early thirties, lower middle class, with a chip on his shoulder? Also, her ex, who now claims that he'd always loved her and wished she was still alive? Yes. He did seem like a murderer."

She pushed her plate away. Her stomach had tied itself in a knot. She kept getting the answers to his questions wrong. She was disappointing him, surely, and she hated herself for caring. "You probably just see murderers because that's what you're used to looking for."

"And you?"

She pulled out her wallet to add a ten to the table. Aviva would be getting a good tip. "Same."

She left, but Graham was on her heels. She could only think of one way of shaking him, so she got in her car and drove back to Hudson's.

CHAPTER EIGHT

*T*he movie had ended, and Taylor felt good. She was
glad she'd called Owen, and she'd learned some
useful things. And maybe the conversation had been good for
him too. It was only Graham who had unsettled her. Not Owen.
He had needed someone to listen, and she'd been there.

Now, nestled in Hudson's arms, she felt safe and loved, and
maybe, dare she say it, comfortable? Such a simple thing, but so
hard to find.

He kissed the side of her forehead in a lingering and tender
way. "Shall we?"

"Definitely."

She slipped in the bathroom to brush her teeth.

When she came out, Hudson had a disappointed look on his
face.

"Mom called."

"Oh?" Taylor had already changed out of her jeans and T.

"She was at Brenda's, and they walked down to Loggers.
They were planning to walk back again, but Brenda had too
much." He attempted a chagrinned laugh. "Why do you have to
look so good?"

Taylor's face warmed under his admiring gaze, and she tossed her hair over her shoulder.

"Brenda is sloppy. Too far gone to walk home, so mom was wondering if I could pick them up. I'd tell her to get a taxi, but this is Comfort."

"We can't just leave them there." Taylor shrugged. She meant it. Though she'd rather pull the down comforter over herself and her lover, she wasn't going to leave two retirees at a bar with no way to get home. "I can come, right?"

"It's cold…" He looked her up and down, eyes lingering on the lacy, ivory bralette.

"Give me just a second and I'll be ready." She padded back into the bathroom to get dressed, making sure to touch up her makeup.

THOUGH IT FELT like Hudson lived far, far out of town, it was a quick drive to the local bar where Taylor had expected some kind of scene. A fight or the ladies getting kicked out. Instead they found Hudson's mom elegantly tipsy, and her best friend almost passed out in a booth. His mom stood and extended her hands. "Darling, thank you so much for coming."

"Anytime." Hudson didn't look bothered. His eyes were soft with real affection.

"Taylor, darling, sorry for interrupting your night."

"No, it's okay. I understand completely." Taylor hadn't grown up with drinkers, but it was clear that "Auntie" Brenda was in no shape to walk home.

"She's fine for the moment." Cheryl gave her friend a sad little look. "You made it all the way down here, you might as well get yourself something."

Hudson shook his head. "Let's just get you where you're going."

Taylor looked away while Cheryl and Hudson helped Brenda out of the booth. It seemed intrusive to watch her like this.

Glancing around the room, she spotted another older lady losing herself to drink. In a far booth the tiny frame of Lorraine Love sat not nearly as still and serene as Taylor was used to seeing her. She waved her hands above her head, and her usually weak voice managed to carry all the way to where Taylor stood.

"No. No. No." She repeated the single syllable over and over again. "This murder has nothing to do with that last one." Lorraine was speaking to a tall, thin man, and though Taylor could only see the back of his head, she had a feeling it was her faint but pursuing journalist Graham. "It was the work of a madman." The word madman reverberated through the bar stopping even Hudson who turned with brows furrowed.

"Can I have a minute?" Taylor asked Hudson.

He made an unhappy grunt but didn't try to stop her.

She sucked up her courage—it shouldn't have been hard. There wasn't anything intimidating about Lorraine, right now. But the feeling that sober Lorraine gave her lingered, and she was nervous about approaching. Nonetheless, someone had to get her out of the bar.

The walk to the booth felt endless, but she got there, eventually, and cleared her throat. "Pardon me."

Graham was seated across from Lorraine. He turned and his friendly face lit up. "Taylor Quinn, Amateur Girl Detective."

"Taylor Quinn owner of Flour Sax Quilt Shop," she corrected. "Lorraine? Are you ready to go?"

Lorraine stared at her, not comprehending. "This man has it all wrong. He thinks Comfort is a hotbed of homicide. Some kind of Cabot Cove. Or Kembleford."

Taylor smiled at the references to Murder she Wrote and

Father Brown. She had a feeling that's how Graham wanted to paint Comfort in his article.

TAYLOR HELD OUT HER HAND. "Are you ready?"

"I told him it is nothing of the sort," Lorraine said. "Bad things happen everywhere, but what happened to Shawna was something else entirely."

"Please continue," Graham gave all his attention to Lorraine, but Taylor was acutely aware of him. His floppy hair hung just to his eyes. His chin was stubble free, though he didn't have a baby face. And he had left his winter coat behind, now wearing a crumpled corduroy jacket over a button-down shirt but no tie. It was a look, and Taylor wished she didn't like it so much.

"I think she needs to go home. Lorraine, do you realize who you're talking to?"

"He said he's a journalist, and I hope it's true. This murder was the work of a madman." Lorraine was whispering now. "An evil, psychotic killer. No young female is safe in this town. He's come back. Just like when I was a girl."

"All right that's it." Taylor slid into the booth, hooked her arm through Lorraine's, and attempted to pull her out.

"Slow and steady." Graham held out a hand, his voice calm and rational. "I know you don't trust me yet, but you definitely want me to be the one hearing this and not one of those other yahoos. Speaking of, I think I saw a guy from *Yahoo* news earlier. You wouldn't want this story to break on *Yahoo*, would you? This is a local story and belongs on the local paper. None of that half-baked browser nonsense or, God forbid, *BuzzFeed*."

"There's no story here. She's just..." Taylor tilted her head indicating, she hoped, that the older woman was drunk.

"Okay." He held up his hands in surrender. "But before you drag her out, make sure you know exactly what you want to find out before you drop her at home to sleep this off."

Susan, the waitress that Taylor knew best, joined the table before Taylor could drum up a response.

"Hey, Hun," she said. "Hudson told me to let you know they're out at the car. He doesn't want to rush you."

"Thanks." Though Susan claimed Hudson didn't want to rush her, she knew better. He was itching to get back to his warm, comfy bed. And so was she.

Wasn't she?

"Lorraine did you drive here?"

"I certainly didn't fly," Lorraine snorted when she laughed. A sober Lorraine would never have.

"I can give you a ride home, if you need." Graham pointed at the empty pint in front of him. "Just a Coke."

Taylor hesitated. Getting a ride from Graham was a foolish idea. All she needed was to take Lorraine back home.

"I'm not worried about myself. I'd better drive her home in her car."

Susan had lingered, probably waiting for a message for Hudson, and chimed in, "Don't worry, I've called Tansy already.

There was no way Taylor was going to leave the very inebriated Lorraine Love alone with a reporter, even if he did have a disarming smile that reminded her of Clay's. "I can wait." Taylor took out her phone. She texted Hudson to take the ladies back to Brenda's while she waited for Tansy and asked him to come back for her.

"Can I get you something while you wait?" Susan asked.

"Sure. Coke. Jack and Coke."

Susan scribbled it on her pad and moved on to the next table.

"Young people don't like to listen." Lorraine had kept talking to Graham while Taylor and Susan spoke, and was in the middle of what Taylor hoped was an entirely different complaint now.

"Tansy doesn't. Shawna didn't. This one won't." She gave Taylor a disapproving stare. "But this has happened before. In

1975. She doesn't believe me because she doesn't know about all the girls that died before." Lorraine held out her arm, pushing the long flowing sleeve of her silky blouse up. "They were all stabbed. Like I was." Deep gashes, poorly mended, covered her upper arm.

Taylor swallowed nervously. Her mom had been a little girl in Comfort, Oregon in the 1970s. Grandma Delma and Grandma Quinny had been young moms. None of them had ever mentioned a string of murders from that era. It hadn't come up even once.

Graham set his phone in the middle of the table. "I'd like to record this, Lorraine. Do you give me permission to record what you're saying?"

"Yes, please do. Shawna wasn't killed over a blanket or a blog or anything like that. She was killed because nobody ever caught The Cutter."

Taylor's phone buzzed in her pocket, and she jumped, bumping into Lorraine.

From under the table, a foot pressed the top of hers, a surprisingly comforting gesture. "Sorry." She took her phone out and read the text from Hudson. He said he'd be right back and have a drink with her while they waited for Tansy.

He was a really good guy.

Graham's face was locked on Lorraine. His body was tense, shoulders high, and he leaned forward, listening with every fiber of his person.

Lorraine took a long drink from a tumbler full of brown liquor. She wrinkled her nose and opened her mouth to say something else and then she passed out.

Graham exhaled, as though he'd been holding his breath, and pulled his phone back to himself. "Damn."

"Forgive me if I don't agree." Taylor's voice was a whisper.

"Interview with the lone survivor of a serial killer who was never caught? Come on, have some sympathy for a journalist."

"I grew up in this town. My parents grew up here. Some of my grandparents did. I've never heard of this killer before. Not once in my whole life."

"How many people live here?" He stretched one arm across the back of the booth.

"About two thousand."

"And you think you know everything about every one of them, huh? No one has secrets from Taylor Quinn."

"It's not that..." She blushed. Why did he make her blush? "But, come on. A serial killer is the kind of story kids hear. I know the story about..." she paused, trying to drum up the most lurid story possible. "Oh! I know! I know the story of Jeremy Mitchell who ran off with um...with what was her name? Graham something."

"I'm Graham." He lifted his eyebrow. That flirty thing he had done before.

"Shh...I'm trying to remember." What was that girl's name? "Um...Lauran Graham? No, that's the Gilmore Girls...Wait. Gilmore. She was the youngest Gilmore, I think Sarah. But whatever her name was, she was only fifteen and he was like forty. He only got five years for it, the bastard."

"That's a pretty good story. How long ago?"

"When I was in grade school." Taylor fanned herself with Lorraine's napkin and wished her drink would come. It was too hot in Loggers tonight.

"It's not like someone told you that story. You were actually around when it happened." He tapped her foot again with his, but she wasn't sure if he'd meant to this time.

She sat straighter, excited as she remembered another story. "One of Hudson's uncles was killed in a duel."

Graham laughed. "Hudson's your boyfriend, hey?"

"Yeah." She pulled her feet closer to the bench.

"Who were they dueling over?"

She quivered in excitement, though she knew for a fact this

story was not that exciting. "They were dueling over a dog. He'd run away, I think, and the guy who killed Hud's uncle claimed the dog had always been his, but the dog was an expensive breed, with really clear markings. They met at dawn and everything."

"Who told you that story?"

"Hudson…"

His eyes lost a little of their shine. Maybe. "Ah. Well, I'm not saying you're not the repository of all tales ever told in Yamhill County, but there might just be one or two out there you don't know yet. It's a big area, even if Comfort is small."

The atmosphere was tense. She found herself breathing faster than she wanted to.

Graham looked away.

Lorraine, head on the table, snored.

Graham chuckled.

Taylor relaxed.

And in another moment Hudson was there, pulling a chair up to the end of the table.

"I don't think I can weasel anything out of her tonight," Graham said. "If you two want to go, I can wait till her daughter shows up."

"Thanks, man." Hudson offered his hand.

Graham shook his hand, but seemed to be sizing the other man up.

Taylor didn't mean to compare the two as she drove home with her young, handsome, strong, fit, devoted, and kind boyfriend.

But she did.

And though the math didn't add up in any logical way, Graham came out ahead.

Hudson drove her to her own little house on Love Street. "Bad news." He put the truck in park. "Mom refused to go home with Brenda so she's at my place. But please come by any time you need to escape the paparazzi tomorrow."

"I love you," she didn't like the sound of the words as they came out. She didn't trust them, so she kissed him.

She did love him. She was sure she did.

CHAPTER NINE

$\mathcal{T}$aylor went straight to Hudson's the next morning with donuts. It felt right, after all, Brenda and Cheryl had done it the day before.

Plus, she had some questions she wanted to ask Cheryl, and she knew exactly what she wanted to learn from her.

Brenda showed up moments after Taylor, looking fresh as a daisy despite her bad night.

"Hair of the dog." She laughed with a wink for Cheryl.

"She means a vitamin infusion. How early did you have to get up to get a drip already?"

Brenda put her finger to her lips. "I'll never tell."

Hudson poured them each a tall cup of black coffee.

Taylor brought out the cream and sugar. She plastered the friendliest smile she could on her face and dove right in. "Comfort, Oregon. 1975. What do you remember?"

"I was only thirteen," Brenda said with a smug grin. "I'm much younger than Cheryl here."

"I was old enough. And young enough too." Cheryl pursed her lips, but her eyes were smiling.

Hudson piped up. "She was about eighteen. What's up Taylor?"

Taylor hadn't discussed this with him on their drive home, though she had been tempted. He'd heard enough, or so she'd thought.

"I want to hear everything you remember about a string of murders and someone called 'The Cutter.'"

Brenda rolled her eyes.

"You've been talking to Lorraine Love," Cheryl said. "God bless anyone who does that."

"That's not much of an answer." Taylor quirked her eyebrow. "Having memory troubles?"

"Lorraine's alcohol problems go way back. She got herself in a little trouble a long time ago and has always tried to pin the blame on some mysterious bad guy." Powdered sugar fell on Brenda's bosom as she took her first bite from a lemon filled donut.

"No one died mysteriously in 1975?" Taylor pressed. She wasn't going to give up. She wanted to corroborate or disprove Lorraine's claim.

"We're not saying no one else died then. I'm just saying the idea of a string of slasher murders is a fiction entirely existing in Lorraine's head. You know it's why she married Phil Dorney don't you?" Cheryl piped up with support of Brenda. "If you've met her at all you've got to be aware that he's not her type. He's smart, but not book smart. He was handsome when he was young, but not sweep-women-off-their-feet handsome." Cheryl glanced at Hudson. "But he is big and strong. And young. A few years younger than her, in fact. Perfect for the kind of woman who wants someone who makes her feel safe."

Hudson turned away.

"If there wasn't a killer, what did Lorraine need protection from?" Taylor ignored the pointed comments about her relationship with the handsome, strong, young, and not necessarily book smart Hudson.

"I suspect she wanted protection from herself." Cheryl broke a glazed chocolate cake donut in half. She took one tiny bite out of the half she held.

"She claims it was a serial killer. Who did she say the other victims were?" Taylor picked up the other half of the chocolate donut and ate it in two bites.

"Oh gosh," Brenda dusted the sugar off her blouse. "There was the girl a few years ahead of me in school. What was her name? She was a junior in high school, I think. She went away in early fall and never came back. Mom always said she must have gone to have a baby."

"But Lorraine said she was stabbed to death? That's a bold claim with no body."

"Oh, some girl in Portland died around the same time, and Lorraine always said it was the same girl."

"But I thought The Cutter was supposed to be in Comfort?"

"As Lorraine claims, the girl was killed here and taken to Portland where she was dumped." Brenda moved her coffee cup back and forth, inhaling the aroma.

"But what about the girl's family? Did they file a missing person's report or something like that? Surely if they had sent her away to Portland for a pregnancy, they would have quashed any claims she'd been killed." Taylor tapped the side of her mug. This was her first attempt to conduct an interview in a way that might impress...she glanced at Hudson. No. She just wanted to do a good job. Not impress anyone.

"Lorraine hadn't built up her story yet, when the girl—what was her name, Cheryl? This is driving me crazy."

"Wasn't it that Baker girl? One of Ernie's relations, I think." Cheryl smirked.

"Oh." Taylor frowned. Grandpa Ernie wasn't on her list of

eyewitnesses. She barely trusted his memory of last weekend, much less the summer of '75.

"No, not the Baker girl. She really did get herself pregnant, but she stayed in town, and that wasn't in '75, it was maybe a year or two later." Brenda drummed her sugar covered fingers on the counter.

"Probably no one important." Cheryl shrugged.

"Everyone's important to somebody, Mom," Hudson interjected. "I've got a job this morning, but you three feel free to do whatever it is you're doing." He kissed Taylor on the side of the head.

"Darling." Cheryl held her heavily ringed hand in his direction. "Let's do dinner tonight. Berry Noir, maybe?"

"Sure, Mom." He gave her hand a squeeze, then left.

Cheryl shook her head. "I don't think that family was from around here, and they didn't stay long. That's all."

"What happened to them?" Taylor asked, giving herself the other chocolate cake donut.

"The whole family moved. You can't expect me to remember when, can you? It was years ago. They used to live in one of the flour mill houses. You know the cinder block houses toward the edge of the town."

Taylor knew the houses. Comfort's own version of low-income housing. Originally built by the company to rent to their employees.

"Okay, this unnamed girl whose family moved away sometime after the fall of 1975 is one victim. Who else? I believe it takes three to be a serial killer. And can I top off your coffees?"

Both women held out their mugs.

Brenda chewed on her lip, deep in thought. "The schoolteacher, right?" she asked Cheryl.

"Yes, that's right. Everyone said she died in a car accident coming into town. She went through the windshield and was covered in cuts from the glass. Cars were different back then, and she wasn't wearing her seat buckle."

"I see. One girl left town, and a teacher had a car accident. When did Lorraine get attacked?"

"She got into trouble around New Year's." Cheryl dismissed the idea of an attack with her tone of voice.

"Anyone else or just those three?" Taylor asked.

Cheryl drew her brows together in concentration. "There was one more. Who was it?"

"You can't have forgotten." Brenda had a look of mock astonishment on her face. "It's the only one that was real."

"I didn't forget," Cheryl raised her voice. "I'm just trying to remember her name. And I was going in chronological order. First, the girl who went away, then the teacher when the roads got real slick with rain. Between the teacher and Lorraine, there was the student at the Comfort Arts and Crafts College."

The way she misstated the name of the college irked Taylor. It was a wonderful school with a great reputation in the arts world, but Cheryl made it sound like a joke.

"She came from Portland, so none of us knew her. Hadn't been here long, but was found in her dorm room, stabbed to death."

The blood drained from Taylor's face, leaving her dizzy and cold. "Let me guess. She had a pair of sewing scissors in her back?"

Cheryl leaned across the kitchen island. "Close. In her heart."

Taylor's hand instinctively went to her own heart and fluttered there.

"The sheriff said it was suicide," Brenda said.

"Was there a note?" Taylor's voice was hoarse.

"Oh, I don't remember. It was so long ago." Cheryl waved it away.

Taylor took a deep breath and held it for a moment, then let it out, slowly through her nose. "A girl who hadn't lived here long, disappeared. Probably unrelated. A teacher was in a car accident, also unlikely to be related. But this girl, she was stabbed in the heart with scissors. Was this also in the fall?"

"It was over Thanksgiving weekend. The school was fairly deserted. She's lucky someone found her."

Taylor didn't feel like "lucky" was a good description for the poor forgotten student. "And then what happened to Lorraine that winter?"

"I don't think anyone knows what really happened to her. She had some friends who rode motorcycles back then. Probably Hells Angels, I wouldn't know." Brenda said with a shrug.

"Sure, at thirteen, you were just a kid."

"Lorraine was young back then. Much too young to be with bikers. But she was off with them a lot. Her parents were fit to be tied. You know the Love family. Very careful of their reputation. One day Lorraine came home all bandaged up and said she'd been attacked."

"What exactly did she say happened?"

"Who can remember?" Cheryl lobbed the question to Brenda.

"It was the seventies and she was a wild teen. She'd been drinking for sure, maybe even drugs. It was probably a bar fight. She'd gone to the hospital and got herself fixed up before she came home, so whatever happened, she'd been well enough to take care of herself."

"Maybe someone else took care of her," Taylor suggested.

Cheryl held out her coffee cup for another refill. "Maybe so. She wouldn't stop talking about it. She graduated high school and left for college, but every time she came back, she'd bring it up. It was just like a Love to invent a story to save her reputation."

"At what point did she start tying these other deaths into her story?" Taylor asked.

"Right away. Like, as soon as she came home, she said she'd

been stabbed with scissors. Said that the other two women had been as well. She just wanted people to see her as the victim of a great tragedy, instead of as a kid who'd made really bad choices."

"We all liked her better when she was just a party girl. Made her more human. She got really stuck-up afterwards."

"I think she may have cracked. Drugs, alcohol, that smart brain of hers. It happens sometimes. There's other Loves with mental illness. I mean, take that story they tell about the miller's daughter. If that's not a case of mental illness, what is?"

Not for the first time, Taylor wished she'd paid attention during her tour of the mill a few weeks back. She still didn't know what that story was about. "Whatever set her off, the murder of her volunteer must have brought it all back to mind. So terrible for her." Taylor felt deep sympathy for the woman. If Lorraine had lost her ability to reckon with reality because of alcohol or mental illness or just trauma in her youth, then the loss of Shawna in such a gruesome way must have been utterly devastating.

"Unless," Cheryl said looking a little coy, "her mental break made her murder Shawna. After all, she was just sitting at that desk doing her little studies when you popped in and found her friend's body, no?"

Brenda pursed her lips and nodded enthusiastically. "Maybe these stories all these years have been Lorraine's cry for help. Maybe she's been begging someone to stop her."

"You think Lorraine is The Cutter?"

"Why not?" Cheryl asked. "After all, cutting usually refers to self-harm, doesn't it? She says she calls him that because he used scissors to kill, but it could just as easily be her saying she did it to herself, and maybe the others as well."

Taylor's stomach hurt, and not just from too many donuts. It was so easy to tell salacious stories on a sunny morning, or to make light of tragedy that didn't directly touch you. To Cheryl and Brenda, this was some kind of dry humor. A macabre joke. They didn't mean it at all.

Lorraine, with her small frame and delicate constitution, might seem the least likely person to overcome someone and stab them with scissors. It would take strength to get that job done. But it felt painfully possible to Taylor because adrenaline could make people capable of great feats of evil. "Thanks for all the insight." Taylor hoped she'd managed a grateful smile. "I appreciate the information, and I hope I can use it to help Lorraine at least a little bit. I'm sure whatever happened all those years ago has nothing to do with Shawna's death."

"It's got no more to do with that small string of sad events in 1975 than it does with that fraudulent old blanket you guys have over at the museum," Cheryl added.

Taylor sighed. "What are people saying about it?"

"I'm no expert." Brenda spoke in exactly the tone of voice people use when they really did think they were experts. "But I am the Comfort Middle School home-ec and history teacher. And if you ask me, that's supposed to be a button blanket. Probably modern made of old materials. And the reason it was at a quilt show was because whoever made it knew they hadn't done it right and abandoned it. And whoever found it didn't recognize what it was."

"That would explain the loose little threads all around the appliqué, but button blankets are supposed to be wool. And the colors are wrong. Cream and black instead of black and red." Taylor chewed on the idea. Button blankets were used in traditional Pacific Northwest Native American ceremonies.

"I said it wasn't a good one," Brenda chided. "Grandma Kaya had one that someone had made for an uncle on that side of my family. Same fish and tree as yours, but red on black as it should be. Beautiful mother of pearl buttons. That one you have is all wrong, but that doesn't mean someone didn't try to make a ceremonial blanket cape out of whatever materials they had at the time."

"It certainly doesn't. Thank you." If it were an attempt at a ceremonial button blanket, Taylor would have to take back the snide thoughts she'd had every time someone had called it a blanket rather than a quilt. "This gives me something to discuss with Lorraine and Erika, the expert from the college, though I think they ought to have talked to you after all."

"Nah. I don't want that kind of attention. Looks dangerous." Brenda gave a wink.

"Definitely stick to the blanket when you talk to Lorraine," Cheryl admonished. "Steer clear from that cutter story. It won't do anyone any good to get her off on that."

TAYLOR WENT STRAIGHT from her successful interrogation to Flour Sax where she was over an hour late for filming.

"I know we decided to continue," Roxy said as she shut down the camera after a moderately successful session. "But if you're heart's not in it, you don't have to keep trying."

Taylor stared at her friend, only half hearing. She wanted to get straight onto the interview of her next two witnesses—Grandma and Grandpa Quinny. "It was an off day. I am getting better. I mean, we've been at this a couple of years now and have definitely improved, even if our numbers haven't."

"You are doing better." Roxy offered that energizing smile of hers. "But you don't have to keep doing it. This quilt store was a success long before YouTube, and it can keep going without the show. I'm sure of it." She sucked on her bottom lip. "I have some ideas, if you have time to talk."

"I want to hear them." Taylor maintained eye contact and nodded encouragingly. Even with her mind otherwise engaged, she wanted Roxy to feel listened to. "Can we find a time for a meeting?"

"Sure." Roxy's smile dipped into frown zone. "We've still got an hour before we open. We could talk now."

"Can't. I'm sorry! I've got something else. You and Clay have the store today, right? No point in my being here at the current level of sales."

"Yes, we'll both be here."

"Great! Let's find a time to talk...soon." Taylor slung her bag over her shoulder and left. She did need to talk, and she did need ideas. She couldn't let the failure of the expo destroy her business. But if murder was bad for business, serial murder was worse, and her heart burned to get to the bottom of Lorraine's claims before the press started talking about it. She hadn't spotted the reporters anywhere this morning, but it was getting later, and they'd probably be on the prowl soon.

She glanced around and told herself she was not hoping to find Graham Baxter waiting for her.

TAYLOR'S PATERNAL GRANDPARENTS, affectionately called Grandpa and Grandma Quinny by the family, were safe at home in their 1990s McMansion version of a farmhouse. It was charming in the Disneyland sort of way. You knew it wasn't a real farmhouse, but you still wanted to be there as often as you could.

Unless, like Taylor, you were feeling resentful of their officious generosity. Her shoestring cousin Coco was the current recipient of said generosity, and Taylor wondered how long the girl would want to live with the Quinns while also taking care of Grandpa Ernie.

Grandpa Quinny was out in his barn doing the things you

do on behalf of your strawberries in November. Grandma Quinny was in the kitchen.

The large farm table that stood in place of a kitchen island and had been purchased at the antique mall across Main Street from the row of quilt shops, was covered in scones and the room smelled of fresh baking and hot coffee.

An episode of Real Housewives played on a little TV that hung from a decorative pillar.

"Darling," Grandma Quinny crooned, wiping her hands on a towel. "I'm so glad you just let yourself in." Grandma Quinny's tone implied a call would have been appreciated, but Taylor knew, in her heart, that she was welcome. In fact, Grandma Quinny regularly reminded her that there was room in their 4000-and-some square foot house for Taylor and Ernie to make themselves permanently at home. Taylor wasn't sure Belle and Jonah were included in that invitation, but she knew that all four of them would rather have their sense of independence than all the comforts this particular farm offered.

Grandma passed her a mug of coffee. "It's decaf, love, I'm so sorry. I know how you kids are with coffee, but I've had all I can take this morning."

"It's perfect, thank you," Taylor said wrapping her cold fingers around the mug. "I've had enough already too."

"I hate to rush you, but you'd better tell me what you're after." Grandma Quinny pulled a lump of dough from a big stainless mixing bowl and began to shape it, folding it gently and patting it over and over again. "Has something happened? Is Ernie okay? I can't remember the last time you just came by to chat."

"Sorry." Taylor hid behind her large ceramic mug for a moment.

"That wasn't a reprimand. But I do want to make sure that you get what you need so that you'll come back again." That comment did hold a hint of reprimand.

Taylor took a deep breath and then spit it out. "I won't beat around the bush. What do you remember about the fall and winter of 1975?"

Grandma Quinny tilted her head. "Hmm…1975? Let's see. Your dad went to kindergarten that year. Nothing much changed for the big kids. Your Aunty Beth was a preschooler. My sister had just moved to Depoe Bay."

"Was that hard for you?"

"I did feel lonesome, thank you for asking. That beautiful coastal town felt like it was on the other side of the moon." She sliced the fat square of dough into even triangles. "It's hard when a sister moves away." There was no malice in her tone. It wasn't some kind of judgment about when Taylor had moved away leaving her young sister behind. Just sadness and longing. Plus, Taylor was sure Grandma Quinny didn't think of Belle as her real sister.

"What was Lorraine Love like back then?"

"Lorraine was a young girl. High School, I think. Sixteen, possibly. Something like that. She had a slick car. Those Loves have always had money." She paused in cutting the scones. "Lorraine ran with a wild crowd back in 1975."

"I've heard about The Cutter, Grandma. Can you tell me about that?"

Grandma Quinny sighed with exasperation. "Oh that. People always want to make small towns sound like dens of secret crime and violence. If you've been around for a few generations, you know it's just family. All families have their rough times. The people in the cities, they want to justify their dangerous neighborhoods by saying it's just as bad everywhere else."

"Grandma, what does this have to do with The Cutter?"

"I'm getting to it." Grandma Quinny waved her hand, fluttering away Taylor's impatience.

"Sorry." Taylor helped herself to a scone.

"Just one. They're for the church."

"Carly from Bible Creek Quilt and Gift says hi," Taylor said remembering the message from what felt like years ago.

"I've seen her more recently than I've seen you, young lady."

"Can you please tell me about this Cutter thing?"

"Some people don't believe The Cutter existed. Some people do. I admit, if it was just Lorraine and the first girl, I would have my doubts as well. Nobody ever tied the body in Portland to the missing girl from town. The family wasn't from here, originally, so there was no one to report back after they moved away."

"What about the car crash?" Taylor picked small bites off her scone. She hadn't really been hungry, not after all her donuts. It was just her lack of control around such warm, fresh baked goodness.

"That's where things get interesting. If you read the medical examiner's report, which many of us did." She glanced up at her TV and laughed. "Listen, we didn't have reality TV back then. We had to find our entertainment where we could."

Taylor pressed her lips together to suppress a laugh. It was so like her grandma to read an ME's report for entertainment, and yet it was an awful lot like herself too.

"She had cuts and wounds that were not consistent with the glass from the broken windshield, and nobody ever could explain it."

"And the suicide?" Taylor asked. If Grandma Quinny took something seriously, it tended to be serious. She hadn't expected this.

"Have you ever heard of anyone committing suicide by stabbing themselves in the heart?" Grandma Quinny made heartbreakingly deep eye contact.

Taylor shook her head no.

"Exactly."

"Hudson's mom," Taylor began, but Grandma Quinny rolled her eyes.

"Don't listen to a word Cheryl has to say. That woman makes up more storylines than Andy Cohen."

"Maybe so, but everything else she said matches an awful lot of what you just said."

Grandma Quinny shrugged. "They say if you have an infinite number of monkeys typing infinitely, one of them will write Hamlet."

"The murder of the museum volunteer has brought up the past for Lorraine, and I'm worried about her."

"I see. I suppose I'll have to go visit her, won't I?"

"I mean...you can," Taylor said, "but that wasn't exactly what I was thinking. It's just there's a lot of press here. They're hovering around the quilt store. They're looking for people to talk about what they're calling 'a string of murders in a small town.'"

"What did I just tell you? People find a nice place like Comfort and they want to ruin it. We're no more a hotbed of murder than Disneyland. People die everywhere, from all sorts of causes."

"Grandma Quinny, something just occurred to me. The Cutter—if he was real—was killing when Lorraine lived here before. And if it has started again..."

Grandma Quinny's lips pursed and eyes narrowed. She clucked. "Don't try to pass off Cheryl's ideas as your own."

"Sorry," Taylor bowed her head a little.

"Now, help me box up the scones that have cooled. They're going to freeze them at the church, so they have something nice for the ladies' coffee every fourth Thursday. Speaking of, next week is the fourth Thursday."

"Next week is also Thanksgiving," Taylor said. "Surely you're not going to go have coffee at the church instead."

"No, but I am having Thanksgiving and I didn't want you to forget. Will it be two seats at the table? Or three? Or maybe more?" She lifted both eyebrows and nodded, clearly hoping

Taylor had convinced half the town to come to the farm for dinner.

Taylor sighed. "Just me and Grandpa Ernie this time. The Langs get Belle and Jonah, and Cheryl gets Hudson."

"That's fine, dear. We're blessed to have you both at our table.

On her way out, Taylor spied Jonah, Belle, and the real estate agent touring a large, old farmhouse two parcels down from the Quinn family strawberry farm.

That would be an interesting choice of location for a party house full of wild, rich, gen Z influencers. She had a feeling neither the Quinn family nor their immediate neighbors would be excited about it.

CHAPTER TEN

*C*lay sat at that comfortable and sheltered desk tucked under the stairs. He leaned back in his wheeled chair so he could look through the open railing. He had a clear view of the sales floor of Flour Sax Quilt Shop from that angle, though at the moment there wasn't anything to see except Roxy.

He smiled. Roxy was plenty to look at.

He'd liked her spunk and vibes immediately. Her smile filled the whole room even though she was probably the smallest woman he'd ever dated.

She had a way of making his slightly less-than-average stature feel tall. And he loved running his hands through those glorious brown curls.

Once, at her place, he'd seen a box under the sink that indicated those curls weren't naturally brown anymore. But who cared? He didn't think he'd ever dated a girl whose hair was her natural color. And anyway, as he was inching closer to forty, his own sandy brown hair had a little silver in the temples too.

She was turned away from him at the moment, balancing delicately on her tiptoes, her small bottom firm in her tight jeans. He longed to stand behind her with his hands on her waist. He didn't want to interfere with her work or steal a moment of affection. He knew her weak leg could give out and he hated the idea of her getting hurt or even just embarrassed. But she finished what she was doing with only a slight wobble. And he found himself sighing with relief.

It was the only relief he felt.

The worksheets opened on his computer were nothing but stress.

He pulled out his list of ways to get young girls to the shop. He needed a laugh. The idea of throwing beautiful girls at a little ego-tripper like Jonah had become an obsession. Thoughts of it haunted him when he tried to fall asleep at night, or as he drove the long empty roads to a town with real stores.

He had dismissed the idea of a wine and sewing party like the wine and painting parties because his target market was under the drinking age.

He'd also dismissed anything reaching out specifically to current high schoolers because he was not a creep.

The only place he could think of to nab his niche target was that craft college at the end of Love Street. He thought of offering classes in the shop and seeing if the college might grant credit for them. The thing was, those arts students seemed so serious. He wasn't sure an artist like that could really lure the kid away from the irritatingly brilliant Belle.

But if he could get young people to start coming to the shop, it would do more than just prevent his early grandfather status. Things were looking really bad for Flour Sax. Money seemed to be pouring out and trickling in. What they needed was one huge shopping day with hordes of people. If only there was a way to get all those fans of Jonah's to the store at once. Like maybe a meet and greet. On the holiday weekend....

He was caught up in these thoughts when Roxy joined him

at his desk. "What've you got there?" She picked up his list with a frown.

"You'll laugh," he said.

"I could use a laugh."

He pulled her to his lap where she sat happily and comfortably. She really was a good fit. "See," he said, "quilting is still kind of an old lady thing."

"Hey now," she laughed.

"Knitting, crocheting, and macrame all had their time in the sun for the Millennials. Gen Z, those kids younger than Millennials, think Millennials are dumb, which means they're ripe for picking up a new hobby. And I'm trying to think of how to get them to pick quilting."

"Why would that make me laugh?" Roxy squinted at the paper. She had cheaters on a beaded chain around her neck but was loathe to put them on.

"Well...see...it's because I don't want to be a grandpa."

A laugh bubbled up, making her quiver deliciously on his lap. "What?"

He hadn't meant to tell the truth, but he didn't consider himself a liar and, in the end, he did think she'd probably laugh. Or at least he'd hoped so. "Jonah and Belle..."

"Ooh!" She immediately understood. "I hope they don't rush into kids either. But do you think quilting will be the distraction she needs?"

"It wasn't Belle I was thinking of distracting."

She swatted him on his arm. "You're a rotten person, did you know that?"

He leaned in and nibbled her neck.

"You want to turn my boy into a cheater." She swatted him a little harder, but also nestled into his embrace.

"I don't really want to...but if they didn't stay married, would it be so bad?"

"Young man," Roxy spoke in a firm, motherly voice. "I admit you made me laugh, but divorce is terrible. And as much as I think the kids rushed into marriage, I wouldn't wish divorce on anyone."

CLAY HELD his hands up in surrender. "Roxy, you are dating someone who is often selfish. But I don't want to hurt them either. I just, well, I mean can you picture me as some kid's grandpa?"

"Have you talked to the college about this idea?" Roxy poked the paper, graciously changing the subject.

"Not yet."

"It's a good one. Sales have been pretty terrible, haven't they?"

Clay shut his computer so she couldn't see the actual numbers. "It's been rotten. I'm starting to worry."

"What about the YouTube money? That's got to help."

He shook his head. "Not much of that left. Taylor invested heavily in that quilt expo. I don't think she wanted you to know."

"But there were hundreds of thousands of dollars, weren't there?" Roxy hopped off his lap and began to pace, reading his notes over and over again.

"I don't know what was there before she gave me the books, but she ran a whole lot of big radio ads in the city for this thing. It was costly, and with the murder, it just didn't pan out."

"Shoot."

"And you are great gals, but the show is not making money anymore. I don't know if it's Taylor on the screen or something YouTube has changed. Belle doesn't seem to manage it the way she used to, though we do appreciate Jonah is still editing. But the viewers are gone. The ad revenue is peanuts."

Roxie cleared her throat nervously. "Belle passed that off to me, the business stuff. I could be part of the problem."

"Whatever the cause, the money went out and it hasn't been coming back in. There's a savings, but it's nothing particularly impressive for a store like this."

"She keeps getting new stock in." Roxy turned to look at the most recent delivery in dismay.

"Yeah, Taylor's been known to try to solve problems by shopping."

"That's not fair."

"It's the truth, and the sooner she realizes it, the sooner things will turn around for her. I'd hate to see what her personal finances are." He grimaced. He'd been burned by her personal finances in the past.

"The house is paid for, at least. I remember when Laura paid it off. We had a real bender at Loggers to celebrate."

"Ernie's had a lot of expenses lately." Though Clay sometimes found himself missing his life in Portland with Taylor, he daily woke up thankful they didn't share a checking account anymore.

"She'd never do anything to risk her family business." Roxy walked to the cartons, ran her hand across them and then walked back. Her love for the Quinn family and the little shop was written in her big, weepy eyes. "It's not at risk, is it?"

"I don't think so. Not yet. She's not going to get rich from it, but she can hang on for a while. At least I hope."

"I could cut back my hours," Roxy said. "Jonah would probably help me out."

"You don't have to. She can afford the two of us. The apartment's most of my salary, anyway, and I've only been turning in a few hours a week. Just enough to keep me in ramen till things turn around."

"That's terrible. You can't live like that." She settled onto his knee again.

"I exaggerated but it's still kind of true. I mean she's giving me free housing. I don't have anything to complain about."

She looked up at the ceiling. "How much would it save if she didn't have to run electricity and water to the apartment as well as the shop?"

"What are you asking?" Clay liked the way this conversation was heading.

"Why don't you move into my place? I'll feed you wholesome meals and that might make up for becoming grandparents a little sooner than you had hoped."

"I don't hate that idea. I wonder what Taylor would think."

"I'm sure she's over you. She's madly in love with Hudson. But I do think that all of our togetherness might be a little rough on her."

Clay suppressed a grin. He didn't mind her suffering a little considering the way she'd broken his heart. "Hey, maybe she could actually rent the apartment. Instead of costing her in utilities, it could bring in some income."

She shook her head. "I doubt she'd want some random person to have unlimited access to her shop day and night." She paused, then spoke more optimistically. "The kids might like to have their own place. They can't live with her forever."

Clay thought of the relief he had seen on Taylor's face the moment she realized she had someone to help her care for Grandpa Ernie. But he didn't correct Roxy. "Maybe so." He kissed her cheek.

She stood and stroked his sandy-brown-with-hints-of-silver-hair. "If you moved into my apartment for a while," she said, "you could probably handle her books, and take other clients too. And then who knows what would happen."

He smiled, but he hadn't liked the use of the phrase "for a while." If he moved in with Roxy, he sure would like to think it would be for a long, long while. Maybe even long enough to become actual old grandparents. He was just beginning to enjoy the vision of himself in a recliner watching football while a silver-haired Roxy brought him a tray of cookies, when Taylor came in. She looked preoccupied, so he turned to his work. He wasn't going to add to her burdens at least.

But right on her heels were three journalists who must have been hiding in the shadows.

CHAPTER ELEVEN

"*T*aylor!" The female reporter, who looked to be about Taylor's own age, held the other two back with her elbow. "Taylor, can I buy you a cup of coffee?"

Taylor looked from reporter to reporter. Graham's lips curved sheepishly. She suspected he got away with murder because of that crooked smile. The older man scowled, like he knew he had been cut out.

While a wiser woman might have said "no comment" and walked right out the back door, Taylor liked the girl holding back her male rivals. "Sure. Let's head to the diner."

The scowling man straightened up, and Graham nodded.

"But I won't say a word if either of them comes in after us." Taylor frowned sternly at the men.

"Perfectly reasonable," the chosen reporter said.

Graham looked like his feelings were hurt. The other guy's face resumed its scowl. Both men left the store at the same time the women did.

. . .

THE WOMAN SITTING across from Taylor was dressed in a boxy, oversized blazer and a pinstripe shirt buttoned to her neck with two glittering brooches on each collar. She wore huge, clear plastic framed glasses and shiny blue eyeshadow. She crossed her arms on the table and stared intensely at Taylor. "I'm Ramona and I'm so glad you were willing to let me buy you a coffee," she said. "I think you have an important story to tell, and I think *Delilah Online* is the right media for you."

"*Delilah Online?*" Taylor asked. "I think I've heard of it. What..."

"*Delilah Online* is a feminist news blog," Ramona interrupted. "Usually we wouldn't track someone down like this, but I actually live in the area. I'm an English professor as well as blogger. Over in Monmouth. When I heard there was another murder in Comfort, I just had to come talk to you."

Aviva, the young waitress who was a friend of Belle's, came to the table with glasses of water. "Can I take your orders?"

"I'll have a coffee, two creams. You know how I like it." Taylor pretended the fourth cup of the day wasn't going to make her anxiety skyrocket.

"Can't I tempt you with a sandwich?" Aviva leaned in close. "Jess made a brisket yesterday that's to die for."

Ramona interrupted. "I'll also have a coffee, black. And yes, bring us two brisket sandwiches."

Taylor waited till Aviva had scampered away before asking, "What made you want to speak with me?"

"That's a great question. I've been following the tragedies here in your town. They began with the loss of your mother. Everyone knows about that, thanks to Jonah." Ramona blushed, slightly, as she said his name.

Taylor would have thought this feminist blogger was too old to have a crush on a kid like Jonah, but there was no telling.

"Then there was a string of murders, and your name just kept popping up," Ramona continued. "In the first case, you were good friends with the victim's family and seemed to be deeply enmeshed in the problem. With the second one, you were present when he was killed."

Taylor nodded, wishing her coffee would come to keep her hands busy.

"The fourth murder, I mean Taylor, you hired the woman who died." Ramona stared at Taylor, almost a challenge. "How do you feel about all of this?"

Taylor returned Ramona's unflinching gaze. She wasn't a reader of *Delilah Online*, though she knew it was sort of a woman's magazine with a liberal political point of view. Not a perspective she came across often in her small-town Oregon quilt shop. "Are you asking me how I feel about my mom being murdered?" She stated it frankly, not wanting to play games or get trapped into saying more than she would have willingly offered.

"That sounds like a good place to start. Talk me through what your experiences were like."

"I'd rather not," Taylor said. "What kind of article are you trying to write?"

"I want the world to know your name. You're a proper amateur detective spurred into action by personal tragedy. Books by the dozens are published every day on this premise, but the reality is rare. I think the women of *Delilah Online* need to meet you."

Taylor sat with her mouth closed. She had no interest in being introduced to the world as an amateur detective with a lurid life story. She had no interest in fame based on the loss of her mom. And she had a feeling that publicity like this would make it a lot harder for her to do any kind of snooping. "I don't think I have anything to tell you, except that a lot of people die all the time, all over the country, and a lot of people care about it. I am unfortunate enough to have a brother-in-law who made himself a little bit of fame online. That's all."

"Brother-in-law? Jonah and Belle are really married, huh?"

Taylor bit the inside of her cheek. She hadn't meant to give this woman any kind of headline. "It's a matter of public record."

"Married officially. The Juvies aren't going to like that." There was a quirk to Ramona's smile that irritated Taylor. This woman wasn't here to talk about Taylor's tragic backstory or her skills as an amateur detective. She was an old Juvie wanting to cash in on the local star for her own fame. There was no way Taylor was going to play into that.

Taylor lowered her voice and leaned forward like she had a big secret. "Have you heard of the mystery quilt? This murder has a twist."

Ramona rolled with the change in subject. "Tell me more."

Taylor lined out the known history of the quilt and that Shawna had shared information online that it might be a case of insurance fraud. "Millions of dollars at stake. Dangerous for anyone to write about."

Ramona's mouth made an O of interest. "Indeed? Do you think I could see this quilt?"

Taylor pulled out a pen, jotted the name of the museum on a napkin, then slid it across the table. "You can always ask the curator at the museum. I'm sure she'd be happy to work with a legitimate journalist like you." Taylor sipped her water innocently. She waited longer than the twelve seconds that would usually open someone up, and then she kept waiting.

Ramona fidgeted. "Maybe I should call her now."

"Sure, why not? A dead female journalist, a piece of folk-art fraud. These things seem like they'd be much more interesting to the Delilah Online audience then the sister-in-law of some kid on TikTok."

Ramona nodded. "I think you might be right. You'll excuse me." She laid some cash on the table and slipped out.

Taylor kicked herself. She'd let her annoyance at Ramona's response to the mention of Jonah get her off her game. Her whole goal today had been to keep the journalists away from Lorraine, not send them to her. She had a feeling this was going to come back and bite her.

Aviva showed up at the table with the huge, juicy sandwiches Ramona had just ordered. "Is she coming back?"

"I don't think so." Taylor pushed the little wad of cash towards her. "But she left you this."

"Thanks." Aviva picked the bills up and smoothed them out. "So…" she looked around, the diner was fairly busy. "Let me know if you need any help, okay? I mean with the murder, not the food. Though obviously, I'm your server today, so let me know if you need anything for the food too, right?"

"Got it. Thanks."

Aviva sauntered off counting the bills. Taylor shook her head. Aviva was a good kid, but there was no way she was inviting her into this mess.

Moments later, as Taylor was spreading a little extra mustard on her sandwich, Graham seemed to just appear in the booth with her. He offered his lopsided smile that gave Taylor an uncomfortable twitch in her heart. "Sandwiches this time. Perfect. I knew if I stuck to you, it would benefit me in the long run." He picked up Ramona's abandoned lunch and took a healthy bite.

"Let me ask you something," Taylor said.

Graham wiped his mouth with a paper napkin. "Shoot."

"Who's that other guy, the short one?"

"That's Gus. He's with a college paper. Editor-in-chief. You must really rank, since he didn't send a student."

"Pity the College of Art and Craft doesn't have a journalism department if this is such a big story." Taylor took another healthy bite of her sandwich.

"If? We've got a thirty-year killing spree here with The Cutter." He lowered his voice and leaned forward. The table seemed to shrink between them. "How seriously do I take our dear drunk friend?"

"I've only known her a few days longer than you have." She hesitated to spill secrets Tansy had told her in confidence. "And as you know, until last night, I'd never heard of anyone called The Cutter."

"You've had some time. What have you learned?" He dug into the sandwich again, his hair flopping in his eyes as he ate.

He was a flannel shirt wearing anachronism. Something from the 1990s come back to life. And he believed not only that she could have found out important info on the case in such a short time, but that she should have.

She hated that she found his confidence in her sexy, especially when she had a legitimately kind man at home. Well, at his home, but the idea was the same. Hudson didn't want her messing around in dangerous murders, but he was so nice. So thoughtful and wise for a kid his age. Hudson was the Rory Williams to Clay's Doctor Who.

Not Clay.

Graham wasn't her ex, Clay Seldon. And he wasn't Matt Smith's iteration of the sci-fi time traveler, either. He was, in fact, a stranger who wanted info from her for an online newspaper article.

And yet, she knew she was going to give him what he wanted. Maybe not right now, but she could feel it in her bones that she'd give him whatever he wanted.

"Not much, to be honest." She sat up a little straighter, proud of herself for not spilling all her carefully gathered beans.

Graham finished off Ramona's sandwich, and washed it down with her coffee too.

"What's in this for you?" Taylor asked.

"It's a living." Graham shrugged.

"If all you wanted was a living you could do anything. Why do this? Do you see journalism as a kind of vigilante justice? Or are you one of those who see yourself as a light in the darkness, educating the ignorant masses?"

"After that movie, *All the Presidents Men*, all journalists have seen themselves as investigators. We're out here trying to do the Lord's work. Hunting for our own Deep Throat, if you will." He leaned back in the booth smiling down on her, almost. He liked the questions, both getting them and answering them.

"Is that why you went into journalism? Because you wanted to catch criminals, but you didn't want to have to carry a gun?"

"Who says I don't carry a gun? I work for *Oregonlive.com*," he said it like a joke, but she wondered.

The corduroy jacket he wore over his plaid flannel was baggy with plenty of room for a side holster. And in her part of the state, concealed carry was usually a badge of pride.

She pulled her feet in closer to her bench seat, almost unconsciously. She'd lived in Portland long enough to lose a little of her small-town Oregon way of thinking. The idea a sitting across from a stranger who was packing made her nervous.

"What did *Delilah Online* want to know from you?" He went to take another drink of coffee but stopped short and looked in it. "Empty. Worth getting the server back—for coffee or info?" he asked.

She ignored his question about Aviva. "Do you want my honest opinion as an amateur detective, or do you want me to give you the same line Ramona gave me?"

He let out a short bark of laughter. "Amateur detective stuff, please."

"I think She's a big fan of my brother-in-law, Jonah Lang. You may have heard of him, if you happen to have a TikTok obsessed teenager in your life."

"Who hasn't heard of Jonah Lang? Our own little Oregon-influencer-darling."

"Ramona works for a feminist blog, and she's some kind of

professor at Western Oregon, but I think she's a Juvie. I think she saw an opportunity to come to Comfort to confirm some rumors about the kid and, if she was lucky, get to meet him."

"I wouldn't be surprised if that's what Gus's after too." Graham tried to catch Aviva's eye, but she was busy with a different table. "Jonah's career online has been fast, furious, and unexpected. Though it started with your mom's outtakes, it's deeply invested in murder now."

"I'm surprised Nike didn't fire him before he could quit." Taylor sipped her coffee and quietly pondered Jonah, Nike, and murder. Maybe he'd realized it was only a matter of time before the shoe company cut their ties.

"I don't know what story Jonah's telling you, but they did fire him. Murder is not on brand for Nike."

It was like a punch in the gut, but Taylor tried not to let it show on her face. Of course, Jonah had lied to her and Belle. Or maybe just her. Maybe Jonah and Belle had both lied to her. It was what kids did, when they got in over their heads. And this was just another reason Taylor was sure they were too young for a lifelong commitment like marriage.

"Want to talk about the mystery quilt?" Graham asked.

"I thought you were in Comfort for the murders."

"I don't know what I'm here for. Not anymore." Graham leaned forward on the table and looked at her from under his floppy hair. He was making real eye contact with his big, dark eyes, not that polite "look at their nose so you don't overwhelm them" thing they teach you in business communication classes. "You come to town for one thing as a journalist and you start to lift rocks. You never know exactly what you'll uncover."

Her heart was spinning somewhere in the vicinity of her throat. She was breathless, for just a second. "The Cutter," she stated.

"Sure, The Cutter." Graham lifted an eyebrow.

Taylor cleared her throat and pushed her mug away. Her

stomach was a little too twisty to finish her lunch. "The lady that introduced you to The Cutter is the same one who has the mystery quilt. We can head over there, if you want to, but Ramona will be there already."

He didn't break eye contact but nodded in agreement. "I'm in no hurry. You tell me what you want, and that's what we'll do."

CHAPTER TWELVE

*T*hey went to the museum despite the possibility of running into Ramona and fairly sure that Gus would follow them. They were not disappointed when they arrived and found they had the museum and Lorraine to themselves.

Graham had an impressively deferential attitude towards Lorraine, and whether it was that or the disarming smile that had sucked Taylor in so quickly, Lorraine responded warmly to his questions.

She took them back to the outbuilding and let them examine the quilt again. It was spread over the table where Shawna had died, as though it wanted to comfort the space somehow.

Taylor felt a warmth toward the old quilt, though she knew it was just fabric, and didn't have any feelings.

Lorraine passed out the white cotton gloves. Graham donned his as though examining historical textiles was a regular thing in his gig for the newspaper.

Taylor did the same.

Lorraine presented them with tiny magnifying glasses. "We ought to examine this closely," she said, almost purring. "I've had a report back from my friend, the expert, Erika. The backing and field fabric are a linen and cotton blend. Without a laboratory, we can't be sure that it's old enough to have been an English Regency era sail, but from the content of the fiber, we know it is an era-appropriate possibility. They did not use that blend for a significant amount of time, so the window for the age of fabric has been narrowed."

Taylor ran her cotton-covered finger across the rough surface. It was sturdy, even after all these years, or at least you could tell it had been sturdy. Not something a lady would usually choose to do decorative work on. The pieces of fabric that had been turned into appliqué were a much softer material, as though someone had repurposed clothing that had been worn for a long time.

Lorraine also traced one of the feathers with a finger. "This material was easily identifiable as wool, but more than that, Erika didn't say. The call had been primarily about the linen. She was extremely excited."

"Were you able to contact the Chachalu Museum at the Confederated Tribes of Grande Ronde?" Taylor found herself using the formal name for the reservation, almost like she wanted to catch Graham up on their previous conversations.

"Based on the design alone," Lorraine said, "it could easily have tribal roots, however, if that's the case, it would be much newer than we hope."

Graham scratched his head with his cotton-gloved hand.

Lorraine tsk'd.

He looked sheepish and apologized as he pulled the glove off.

"It might look as though there isn't much more we could do to destroy this," she said, "but that is all the more reason to be careful going forward. If a Native American woman from a local tribe did this beautiful work, then it should be honored, even if it's only a hundred years old. I've spoken with the curator at their museum. She's very interested." Lorraine's wistful tone suggested she really did hope it was European in origin. If it was native, it ought to be repatriated.

Taylor felt a pang at the thought. It was theirs, they found it...right? She shook her head. She knew that was wrong. It was far from hers. It belonged to a museum, but it should live in the right museum.

"If a European woman made this while in Oregon, from materials that were new at the time, it is irreplaceable," Lorraine continued.

"Where's the story in this?" Graham stepped back from the table and crossed his arms. "Did Shawna die because of this?"

Both women stared, their mouths pressed shut. Taylor didn't want to answer that question, not when she was feeling so warmly about the quilt.

"Or is this about something that was stolen from the Confederated Tribes? That's also a good story," Graham offered the second option.

"The difference between what the media considers a story, and what we in academia consider of note, is fascinating."

Taylor let their talk float over her for a moment. She was lost in thought. If this were a button blanket, surely it was more than a hundred years old. The button blankets she was familiar with were made of wool trade blankets, usually red wool on black. This could have been a very early iteration, made from what was on hand, before the traditional form had been established. And the mother of pearl buttons that would have adorned it had long been removed.

If this was a case of theft from the tribe, then it was more than the charming local story of a lost treasure found. They still might have something of true local significance.

"Carly from Bible Creek Quilt and Gift shared photos of this with numerous quilt groups online. But has anyone shared it with local members of the tribe? A family member might recognize it more easily than the museum curator."

"I sent the photo to the museum and they have shared it among their community. Unfortunately, an item like this would have belonged to a simple, humble family."

"Not a button blanket. And not an early one." Taylor turned up the corner of the blanket. "This predates the formalized button blanket style. The materials may have been discarded, and humble in origin, but they were repurposed into something beautiful. And if all those little threads across the surface had once held mother-of-pearl-buttons, then this was once a highly significant ceremonial robe, created to bestow great honor on an important person."

Graham let out a low whistle. "There is a story in that."

Lorraine's eyes narrowed and she seemed to look into the great distance silence for a very long time. "Yes," she said. "But would someone kill over it?"

Taylor had no answer for that. If the piece had been lost generations ago, no one would kill over it, because no one would have known it existed.

And if it had been carefully protected and loved for generations by a family, then it would not have shown up, incorrectly identified, at the quilt expo.

"No," Taylor agreed, feeling strongly that she was right. "If this is a ceremonial button blanket from a local tribe, no one would have killed over it."

"And yet," Graham reminded them, "Shawna is still dead."

The air in the room had grown somber despite the flickering fluorescent light. Without a word Lorraine let them out, shutting the door and locking it behind her.

"That poor child was killed by a madman, and it had nothing to do with the quilt. I know it better than anyone."

They walked back to the mill building in silence with shades of Lorraine's delusion hovering over them. Gus and Ramona stood at the door to Lorraine's office. Ramona was engrossed in her phone, and Gus stared into the distance with a now-familiar scowl on his face.

"This way," Graham said with a nod of his head towards the other side of the building. "I have a few more questions, if you don't mind. I'd like to talk more about The Cutter." He gave the name too much emphasis for Taylor's liking.

Lorraine lifted her chin and nodded. "Good. It's about time someone did."

Taylor walked behind them to The Miner's Daughter Café, but when Lorraine went in, Graham gave Taylor a wink, and shut the door on her.

She supposed if he wanted to walk home alone, that was his business. She had no interest in solving a decades old crime spree that lived only in Loraine Love's head. She skirted around to the other side of the museum to get to her car without being spotted, but Ramona and Gus had been too quick and were waiting for her.

"Ernie Baker's your grandpa?" the short man asked, with little enthusiasm.

Taylor's heart seemed to stop. Grandpa Ernie had to be okay. Belle was with him. "Yes."

"I'm Gus Baker. We're second cousins."

"Of course, we are." Relief that Gus hadn't been waiting with terrible news washed over her.

"Why don't we head to your store and have a chat?" Gus, despite his stature and Eeyore like face had a commanding way about him. She felt compelled to do as he said even as she resented it.

Ramona sidled up next to him as though she were invited, but Taylor only let Gus in her car with her. After all, he was probably family.

. . .

AT FLOUR SAX, Taylor let Gus Baker have her grandpa's recliner. She made them both a cup of coffee in the Keurig, though hers was decaf.

"You probably know by now that I'm the editor in chief of the Amity Evangelical College newspaper. Obviously, I can't ignore the fifth murder in a town the size of Comfort, but if this is a dangerous case, I can't let my kids come poking around in it, can I?"

"I don't have an answer for you."

"I grew up in Willamina," he said. "Graham said he'd talked to Lorraine last night. He said she told him about The Cutter."

Taylor waited. Gus wasn't asking questions, after all.

"Lorraine and I were friends back then."

Taylor stretched her neck from side-to-side. She'd be lying to herself if she continued the fraud that she was not interested in this vintage mystery.

She passed him his mug and pulled up one of the chairs from the student sewing machines. "Go on," she said.

"I don't think Lorraine's crazy. I remember her after her accident. She changed, and there was no way her wounds were self-inflicted."

"And the others?"

"I was a kid," he said. "I didn't have firsthand knowledge of the others, but it's the story I've been chasing my whole life, and it's the first thing I thought of when I heard that Shawna Cross was murdered the way she was."

"Let's be realistic," Taylor said, "1975 was forty-five years ago. Whoever stabbed those girls," she went with his story rather than fighting it, "surely that person would be too old to do it now."

"If he'd been a teenager when he committed the crimes, then he could have pulled it off. And if he'd been a teen back then, the killings might have stopped in our area because his family moved. Who knows how many seemingly random stabbings around the country could be chalked up to him, if we knew how to tie them together."

"You watch too much crime TV," Taylor said thinking of all the episodes of Criminal Minds she and Clay had watched while they lived together.

"I've been a newsman for three decades. I don't need television to know that criminals get away with it every day." He sounded disappointed.

"What would have brought him back to Comfort now?"

"Maybe a lengthy string of murders getting a lot of attention in the media when all his hard work had been forgotten." He grunted and settled into the chair. "I've done a lot of research on murderers. They don't like their efforts to go unrecognized."

"But why kill Shawna? And how did he know where to find her alone? Your theory doesn't hold up to the motive or opportunity test."

"I want to invite you to my office," Gus said. "That's why I came to town in the first place. I want to show you my notes. My wall of newspaper clippings and string, so to speak. It'll make me look like a man obsessed, but it will show you a picture you wouldn't see anywhere else. I can show you the way those victims were connected and exactly how they connect to Shawna Cross."

"No." Taylor shook her head. "You may or may not be a Baker. I don't think it's wise of me to head off with you anywhere right now."

He groaned. "You can bring that big strong boyfriend of yours. I know the East family. Always have. Shoot, I know Hudson. He went to my college."

The look of shock that flickered across her face hadn't been missed.

He shrugged. "Only one year. We gave him a great scholarship. He was part of the debut class for our trades program. But we were too..."

"Religious?"

"We're not as strict as our name makes us sound, but he wasn't into it. Bring him along. He knows where my office is. These are my office hours." He handed her a card. "I don't know about those other two, or why they came here the same time I did, but I knew that what I had to say wouldn't translate well in an email. Will you come?"

"I'll ask Hudson. And I'll ask my grandpa if you're really my cousin.

"Say hi to Ernie for me. My dad and Ernie were first cousins. He'll know who Gus Baker is." Gus stood up slowly as though his back was bothering him and left. Taylor flipped his card back and forth knowing she was absolutely going to go see him whether Hudson wanted to come or not.

FORTUNATELY FOR HER, Hudson was more than happy to come.

After getting perfunctory confirmation that Gus Baker was a relation, Taylor began to formulate her questions for him. By the next afternoon, after checking into the shop and making sure everyone was ready for a busy day doing nothing, Taylor sent Hudson a quick text, and he came by her house to pick her up.

"I see you're taking real ownership of the shop these days," he laughed.

She flinched at his jokey tone. "We're not busy enough for all of us to be there. I don't want to sit around an empty shop, and I certainly don't want to make it so Roxy can't pay her rent."

He interrupted her with a kiss and a squeeze. "That's the truth, but it's not nearly as funny."

They drove straight to the small private college and parked in the guest parking. Hudson led her straight to Gus's office.

They knocked on his door and then let themselves in.

The office was brightly lit, but cold and Gus was slumped over his desk, a pair of sewing sheers sticking out from the side of his neck.

Yamhill County Sheriff's Department sent their finest to the crime scene including Reg, Taylor's old friend. Hudson and Reg greeted each other with that stiff formality men who had dated the same woman at the same time sometimes have. After taking their statements, the deputies let them leave.

On the drive home, Taylor laid out the whole story of The Cutter to Hudson again, filling in the details she didn't have the first time. Then she discussed each of the journalists who had been lying in wait for her.

"But there had been more than just three cars parked on Main Street that first day, hadn't there?" he squeezed in a question.

"It felt like dozens, but if I close my eyes and really focus, I can picture six cars. Imagining at least one of them was a regular customer, there had to be at least two more journalists. Especially if you consider how panicked Clay was. Graham said something about *Yahoo News* and *Buzzfeed*, but I'd figured he was joking. I guess it was just the three who had the commitment to stick around. And boy did they stick." She paused, thinking it was fair to let Hudson talk again, but he didn't speak.

"I'm a little worried. I feel like Graham should be warned. And Ramona. They ought to head back home. Graham at least would be much safer in Portland than here. Because Ramona just comes in for the day, I think."

"If he's a good journalist, he won't want to leave now." Hudson's voice was as stiff as his shoulders. "The story just got good. But I'd worry more about Ramona. Harder to get lost in the city if you don't live in a city."

"Yeah...and she does seem like the kind that would get herself killed trying to get a celebrity interview."

"Should we find her?" Hudson asked.

"I don't want to have to talk to her, but I also don't want her to get murdered." Taylor picked at the decorative hole on the side of her jeans. She really wanted to discuss this murder with Graham. He'd have advice for her.

"Should I find her?" he asked. "I could take you home. That might be the best thing. If it's dangerous for a journalist, it's even more so for you." He gave her a knowing look, his hazel eyes full of concern.

She had grown pretty fond of those hazel eyes, but wished they looked at her with excitement and confidence when they talked about murder. "We should probably tell Jonah and Belle what's going on. Since Ramona seemed to be more interested in them than she ought to be, she could be bringing trouble to my doorstep."

"As opposed to you bringing it there." There was just a hint of a snide tone in his voice. "Sorry. I just can't help thinking how much safer you'd be..."

"If I left these things to the sheriff?"

"It's not your fault that you were the one that found the body. And it's not your fault that these journalists dragged you into it. But did you have to meet with Shawna's boyfriend?"

"Someone had to talk to the guy." Taylor looked out the window. She knew she was bringing risk to herself, but that was up to her, not him.

"Seems to me Tansy Dorney would have been a better bet, if she was really Shawna's best friend."

"I don't know how close they were. Sometimes when someone is gone, you feel a lot closer than you felt before. Her ex mentioned Tansy but didn't say anything much about her."

Her phone rang before they were back to town. She glanced down. It was Reg. "Should I answer it?"

"I'm driving, so you might as well." Hudson shrugged.

She answered.

"Hey Taylor, I know you've already made your statement,

but we'd like to interview you one more time. Can you swing by the office tomorrow morning?"

Taylor agreed and hung up with very little conversation.

Being close to danger was thrilling and being involved in meaningful work felt like a strength.

Grief had overwhelmed her, paralyzed her, even. Involving herself in crime investigation was physiologically the opposite of grief. Her counselor had brought it up once. She'd implied it might not be healthy, but Taylor hadn't agreed. Adrenaline pulsed through her veins right now. It was a high, of sorts, and so much better than the feeling of failure she got from being in the empty store that had thrived under her dead mother.

The idea that Hudson didn't approve was the lone sour note. She reached out for his hand, wanting to be reassured that this steady, healthy man with the good communication skills was real, and did love her.

He wrapped his big, strong fingers around hers and squeezed lightly. The familiar touch of her lover made her breathe a little easier, anyway.

"Sometimes," he said in his low, husky voice, "I just want to whisk you away somewhere safe, far from murder and rain and bad memories."

She shivered.

But not in a good way.

AT HOME that night Taylor made a large pot of spaghetti and turned half a loaf of bread into garlic toast for herself and Grandpa Ernie. She needed the comfort and he deserved a hot meal at home with family.

Jonah and Belle joined them mid-meal. It was a huge relief to have all three of them safely under her roof.

"Be careful," she said after telling them the whole story. "I'm a little worried because Ramona from *Delilah Online* was much more interested in you than me."

"And you don't mind taking risks for yourself," Belle said, "but you don't want to bring trouble to us, is that right?"

"Exactly. I'd be devastated if you got hurt because of me."

"Did you ever think, young lady," Grandpa Ernie interjected, "that the rest of us might be devastated if you got hurt?" He had refused his oxygen before dinner and his eyes looked angry and frustrated, as they would if you couldn't breathe well and got confused easily.

"I promise," Taylor said, "to the very best of my ability, Gus Baker was the last dead body I will ever find."

CHAPTER THIRTEEN

*T*aylor stared at the body of Ramona, the journalist for *Delilah Online.*

She had run to Western Oregon University to see Ramona before she went to meet Reg at the sheriff's office. It was a half hour's drive the wrong direction but would have been worth it. Taylor had wanted to talk about Gus. Wanted to talk about his suspicions. She just wanted to know what Ramona knew, if anything. She had wanted to warn Ramona to be careful.

But the scissors in Ramona's back were evidence Taylor had been too late.

Taylor scanned the office before she called the sheriff, taking pictures of anything and everything that might have useful information on it. It would be a slog getting through each picture, but she wasn't going to miss a trick this time. She took several close ups of the wounds, and though Ramona seemed to be the kind of writer who did her work on the little laptop that was laid on her bed, her desk was covered in scraps of paper.

Torn receipts, backs of envelopes, and corners of junk mail were covered in a clear and crisp block print. Taylor managed to get a picture of everything that was face up, taking extra care not to touch any of it. Maybe she was wrong, but she sure suspected these were notes about the murder.

Taylor managed to fill the better part of ten minutes documenting the scene. Then she called 911. It was only after she tapped the last 1 that the horror of the scene hit her. She fell back against the wall to catch her breath and calm her racing heart. No, death was not normal yet, especially not violent death.

Ramona died in an outfit very similar to what Taylor has seen her in last. A boxy blazer, this time in a high-contrast plaid. High-waisted jeans cuffed at the ankle with chunky shoes. She was funky and young and had been full of hope. Taylor stared at her as she waited for the sound of sirens in the distance.

Reg arrived with Maria, one of the deputies Taylor was becoming very familiar with. Reg and Maria had a sort of camaraderie that Taylor hadn't expected. And though she used the word camaraderie, Taylor knew it had to be something a little more. The two deputies shared glances and light touches as Taylor watched them walk across the University campus that reminded her a little too much of Clay and Roxy.

Reg greeted Taylor with a look of severe disapproval. "Stay out of the way." His firm words were like a slap. He went straight to the body taking his own pictures.

Maria pulled her to the side. "This doesn't look good."

"Three murders," Taylor agreed. "It's terrible isn't it?"

"In the last week, you have been the person that found three different murdered individuals." Maria's eyes held both sympathy and disappointment, as though Taylor was her daughter and a bad one at that. "And each of them was killed with a pair of sewing sheers."

"It's beginning to feel personal." It was the first time Taylor had put it into words, but she meant it wholeheartedly. Someone was trying to terrify her, and in admitting it, she truly understood the crime of terrorism and why it was so evil. She swallowed nervously. "I'm getting scared."

Maria watched Reg for a moment, then turned back to Taylor. "We're going to need to take you down to the station with us. I hope you understand what I mean. And also, you have the right to remain silent."

"Reg, what does she mean?" Taylor's voice came out quiet and hoarse as she held back what she knew would be embarrassing sobs.

Reg was kneeling on the ground next to the body, but he looked up at her with his face stiff and angry. Very similar to the face he'd made when she'd had to explain that she wasn't interested in him romantically. Then he turned to Maria. "I'm calling the coroner. He should be here soon. You and Serge can take Taylor down to the station."

"I'll go with you," Taylor said. "I'll answer any questions you need."

Maria looked forward, not making eye contact as she repeated, "You have the right to remain silent. Anything you say and do can be used against you in a court of law." She recited the rest of the Miranda Rights as she led Taylor to the county issued sheriff's SUV. This trip to the sheriff station was going to be very different than any of the others Taylor had ever taken.

TAYLOR WAS LEFT ALONE in one of the small interview rooms for what felt like hours and hours and hours. She had not handed over her phone, and spent the time texting her lawyer, Amara Schilling, and calling her sister. Neither responded.

She knew Amara was the wrong kind of lawyer, but she was sure she could help point her in the right direction, at least.

The walls of the little interview room were dull cream, unadorned. And the table was a faux wood laminate like the many tables she had sat at as an employee or student. There was nothing about the space that said, "This is it. You're going to jail," and yet every fiber of her being trembled knowing that she was one step away from serious trouble.

But it had just been Reg.

Her old friend.

He wouldn't let them *really* arrest her for a crime she hadn't committed. And he had to know that she would never murder anybody.

It had to be a setup.

As she seemed to have unlimited time, she scrolled through the pictures she had taken at Ramona's. Some were just names and dates. Some were clearly groceries lists. Most were things she didn't recognize as being useful to her situation.

There was an interesting note that included both the Chachalu Museum and Lorraine's name. But the other things in that list were unfamiliar to Taylor. There was a note that listed all of Shawna's family, including Tansy who was identified as a BF. Taylor wondered if BF was intentional. BFF meant a deepest friendship. Perhaps BF was supposed to mean the women weren't all that close. Perhaps, though they were friendly, they didn't truly have each other's backs. But Tansy as a potential murderer had seemed more likely when Shawna was the only one dead.

Taylor went back to the picture that included the list with the museum on it and tried to guess what the other names were, but before she could come up with anything reasonable, the sheriff, himself, came in.

A short, stocky, and powerful man, Sheriff Rousseau had shown his dislike for Taylor in the past. And his presence filled her with fear far worse than Ramona's dead body had. This man had her fate in his hands.

"Maria told me you felt like someone was targeting you with

these murders. Who knew you were going to go see Gus and Ramona?"

Taylor stared in disbelief. He was taking her idea seriously? It seemed impossible.

He sighed. "Taylor, we know you didn't do this. How could you have? No motive. No connection to these guys except the claims that Baker was a cousin."

The Sheriff was fast, if he already knew that.

She continued to stare.

He shook his head. "Gus Baker's my cousin too. On his mother's side. You and I are practically related, Taylor. Now, who knew you were going to go see him?"

"No one. I didn't tell anyone. The journalists all wanted to talk to me, but I don't know who else they were talking to."

"You want me to think it was you?"

"No." She felt trapped in that small benign cage. She knew what she was trying to say, but words were failing. Just because she didn't tell anyone where she was going to be, didn't mean she'd killed someone. "Hudson knew. Maybe he told someone."

"Pushing it onto your boyfriend won't really help your case. I could hold you here. Probably couldn't charge you yet, but I could keep you in the jail, if I wanted to take the easy way out. But I don't want that. I want to make sure no one else gets murdered this weekend."

"I didn't say Hudson did it. I thought maybe he told someone. His mom's been staying with him. We found Gus together, maybe he told her where he was going, and she told someone else."

He gritted his teeth. "Maybe. What about this Tansy Dorney?" he asked, "Lorraine's daughter."

She noted that he didn't mention Tansy's dad. "Do you know Lorraine?" Taylor asked.

"I'm not from Comfort, but this county's not so big. And Lorraine, she leaves an impression."

"I think Tansy's really sad that her friend was killed, but I also wonder if she had professional jealousy." Wondering about that to her boyfriend, or even Graham, was so different than suggesting it to the sheriff. Her stomach turned with guilt. "But," she added quickly, "she'd have no reason to kill Gus or Ramona."

"What kind of profession?" he asked.

"Blogging." Taylor closed her eyes. That was pretty close to journalism, especially since *Delilah Online* called itself a news blog.

"Gus and Ramona weren't bloggers."

Taylor exhaled.

"But blogging is not that different from what Ramona did. And that little college has an online paper." Again, Sheriff Rousseau was quick.

"But she didn't know I was going to see Gus or Ramona. I haven't seen Tansy in days, in fact." Taylor laced her fingers together and squeezed her hands tightly. Tansy needed to know about these murders. She'd already written about the quilt and possibly the murders by now. She was in just as much risk as Graham. "What about Lorraine's theory about The Cutter?" Taylor asked, hoping to get his mind off Tansy.

Sheriff Rousseau dragged his hand through his salt-and-pepper hair. "You sound like my wife. If I have to hear 'What about The Cutter?' one more time."

"Your wife's from around here too?"

"Yep." He admitted it but didn't elaborate. "Listen, we're going to be here for a while," the sheriff growled, but despite his rumbling, angry voice, he looked like he was sorry. He pulled up a chair across from her and fell into it. "Let's get down to brass tacks."

. . .

THE SHERIFF HADN'T GONE easy on Taylor. He had kept at her on and off all day. They never took her phone, but never promised they weren't going to hold her, either. That initial admission that he knew she hadn't done it was never repeated, as though the threat of being kept in jail would be enough to make her remember exactly what they wanted to hear. Several people came and went through the day, but never Reg, Serge, or Maria.

She would have given anything to talk to Reg, at least.

When they finally let her go for the day, Sheriff Rousseau had said cryptically. "See you tomorrow, I guess." There was no twinkle in his eye to intimate it was a joke.

By the time she got back home, she was exhausted, but relieved to find Grandpa Ernie asleep in the recliner in his room.

Belle and Jonah were also in bed already, and though Taylor was angry at her sister for not returning her calls, she didn't want to barge in on whatever those two were up to.

As it was, if it weren't for the numerous dead bodies Taylor had seen over the last few days, and her time in the hot seat, she would have felt sorry for the kids who weren't having much of a honeymoon.

She fixed herself a microwave burrito, grabbed the last bottle of iced tea from her fridge, and fell onto the slipcovered couch in her living room. All of the doors were locked. All of the lights were on. She repeated to herself over and over again that she had no reason to be scared.

But she knew that was a lie.

There was a murderer out there, sticking scissors into people until they died. And the people he was killing were the people she had been talking to.

She picked up the remote to find something to distract herself with. She flipped through Netflix. Row after row of comedy or drama, detectives or lovers. The titles alone were enough to distract her or trigger her, depending on how long she lingered.

She had settled on a cooking challenge when a knock on the door shook her. She sent up a brief blessing for humorous home chefs. They were the reason the sound of the fist on the door hadn't sent her into a panic. At the same time, she found she wasn't jumping to answer it. But whoever was at the door didn't give up easily, and Taylor thought it might be Graham.

Graham, who was most likely to be murdered next.

Her heart beat a little at the idea of letting him in and keeping him safe. And she found herself answering the door almost hopefully.

Because she didn't want him to die.

That was all.

She thought of Hudson as quickly as she could.

But it didn't change the fact that she only answered the door because she had hoped it might be Graham.

Instead it was Erika, the textiles expert from the College of Art and Craft. For a textile expert, she had certainly embraced the drab look of a communist. Her well-worn khaki shirt and trousers highlighted the whiteness of her hair and slight sallow tinge to her complexion.

"I'm sorry to bother you at home, but I was leaving late, and I pass right by your house. Do you have a moment?"

"Yes, sorry, please come in." She welcomed Erika and gestured to the armchair inviting her to sit.

"I won't stay long," Erika said. "I had news about the quilt, and I wanted to let you know."

"Thanks." Taylor tried to drum up enthusiasm for what was the least important mystery on hand.

"As you know, we took a small fiber sample from one of the frayed edges. I don't think we risked the integrity of the piece."

"Sure." Taylor wondered if she ought to offer Erika something to drink.

"I've already reported that the linen is very old, as we thought. But a better lab has had a look at it and refuses to date it any more specifically than "early nineteenth century." Our hope was that it was from the eighteen-tens. But the new information is valid and includes the covered wagon era. This is a significant difference, historically speaking, and a disappointing reversal of opinion. However, the information on the wool is what has really changed the story."

She paused waiting for some kind of response. Taylor couldn't drum anything up. She was still committed to the idea it was a button blanket, in which case it couldn't matter how old the fabric was. It was newer than 1850s and likely belonged to the Confederated Tribes.

Erika continued. "Its over-embroidery disguised the truth. What we thought was well-worn superfine wool, is merely black flannel suiting from the twentieth century."

"Excuse me?" Taylor stared.

"This is an entirely modern work made in part with old materials. Whether the ground fabric is a sail, a covered wagon, or even the tent from a military campaign, we can't know. But considering the age of the appliqué pieces, we are in possession of a modern work."

Taylor sat up. "Then Shawna was right. But do you think it was created to be a fraud, or just submitted to the expo for that reason?"

"We may never know if it was an intentional fraud. We were fooled until a laboratory examined it. The person who submitted it to the expo may have been equally mistaken. These things happen with material history of the common man." Erika glanced at her watch, then moved back to the door. "But just because it's not what the tag claimed doesn't mean it isn't beautiful. It will make a lovely display for the museum."

"It still feels like a Native American piece."

"Even more so now," Erika agreed. "Not likely to be a ceremonial one, but it is beautiful hand work. Well worth displaying at the museum."

"Thanks for letting me know. That's one mystery solved, I suppose."

"Yes. I'm sorry about your friends."

"Thanks." Taylor hardly knew the two journalists who had been killed, but Gus was family, and she felt a solidarity with Ramona, now that she was dead. A woman who'd died trying to get to some kind of truth or other.

"Though this quilt isn't the story Lorraine had hoped for, it's still worth telling. Even if we don't find the creator, we can learn so much about the past studying this piece. I'd love to be able to show the quilt to your grandfather."

"Because of the wool suiting," Taylor said.

"I felt a fool when the lab called back that it was modern. I ought to have been able to tell at a glance. The embroidery does disguise it, but if it's a flannel it could be from as late as the 1960s. Ernie Baker is the proper expert on this, and his opinion would weigh heavily with me."

"I'm sorry. He's sleeping."

"Don't worry, I don't have the quilt. Perhaps you could bring him to the museum, and we could look at it together with Lorraine. I would be honored to be a part of that conversation. I've always liked your grandfather. A truly lovely man." She paused.

Taylor found her eyes filling with tears, and her throat closing a little. Her Grandpa Ernie *was* a truly lovely man.

"Let me give you my number," Erika said. "You can let me know when it might work for you and Ernie."

"Sure." Taylor passed her phone with a grateful smile but found she really couldn't say more.

"Thank you. This means a lot to me." Erika spoke with true warmth in her voice.

When she had gone, Taylor indulged in a few bittersweet

tears. It was lovely to think of Grandpa Ernie's expertise being desirable by this academic expert. It was something sweet to hold on to for the evening.

After Taylor locked all of the doors one more time, checked all of the windows, and moved the furniture ever so slightly, so that if someone did break in, they would trip and make a loud racket, she went to bed. She paused first at Belle's bedroom door, longing to talk to her about both her traumatic day and the good thoughts about their grandpa, but one of the newly-weds was softly snoring, and Taylor let them be.

She was happy that she had something to look forward to, even if it was just taking Grandpa Ernie to the museum to look at the quilt. She would put off the harder conversations for another time.

She didn't call Hudson. She hadn't called him from the Sheriff's station, either. He wasn't going to like it—her running off to meet Ramona. Or Ramona's murder. Or not getting called when she needed help.

CHAPTER FOURTEEN

onah cornered Taylor the next morning. "I've got to get a place for me and Belle. That's all there is to it. She'll still hang out with Gramps every day. She loves it, and he sleeps a lot, so she can still do her research. I promise we're not trying to abandon you, and I don't mean to be offensive," he said. "But I freaking banged my shins up last night when I got up to get a drink. And I know that you are maybe," he had the decency to look conflicted, "still a little messed up from stuff. But I can't live in a booby trapped house. You got to understand, right?" He rubbed his shins.

She stared him down, more intensely than she meant. "I spent all day at the jail being interrogated about a string of murders. The killer is still on the loose and targeting folks who have just talked to me. But sorry your shins got banged up."

"Crap. I didn't know." He jutted his chin out the way young guys do when something is too intense, but they don't want to show it. "Have you thought about moving in with Hudson? Maybe Gramps would be better in a nursing home."

She didn't like that idea, or Jonah calling Grandpa Ernie "Gramps." He hadn't earned the right.

"We can consider it after Hudson's done rebuilding Bible Creek Care Home. I won't move Grandpa Ernie out of town."

"My Aunt Jenny runs an adult care home here in Comfort," Jonah offered.

Aunt Jenny…Taylor wracked her brain. Maybe it was a great-aunt, like an aunt of Roxy's rather than Jonah, because she was pretty sure Roxy was an only child. Or maybe it was one of those cousins one generation up that kids call aunt. She could have asked but she didn't like the way he seemed to think he could make decisions for her family.

"No one's making you stay at my place."

He held up two hands. "Sorry, sorry. I'm not trying to hurt your feelings. But Belle's room is tiny. It's a twin bed, Taylor. And so's the one in my old room at Mom's house."

"Seriously, move out whenever you want. Coco still comes over to stay with Grandpa Ernie, right?"

"Don't get crazy. Gramps can't stand Coco. She hasn't been here in days. Besides, I said Belle wanted to be here. She loves her time with Gramps." Jonah began to pace in that hyperactive way he had. "You heard me literally say Belle will come every day. In fact, that's the reason finding a place is taking forever." He sounded frustrated and tired.

"You guys do what you need to do. I've got a lot on my mind right now." The idea that Belle wanted to be at the house warmed her a little, but not enough to sit around for more of this conversation. If nothing else, Jonah had run into her furniture and it hadn't made enough noise to wake her, so her trap hadn't worked.

"Hey, so…did you ever talk to my mom about Clay?"

The warmth cooled off fast, like jumping in the ocean on a crisp fall day. The nerve of this kid. He dared to ask a favor? "Nope. I don't know what I would say if I did. Her love life? Not my business. Not yours." Taylor strode outside as though she weren't wearing her pajamas and got hit with a cold, cold blast of November morning air. She went to the shed as though she had been heading there on purpose, let herself in and sat on the sofa, well on the edge of it as that was all that was exposed.

Jonah was right.

He and Belle should move out.

But he was wrong too.

She didn't need Hudson in the house to take care of her, and she didn't need to put Grandpa Ernie in a nursing home.

After all, Grandpa Ernie was the brilliant textiles expert who was going to help solve the mystery of the new murder quilt. She grabbed for her phone to text Erika that they could meet at her convenience, but she'd left it in the kitchen with Jonah.

Instead of pouting about it, she decided to take her counselor's advice. She stretched her arms, took several deep breaths, counted backwards from twenty in Spanish, and listed five things she was grateful for that gave her strength.

She took another deep breath, held it in, and thought of love.

Graham's face with his lop-sided smile slowly took form. She pushed it aside quickly. It just reminded her of Clay. That was all. She had loved Clay for a long time. She rested her head on the dresser that was perched behind her on the couch. Would Clay, or Clay-substitutes, always be the first thing that came to mind when she thought of love? Is this what it had been like for her mom, all those years a widow?

No one had ever been able to live up to the memory of her dad.

Taylor's counselor had suggested her own very dependent relationship to Clay had been because he was the opposite of her father. The anti-Todd Quinn. Todd, a big, strong, firefighting hero, who had died in action. Clay, a diffident computer guy who needed a woman to take care of him. It had been suggested, in fact, that she had picked and fallen in love specifically with a man she knew would guarantee to be a disappointment.

Or possibly, he was so different from her dad, that she hadn't been afraid he'd die.

But Hudson wasn't like Clay. He wasn't an anti-Todd Quinn. He was the real deal.

She pictured her longtime boyfriend with whom she had a committed, intimate relationship.

His broad shoulders.

His balanced mental health.

His strong hands.

But though he stood there in her mind like a paragon, all she could recall was his voice saying he wanted to take her away from Comfort, for her own safety. And that didn't feel like love.

She felt around for her phone again, only to remember she didn't have it. She'd have to face the family eventually, so she went back to the house. Seconds after stepping inside, her phone chimed a text, and she jumped. It had been a few weeks since she'd stopped jumping every time her phone made a noise. The relief at not having all of those surprise Snaps from her mom was huge. This time, she was just afraid it was Hudson and she'd have to find a way to explain all that had gone down since they'd spoken.

But it wasn't. It was Tansy. *Owen wants to get coffee. I can't go alone. I'd just cry the whole time. Come with?*

She didn't have to think about it. She'd like to ask the ex-boyfriend a few more questions, especially with Tansy there to correct anything he might try to live about.

"Baker's Dozen in Willamina." Tansy named the little bakery in her town. One that Taylor was pretty sure was owned by someone related to both her grandpa and Gus. And her, actually. She sometimes forgot to add herself into those equations.

It wasn't a long drive, though sometimes the stretch of farmland between towns felt like it went forever. She wished it did, that she could drive south or east to eternity and never run into another person. But she pulled into the little bakery parking lot anyway. Those moments where she wanted to run from it all were fleeting. What she really wanted was to make sure no one else was killed. Ever.

Tansy and Owen looked cozy in the little living room-like seating area. They both had coffee and donuts. Taylor joined them without ordering anything for herself.

"I invited her so I wouldn't spend our whole conversation weeping." As she spoke, Tansy wiped her eyes.

"Hey." Owens' eyes were red from tears as well. "I just wanted to see someone, anyone, who loved Shawna."

"I get it." Taylor meant it. This thing called grief? She and it were intimate. "How are you holding up?"

"Not well. I still can't believe she's gone. Completely gone. It doesn't seem right, or fair."

"I wish I could have one more day with her, to tell her how much I really appreciated her," Tansy's voice was a wistful whisper.

"I wish I could have the rest of my life with her. But I might not have gotten to, and that's even harder. I might have messed things up so badly, she'd never have come back." His eyes implored Tansy to correct him.

"I don't know...." Tansy looked down at her creamy ceramic mug. "But she had changed."

"Not deep in her heart, after all those years. We met when we were sixteen." This, he said for Taylor. "I was in Yreka. I thought she was the most amazing, brilliant person on the planet. My parents told me she was probably an old man pretending to be a girl. When we met the first time, my dad came." He stared out the window for a moment. "It all seems so long ago. We were so scared of what the internet could do, what kind of monsters were hiding on it."

"Hiding on the internet.... You said she'd met someone new

online," Taylor mused. "Do you think he could have something to do with her murder?"

"I don't think she'd met him in person yet." Tansy's soft, sad voice was hard to hear.

"She didn't like meeting people," Owen said. "She wanted to be able to edit everything she said. To type her thoughts out, look at them, correct them. Be the perfect version of herself. But I loved her real self. All of her."

"I know…." Tansy reached for his hand.

He grasped her hand in his and held tight, like she was a life preserver.

There was a passion in the grip that gave Taylor a little sympathy for Tansy's husband, Logan. If these two really turned to each other for comfort it could go badly for him. "What dating service did she use?" Taylor asked.

"Hm?" Tansy broke away from her moment with Owen, though she didn't let go of his hand. "I don't know. She didn't say. Might have been an interest-based message board, even."

"I bet it was," Owen agreed. "Because she didn't really want someone else…she couldn't have."

Tansy lifted his hand to her lips and kissed it. Then she stared at it for a moment and let go. "Sorry. I have to get out of here. I need…maybe I need to go to my dad's for a little while."

"Where are the kids?" Owen asked.

"With Pyper. She took the day off. She knows how hard this has been for me. Pyper's such a great kid." Tansy stared at Owen with a look of disappointment in her face, but Taylor was pretty sure she was only disappointed in herself.

Owen stood as well. "I probably ought to head home."

"Where is home again?" Taylor asked.

But Owen slung a computer satchel over his shoulder and left without answering.

Taylor wasn't uncomfortable with their emotions, or with their mildly inappropriate intimacy, but she wasn't sorry she'd come. There was every chance that Shawna had been catfished by a killer, and she knew a group of enthusiastic online detectives she could turn to for help.

Before she left, she texted Jonah her questions. If anyone could find out who Shawna had met online, it was the Juvies.

CHAPTER FIFTEEN

*O*nce home, Taylor was itching to make further progress on the investigation, so she bundled Grandpa Ernie up to take him to the museum to see Erika. She wasn't avoiding work, avoiding Hudson, or avoiding her sister. She was just enjoying her Grandpa's company as he performed a valuable task for the experts at the museum.

A cold wind was cutting through town now, and it was no day to walk, even if Grandpa Ernie could. She hated that there was no point in bringing him to the museum without his portable oxygen, but he'd been sweet as a lamb about bringing it.

"Your mom loved Thanksgiving." They had driven about a block in silence when Grandpa Ernie blurted that out.

"Stuffing with gravy was her favorite," Taylor mused.

"But she'd never eat the cranberries."

"I always miss her so much at Thanksgiving." The longing for her mom during the big family holiday had been almost desperate the last two years, and it didn't feel like it had gotten any better yet.

"You should make the turkey."

"I wish I could, but there'd be no one but me and you to eat it. We'll go to Grandma Quinny's and be part of her big party instead." Taylor hoped Grandpa Ernie would like the idea better than she did.

"That Quinn's a good feller. Too bad about his son."

"Who's that?" She wasn't sure which of her uncles was on Grandpa Ernie's bad side now. With six kids, all married, there were any number of Quinn sons to pick from.

"Todd. He always was trouble. He's going to slip up one of these days and break Laura's heart."

Grandpa Ernie's portable oxygen was in the back seat. Taylor had hoped he was with it enough that they could get away with putting it on in the museum. Her heart sunk. It sounded as though he had slipped and thought he was talking to his long-deceased wife, Grandma Delma.

"He's a good boy," Taylor said, pondering the statement. Her dad, as a "boy." He'd died when he was just about her age, younger than Clay, but older than Hudson. Maybe not literally a boy, but still…so young.

Grandpa Ernie shook his head, then stared at Taylor from under his bushy eyebrows. "No matter what anyone says, you've got to respect your father you hear me?"

"Yessir." She didn't know if she was Delma, to him, or Laura, or her own self. But she knew her grandparents hadn't approved of their only daughter's early marriage. At eighteen, she'd been even younger than Belle, but Taylor's parents had made it work. They hadn't even had Taylor till they'd been married a couple of years.

"I was thirty-two years old when I met your grandmother," Grandpa said.

He moved in and out of reality so easily, Taylor wondered if she'd been the one confused earlier, rather than him. "And we still didn't rush into things. At eighteen I was fighting in the war with Korea. When I came home, I started a business. Hard work. That's all I knew when I was young." His face began to sag as they pulled into the parking lot of the museum. "Our Belle shouldn't have gotten married. Just like Laura." He gave Taylor a comforting pat on the shoulder as she helped him out of the car. "I'm glad you're a smart one. No rushing for you. Plenty of time. Grandma Delma was thirty-five when she had your mother. You've got plenty of time."

Taylor knew that her very Catholic Grandma Delma had longed for more children. Both she and her doctors had chalked up their inability to have more than one child to her age. While Taylor agreed in theory that she had plenty of time, she knew she didn't have forever.

"Don't rush. Hudson's just a boy. Not even thirty. Whatever you do, don't rush into marriage with that boy."

"Yessir." Taylor gave him a kiss on the cheek. She didn't like that she couldn't trust her own heart right now, and it was nice to know that at least one person didn't think she needed to hurry to figure it out.

Erika and Lorraine met them in the metal outbuilding. The quilt was stretched across the stainless-steel table again, but it looked tired. The fluorescent lights, which had been so cheerful the first time she had come, seemed to flicker, unsure of themselves now. And buzzed. They buzzed so loud this time.

"Thank you for meeting me, Mr. Baker," Erika spoke with reverence. "Many years ago, I was a student of your wife at the college, and it's an honor you'd come here."

Ernie glowed, but Taylor worried. She hadn't been able to convince him to put his oxygen on. She wore the backpack for him, since he refused.

"This quilt was left behind at the Cascadia Quilt Expo, and I had some questions about the fabric." Erika introduced Ernie to the quilt.

Grandpa Ernie stared at it with a frown. "What's wrong with the fabric?"

"Nothing's wrong," Lorraine soothed, she also seemed awed by the old man. "It's quite lovely."

"Should be." He nodded and shuffled closer.

"I believe the appliqué pieces are wool flannel, but I'd like to know what you thought."

He turned slowly to face Erika, his face transforming from that glow of pride to a glower. "Where'd the buttons go?"

"We're not sure." Lorraine's voice was a comforting low hum.

"Supposed to have pearly buttons all around it."

"Have you seen this blanket before?" Erika asked.

Lorraine was slipping cotton gloves on.

"They don't make pearly suits out of flannel. It's just old and worn out."

"Probably so," Erika agreed, though she didn't look like she meant it.

Grandpa Ernie picked up a corner with his bare hands and picked at one of the appliquéd leaves, pulling up the edge. "See that? Like new on the back."

"Do you know who made this quilt?" Taylor asked.

He stared at her like she was impertinent. "It's not a quilt. It's a button blanket, but all the pearly buttons are gone. Who's got them?"

Erika caught Taylor's eyes, her face alive with excitement. "Black flannel suiting on white sail cloth, covered in buttons. This is wonderful, but I'd like to know who made it, if you remember."

"Course I remember. What do you think I am? Mother made this button blanket for the county fair and won first prize. Supposed to be covered in buttons like an Indian blanket, but she made it from her daddy's Pearly suit. He was a Pearly of St. Pancras. Proud and good men, the Pearlies. She used a sail from some old boat. She was a British lady. Always missed her home. War Bride."

"Grandpa...." Taylor spoke softly. "Your mom was born in Eugene. Her daddy was a farmer. He came over by railroad, from Pennsylvania. We have pictures of him as a teenager coming over with all his luggage." This wasn't the fight to pick. It didn't matter how many times she explained it, he wasn't going to remember, and yet the idea that he'd forgotten who his own mother was made her deeply sad.

"Mother was a war bride, from England. That blanket's supposed to be covered in buttons."

Taylor mouthed an apology to Erika. "Hey, Grandpa Ernie, thanks for your help with this. Do you want to go to Reuben's for a bite?"

"You ought to get that blanket home. Don't know how it ended up here."

"I'm letting the museum borrow it for a special display. I loaned them some others from Grandma Delma too."

He nodded but didn't look happy.

She took him back out, but required he wear his oxygen before she drove to the diner. The drive was silent. Her Great Grandmother, Alva Hycox Baker wasn't an English war bride, and she probably hadn't made that blanket either. She couldn't have been a war bride because the timing was wrong. Grandpa Ernie's parents had gotten married during the depression. After World War I, but before World War II. As far as she knew, no one in Comfort would know enough Baker family history to piece together the real story he had gotten all tangled up in. She could ask Grandma Quinny, but she didn't expect much.

Graham had a booth to himself at Reuben's and invited Taylor and Grandpa Ernie to join him. She was so relieved to see he was still alive that she didn't stop to think about what kind of questions he might pester Grandpa Ernie with.

Conversation was light till the meatloaf and mashed potatoes arrived. Grandpa had been faithfully on his oxygen for at least twenty minutes at that point, and when he ripped the tubes out of his nose, he seemed to be completely with it.

"Taylor is a young lady," he said. "The world might think thirty isn't so young, but it is, and she has plenty of time before she needs to settle down."

"I couldn't agree more." Graham ate slowly, savoring the rich, homey food cooked from scratch.

"So, don't you try and force her into nothing. I see the way you look at her."

"It would be hard to miss," Graham agreed.

"You might not think I know what I'm talking about." Grandpa Ernie picked up his mug of decaf and had a long drink. "But I know just who you are. You're some intellectual elite from the city, come down here to do some exposé. Well, you'll not get it from me. I'll let the dead bury their own dead."

"No, sir. I wouldn't expect anything less."

Taylor's face was hot as could be expected from someone who blushed at far less than this. She shrugged at Graham and attempted to enjoy the side salad. Jess Reuben made her own Caesar dressing.

"The thing is, sir," Graham said, "I came down to write a story about your granddaughter, and in so doing, realized I should be talking to you. Now, I understand you don't want to spill any secrets, and I wouldn't ask you to say anything against family, but there is the matter of The Cutter."

"That who you think killed my little cousin Gus?"

Taylor sat up. She hadn't told her Grandfather about that yet.

"Maybe so," Graham said. "And two innocent girls, to boot."

"You carrying?" Grandpa asked.

"It's a dangerous job." Graham's answer was decidedly noncommittal.

"You staying in town?"

"Airbnb on Reiver street," Graham said.

"You ought to stay with us. Safety in numbers."

"Grandpa Ernie...." Taylor could barely get the words out. Graham staying at her place as her idea, seemed honorable, and maybe enticing, but when Grandpa said it...

"Me and Jonah are there, but he's a kid, and I'm too old. You ought to come. Taylor and Belle aren't safe."

"I'm sure Hudson would rather he take care of the ladies." Graham said it like it made no never mind. Like this wasn't the most awkward conversation Taylor had ever had. At thirty years old she shouldn't be so easy to embarrass, but she knew letting her mind rest on her attraction to this journalist was wrong—it wasn't fair to Hudson. And that was what embarrassed her.

"Hudson's got his own people to look out for. Stay with us tonight and I'll tell you a story for your newspaper that will curl your eyebrows."

Taylor's eyebrows bounced up like they had a mind of their own. "About The Cutter, Grandpa?"

"Not over dinner, Taylor. No business with dinner. House rules."

Dinner was lunch, which was usual for Grandpa Ernie. Graham got the check. "It's on the newspaper. You're a valuable source." He offered his hand to Taylor, and when she took it, she felt like she was on fire, a spark that burned from her fingertips to deep within her heart. He didn't squeeze her hand or stroke her fingers, or even hold it overlong, but it had done its damage. "See you tonight."

"Yes..."

She drove Grandpa Ernie home and immediately called Hudson. "Hey, Hud," she said when she got his voicemail. "We need to talk."

CHAPTER SIXTEEN

$\mathscr{H}$udson stared at his girlfriend. They'd met at his house, just after he'd finished his work for the day. He'd rushed to get to her, anxious as she hadn't replied to any of his messages for the last two days. That last murder had hit too close to home. Taylor's tender gray-blue eyes were deeply shadowed. She'd been worried all day, he could tell. Her fine bone structure, delicate, and always looking a little underfed, in his opinion, cried out for his protection.

But her words. Her words made her face feel like a lie.

"This was yesterday?" He spoke in a low, calm tone, because he was calm. Heartsick, but calm. He struggled with how she could have spent the whole day essentially under arrest without calling him, but it didn't make him angry. It made him sad.

"Yes." She swallowed nervously.

He reached across his kitchen table for her hand.

"I'd give anything to have been there for you." He didn't try to disguise the emotion in his broken voice. It was real. It was longing. This girl—this woman—had been alone for so long in life. He dismissed the years with Clay, knowing she had been the adult in that relationship. His memory took him straight back to the fire that had killed her father. Hudson had been a young kid. About six, but he remembered because the fire had been a house located just outside the fancy development they had just moved to. It was on the other side of the playground, the far side of the big road he wasn't supposed to cross. He remembered every moment of watching the fire burn from the window of his upstairs bedroom. Safe in the big new house he lived in with his mom on weekdays and every other weekend.

That fire glowing red and orange over the tops of the smaller houses that stood between him and his own safe haven, mesmerizing him. It had been so hot, he and his mom and her boyfriend had been evacuated. His mom had driven him far, far away to get ice cream.

On the radio, on the way home, he'd heard that a firefighter named Todd Quinn had died going back in the house to save a child.

The child had lived, of course, or Todd Quinn wouldn't have died a hero.

This is what he thought about as he stared at Taylor. How she'd needed a hero, ever since that day.

In high school, as a tall, deep-voiced freshman, he'd seen her again, the glorious blonde senior, and longed to be that hero.

She'd needed a hero yesterday.

He raked his hand through his hair.

Positioning himself as the hero of her story was narcissism and was a classic trait in men who were only-sons of single moms. He could spot it a mile away in other men and fought against it in himself. He'd had a good counselor when he'd needed it after his own tragedy with his dad, but even thinking about that was him turning her crisis back to himself.

"Let me feed you, at least. Early dinner?"

"I don't know." She looked away, but not at anything in particular.

"I just want you to be safe."

"Life isn't safe. Mom died because she made a fun quilt on the internet. Reynette died because she fell in love."

"But the chaplain of the care home died because he was a criminal. Not all victims are innocent." He found himself wanting to argue her into believing she was in danger—into believing that she needed him.

"That Amish author died because she trusted an older couple to take care of her."

He grimaced. It felt like she was saying his protectiveness would kill her. But it was the very last thing he'd do.

"Who killed them, Hudson? Who killed all three of those writers?" She rested her chin on her hand, her eyes gazing somewhere in the distance, far from him.

"I don't know."

"Did you tell your mom we were going to see Gus?" She asked, her big eyes finally looking scared.

"No. I didn't tell anyone."

She reached for his hand, and after holding it for a moment, squeezed it. "I didn't think so. But I can't let this go. Graham is probably in danger."

That name didn't promise a life of happiness for Hudson. Not that he thought Graham and Taylor had fallen in love at first sight. But the way she looked when she said his name. The way she looked when he was near. About a year ago, she'd agreed that he and she were a couple, that they'd fallen in love, and that they wouldn't see other people anymore. But he'd never been sure, not completely, that she'd meant it. That she loved him the way he loved her. He often wondered if it was just because John Hancock had hooked up with that mathematician, Tatiana. He and John were in business together now, but Hudson wasn't in a hurry to tell Taylor that Tatiana had dumped John and moved in with a tech bro in San Francisco.

Graham's presence in town, and her reaction to him brought all of his insecurities back to the surface.

"How can I help you?" The words hurt to say because he knew her answer would be that she needed support in doing something dangerous.

"I don't know what's going on." She looked over her shoulder. "And I don't know what I can do about it. But right now, it feels like everyone I talk to is in danger. Can you...keep yourself safe?"

He sat up, hurt. Of course, he could keep himself safe. He wasn't worried about himself. "But can't I do something for you? Anything?"

"I'm sure you can. I just don't know what yet."

"I need to eat. Let me make you something."

She looked at her phone. "I'm sorry Hudson, I had a late lunch. And I feel like I should be at home with Grandpa Ernie. It, um...I just feel like I should be at home."

He walked her to the car and kissed her before she got in it, but even her kiss felt like she wasn't there with him. Not really.

He'd been hurt falling for girls who needed to be rescued before, and this felt ominously similar.

GRANDPA ERNIE WAS SNOOZING in his recliner in the living room while Jonah and Belle snuggled on the couch looking at houses on Zillow.

Taylor paced the living room wondering if Graham would show up, and if he didn't, if it would be because he had been murdered sometime after their late lunch.

"It's big, it's beautiful, and it's in budget," Belle pronounced.

"You sound like a preacher, three points, all alliterated," Jonah laughed, "but I agree. I think it might be the one. How many do you think could live there?"

"It's not like the other content houses." Belle was intensely focused on the screen. "Not enough bathrooms...yet."

"Renovation won't be too bad." Jonah's voice shook with nerves.

Taylor paused her pacing to look at her brother-in-law. Could it be that the reality of the expense they were about to undertake was getting to him?

"I think we could easily have six influencers there. It's a big house. Five bedrooms plus an attic and basement we could convert. We'd live in the attic, almost like an apartment and rent out the bedrooms and the basement. It would be simple enough." Belle traced her finger across the touch screen again and again, flipping through photos of the house.

"Sure."

"Taylor, come look," Belle invited.

Taylor joined them on the couch. "I didn't know the old Magary place was for sale." Though everyone called it "the old Magary" place, it wasn't that old. A 1960s midcentury mansion. It didn't boast a bathroom for every bedroom, or have a five-car garage, but it was spacious with the five bedrooms as well as three living areas, a formal dining room, a lavish kitchen. Taylor had always loved the place. She'd been to a party at it once, in middle school. A boy she'd had a terrible crush on's grandparents had lived there at the time. Ross Magary…Taylor hadn't thought about him in years.

"Look at this." Belle swiped to a picture of the top level of the tri-level home. "There's five bedrooms here, but a ton of storage, and the rooms are huge. I think we could add a bath for each, don't you? We'd only have to add three, since there's a master and a full hall bath."

"It seems like it," Taylor agreed. It looked like there was plenty of space between a linen closet and bedrooms that had to be three times the size of the tiny ones in the little house they all currently lived in.

"And it does have that attic. It's over both the garage and that level. It's got to be like a thousand square feet."

"I like it. I think it could work. But get an inspection. It's a cool house, but it's getting up in years," Taylor cautioned, trying not to feel envy over the vast, uncomplicated spaces in the pictures.

"Ug, right?" Belle laughed. It was such a natural and happy noise that Taylor had to look at her. How could she laugh with a murderer on the loose? It seemed impossible to feel that kind of pure joy right now.

The doorbell rang, which was probably good.

Taylor jumped up to answer it.

"That better be your young man." The noise had woken Grandpa Ernie. Taylor wondered if he meant Hudson, or if he remembered he'd invited Graham over.

Taylor's heart beat so loud as she opened the door, she thought the kids could surely hear it.

Graham stood on the other side, his eyes smiling but his face otherwise serious. He had a backpack slung over one shoulder. Before saying hello, he kissed her cheek, like greeting an old friend.

"Come in." Taylor opened the door wide for him. She wanted him to see the whole family was in the room before he kissed her again.

"Mr. Baker, thanks for inviting me over. Never can be too safe." Graham entered as comfortably as though he'd come over dozens of times before.

Grandpa Ernie lowered the footrest of his recliner. "Show me your gun."

"Sorry." Graham held up both hands. "I was just trying to impress you earlier. I don't carry."

Grandpa Ernie stood slowly with the help of his walker. "You're not much good without a gun. Hudson's a lot bigger than you."

"Sorry." Graham dropped his backpack and kicked off his shoes.

"Can I get you something? A drink maybe?" Taylor could feel the pressure of his lips on her cheek still, burning like a brand. She shouldn't want him like she did. Hudson deserved better, and though she'd called him to have a serious talk about their relationship, she'd started with the day at the police station and hadn't been able to bring things around to Graham. Not the way she'd meant to.

She hadn't been brave enough.

"Nah. I'm good." He settled into an armchair. "I didn't cancel the Airbnb, but I wasn't going to miss a story that would curl my eyebrows."

Grandpa Ernie shuffled slowly into his bedroom. "You're going to have to take the couch tonight. Closer to the door." He continued to talk in his room, that little den just off the front room, but they couldn't hear him. When he came back, he had an old wooden baseball bat. "You don't look like you're good with your fists, so you'll need this."

Graham met Grandpa Ernie at his chair to accept the weapon. "Thanks. I bet I could do some damage with this." He gripped it like he was up to bat.

Jonah stared. He was a slender kid, tall and reedy. His eyes were stormy. "Hey Gramps, what's up?"

"The Cutter's back." Grandpa Ernie said it almost like it was a joke.

"The who?" Jonah asked.

"Serial killer from the 70s. Our very own." Grandpa stared down the young man, like he wanted to intimidate him.

"The murders...." Taylor murmured. "Three of them now."

"This fellow's come to make sure the killer doesn't get Taylor or Belle. You're too young and I'm too old." Grandpa Ernie let himself back down into his chair. "Not an insult, young man. Just facts." Grandpa Ernie reached for his oxygen tube and slipped it on. "I can't breathe good."

Graham offered Jonah an awe-shucks kind of smile. "I'm just

here to be near your sister-in-law. I'm sure you're used to it by now."

Jonah lifted an eyebrow then turned to look at Taylor.

"He's teasing. He's a journalist and Grandpa Ernie promised to tell him something about the killer. Or something that would 'curl his eyebrows' anyway."

"Maybe I will take that drink." Graham sat on the edge of the armchair and leaned the baseball bat against it. "I don't think I could take Hudson if we had to fight over her. He's got to be ten years younger than me. But with a bat…."

"Graham…." Taylor stared at him with her eyes wide. Her feelings had been so…personal. Those sparks of attraction had felt so secret. How could he joke around about it to her family?

"He hasn't put a ring on it yet." Graham shrugged. "I still stand a chance."

Taylor went to the kitchen to pull herself together. She didn't like this side of Graham.

But she didn't know any sides of Graham, so how could she claim to like him at all?

She pulled a couple of Hudson's beers from the fridge— some Black Butte porter he'd brought over.

She looked down at the cold bottles, evidence that she was in a committed relationship. She didn't know Graham, but she owed him some gratitude. She might never have realized she wasn't *in love* with Hudson, if he hadn't come along.

She fell back against the fridge door and leaned there, frozen in time and space.

Was that true?

Was she just now realizing that she really didn't love him?

It had been a matter of days, hours even, since the questions first started, and she had already decided?

She straightened up and took the rest of the beers from the fridge. The law said Belle and Jonah could drink at home, even though they weren't twenty-one, and she thought maybe it would be better if they all took the edge off.

Back in the living room, Grandpa Ernie had dozed off, which made talking to him hard, but talking about him much easier.

"Looks like I will have to stay the night," Graham said, "if I want to get this story he's promised."

She passed around the bottles, and the opener, then sat on the floor in front of the TV. "Belle," she asked, "what do you know about Grandpa Ernie's parents?"

"My memory is a steal trap, Sis. I know everything I've ever heard about them."

Taylor didn't doubt it. "Grandpa Ernie got confused today, saying his mom was a British lady—a war bride. Who do you think he was really talking about?"

"His grandma." Belle didn't even hesitate. "It goes back a few years, doesn't it? Every family needs a historian." She said this for Graham's sake. "And I volunteer my eidetic memory for the job. Might as well. Gramps' grandparents met in London during the first world war. He brought her home to the family farm—the one he'd bought when he moved out to Oregon from back East."

Relief was rolling over Taylor. Grandpa had been confused, sure, but not completely wrong.

"Gramps' grandparents had been super young when they got married, like me and Jonah. So, when Gramps was born, his grandparents were only like, forty. When he was a kid, his Grandma lived with them."

"It was Grandpa Ernie's Great Grandpa who was a Pearly of St. Pancras?" Taylor was pleased she remembered the whole title he had used.

Belle's eyes twinkled. "My gosh, I haven't heard that name in ages! Did you used to play with the old buttons too?"

"No. When I was a kid Grandma Delma and Grandpa Ernie didn't live with us."

"Oh, that's right. Gramps had a bag full of these mother of pearl buttons, real old, and he'd let me make patterns out of them. Said they came from his Grandpa's Pearly suit. The Pearlies are like the Shriners, kind of. A charity organization in London. They were really new when Grandpa's great-grandpa was a member."

"I wonder why he was calling his grandma, 'Mother,' today?"

"Dementia can be like that," Graham offered. "Your mind boxes everyone you love up together, to keep them safe. When you want to talk about someone you love, your mind goes to the right place for the name, you can see the right person, but the words get mixed up. It's the same reason my mom used to call me my brothers' names, or even the dog's."

Jonah laughed.

"Fun fact," Graham continued. "Studies show that dogs go into that little loved-ones-only memory file, but cats don't."

"So...he knew the person he was trying to tell me about wasn't his mother, but his brain just couldn't get it sorted out?" Taylor asked.

"Pretty much," Graham said. "He's sure he's saying the right word, because his mind is seeing the right person, but you are all sort of woven together in the fabric of his life story."

"Do you think he still remembers anything useful about the 1975 crime spree?"

"I hope so. If he does, he'll be the first. This town is remarkably young. And close- mouthed." He tapped the side of the baseball bat. "Everyone is so quick to say nothing happened in '75 that I'm starting to think something really big went down."

Grandpa Ernie woke a little, but spotted Jonah with his beer in hand. He glowered at the young man. "Not in my house you don't."

"It's okay Gramps, perfectly legal, plus, he's a married man."

Belle batted her sweet blue eyes at him and tipped back a drink from her own bottle.

"Insolent." He attempted to glower at her but couldn't suppress the love from his eyes. "Glad this one's come down for the night, so it's not just the three of us. Tired of Taylor being up at that house with Boggy's boy. She belongs with her family." He stared at Graham. "You there, see if you can't get Taylor to stick around home more often, will you?"

"I'll do my best, but I was promised a story for my efforts."

Grandpa Ernie took a long, coughing, deep breath. "That story, eh?"

"The one about The Cutter, from 1975."

"Comfort's own serial killer. Figment of that girl's imagination." Grandpa Ernie said. "Delusion runs in the Love family. Sometimes it makes them rich though. Lots of money in that flour mill. Sometimes it makes them crazy. Lorraine's lucky. She's one that it ought to have made crazy."

"What happened that night she was stabbed?"

"Pretty teen girl out with her biker boyfriend. Woke up in the hospital and never did tell anyone what happened. Said it was scissors what cut her and drew all those other poor kids into her story. That one at the college, she's the one what got stabbed with scissors." He paused a long time and his mouth turned down in worry. "That woman at the museum. The college girl who was sucking up to me. She was roommates with the one who died. Wouldn't be surprised if she's the one who done it."

"Grandpa…" Taylor whispered.

"Ask her. Might could be."

"Was Lorraine ever able to say what happened?" Graham redirected Grandpa Ernie's story.

"Sheriff went to the bar they'd been at, but all the bartender said was she had a fake ID and it weren't his fault. And she left willingly with her feller. But there was broken glass in the parking lot that morning. I remember that from the police report. Back then we all read the reports. Wasn't much else to do for entertainment."

Graham pulled the baseball bat up and rested it on his knee. "How worried should I be tonight?"

"Pert worried. Three journalists stuck around to harass my kids, and two are dead."

"Gus Baker, your cousin," Graham said, "had an office full of notes about The Cutter. He promised Taylor he could tie the current murders to the old ones."

"Gus's grandma was a Love," Grandpa said. "Delusional. My grandma was an English lady. War bride, in the first world war."

Taylor sighed, happy that he had been able to put the pieces of that back in order.

"Her daddy was a good man. A Pearly. Cockney men who raise money for the poor. He wasn't a Pearly King, but he was a good man. Never met him. She brought his suit with her from home because her daddy was already dead when she got married. Turned it into a wedding blanket. Delma used to display it in her classroom at the college."

"I don't remember her teaching at the college." Taylor leaned on her elbows as she listened to her grandfather. This wasn't the story Graham had come for, but she could have listened to it all day.

"It was when your mom was a wee thing. Long before you were born. She taught sewing, one class a week."

"And she displayed that blanket in her classroom? The button one?" Taylor asked.

"Yup."

"Erika should have recognized it." Taylor felt a chill down her spine. Why had the expert not recognized such a distinctive blanket, and why had she come over alone that night, just to say the fabric was new? Especially since it wasn't new—it was at least one hundred years old.

"It doesn't have its buttons." Grandpa Ernie coughed again, then fished around for his oxygen tubes, but they were already installed in his nose. "I hardly knew it without its buttons. What'd you do with those buttons, girly?" The last question was for Belle.

"Oh!" Belle looked startled as though she'd remembered something. "Gramps, I'm so sorry. They used to be in that special little bag, but I lost the bag so I put them in the cookie tin with the rest of Mom's buttons.

Grandpa Ernie harrumphed into his mustache but looked calmer. "Those are special buttons, young lady."

"Why'd they get removed from the quilt in the first place?" Taylor asked her sister as she wasn't sure Grandpa ever knew.

"They were starting to fall off. Grandma Delma did it, but it was before I was born. I asked, which is how I know."

"And Grandma Delma let you play with them?"

"I was a bit spoiled." Belle batted innocent eyes at her sister. "And had to be kept busy while Mom worked. The buttons were fun. I could have played with the whole tin, but I was smart enough to know that the ones in the little bag were more important."

"Erika knew," Graham said quietly. "Shawna had already written about potential fraud when Erika came to look at it."

"Erika works at the school," Taylor spoke slowly, absorbing Graham's words into her own budding thoughts. "And would have had access to the quilt and the expo, before putting it in the show."

"But what gain?" Graham asked.

"Academic publishing credits," Belle offered. "The faculty has to have a certain number of published works over a certain period of time. I looked into teaching there. I wonder what the last piece Erika published was." Belle turned back to her laptop.

"But why would she claim the wool was from the 1960s?"

Taylor stood slowly, then walked to Graham's chair and sat on the arm, nudging the baseball bat out of the way.

He put his arm around her back, helping her balance. Excitement skittered across her skin, but she worked to ignore it. She didn't know why she'd moved to his chair, she just had.

"Wouldn't the actual story of the Pearly suits be more interesting than just some 1960s thing?" Taylor was so close to him now that she spoke quietly, as though the others weren't in the room.

"It depends. The idea it was fraud was already out. If her original plan had been to make people think it was remarkably old, that was shot." Graham's voice was lower now, and his breath smelled like mint candy.

"Why kill Shawna?" Belle asked, her voice loud and interrupting what had started to feel like a moment.

"Maybe her grandma on her dad's side was a Love," Graham chuckled. "Is everyone in this town really related?"

"Close enough."

Jonah had been silently engrossed in his phone through most of the conversation, but he looked up now, a smile on his face like he'd just won something. "Juvies. They might drive me crazy, but they come through in a pinch."

"How's that?" Graham's arm shifted as he leaned forward, tipping Taylor closer to him.

"I asked what they knew about the prof, and they came through. Erika Wainwright, professor of Fiber Arts and History of Fiber Arts at Comfort College of Art and Craft was roommates in 1975 with a Connie Shirley, who committed suicide in an unlikely manner."

"So…she's killed before," Taylor whispered.

Graham's fingers tightened on her waist as though he wanted to hold her safe.

"The Juvie's don't know, but Erika's been teaching at Comfort College of Art and Craft for the last fifteen years.

Before that she was an artist who had a few shows. Married to a lawyer, so she didn't need to push herself too hard."

Graham laughed.

"What was her last publishing cred?" Belle showed no hint that she envied the Juvies as she asked.

Jonah peered at his phone. "Some article in 2017. She must be due for her next one. That's quite a while ago."

Graham laughed again. "Years and years."

"I never said that girl killed her roommate," Grandpa Ernie piped up loud and clear. "And none of this is the story I promised you."

"We're all ears, sir," Graham said.

"I said Lorraine Love was delusional and that it ran in the family. Always proud that my folks weren't from around here."

Taylor chuckled quietly. The Baker family had moved to the area around 1910, and Grandpa Ernie still considered the family "not from around here."

"Lorraine was trouble. She was fast. And though she was tiny, she was a tough one. Those men she ran with were bad and dangerous. One of them hurt her, I'm sure. Maybe at that bar. Maybe not."

They waited in silence.

"Two weeks after her accident, the body of her feller was found in the creek. His motorcycle was crashed off the side of the road, and he had his own switch blade stuck in his neck."

"Lorraine?" Jonah asked.

"Maybe. The body had been there a long while when they found it. Maybe he'd got real drunk and crashed. And maybe he'd got real mad at her and cut her up after the crash. Maybe she'd wrestled the knife away, tough little thing that she was, and stabbed him in self-defense. But then, how'd she get fixed up? Hitchhiking? No one ever admitted picking her up. Didn't have no cell phones back then. And it was a long walk for a girl like her, back to the hospital. Especially all cut up like she was."

He looked around the room in triumph. He was right. This was some story.

"It was a biker gang." Belle spoke like she had a puzzle to solve, not like she'd just heard a ghost story. "And she was their young muse, for lack of better word. They would have used her and abused her, but not wanted her killed. She wasn't alone with her boyfriend on Bible Creek Road. The whole gang was out riding together. He crashed, cut her up, and the gang intervened. Stabbed him and hauled her to the hospital. Or maybe she did stab him, but all the same, her gang hauled her to the hospital. They wouldn't let a kid like that die."

Grandpa Ernie nodded proudly. "Smart girl. That's what I always said."

"And then she started up with her delusion." Taylor leaned into Graham's chest, comfortable sitting with him, in that exciting way that only new infatuation can bring. "And the more she talked about her idea of a serial killer the more the town had to hush it up, to protect her."

"Because we all knew she'd done it," Grandpa Ernie agreed. "Most likely she done him in self-defense and the others only caught up as she was laid there dying on the road. The gang scattered after that. Left town."

"Did no one try to tell her what had happened?" Jonah asked.

"Nope. We know what the Loves are, and it could have cracked her. Poor kid. Tough kid, troubled kid."

Taylor closed her eyes and tried to picture Lorraine Love as a kid. She was slender in that way that left no youth in your face —the aging kind of skinny that made a person look elderly. But she wasn't elderly. A little quick math said Lorraine Love wasn't quite sixty yet.

"I won't publish this Ernie," Graham said. "What else you got for the newspaper?"

"Good man." Grandpa Ernie stood again, slowly and

painfully, and took himself to his room. The door shut with a click.

"But what do we do about Erika Wainwright?" Belle asked.

"Nothing, yet," Graham said. "Ernie hired me to keep you all alive one more night, so don't do, say, or post anything tonight. We'll figure it out, but right now, we'll just stay alive."

Jonah nodded, immediately accepting Graham's authority.

"Let me get you some bedding." Taylor stood and stretched, arms over head. The idea that she wasn't needed to keep everyone alive had given her body a quick release from her stress and suddenly she was very sleepy.

"Thanks," Graham stood. "Which way to the bathroom?"

Belle pointed him upstairs but stayed with Taylor. "So....?"

"Grandpa Ernie invited him, I swear."

"But Gramps didn't sit on his lap all evening. What about Hudson? He's a really, really good guy." Belle blushed a little. A few years ago, when they'd met Hudson, Belle had teased about wanting him for herself.

"Hudson is a really, really good guy."

"Don't tell me he was your three-year rebound from Clay."

Taylor looked away from her sister, that same guilt flooding her. "We've been exclusive for less than a year."

"Hudson was your rebound?"

"I guess." Taylor sat in the armchair.

"Who even is this guy?" Belle jerked her thumb toward the stairs. "Please don't do anything stupid."

"Graham Dawson. Ask the Juvies who he is. And he's sleeping on the couch tonight. I did not invite him here myself."

"Please finish with Hudson before you move on. This is a really small town."

Taylor scrunched her face up in frustration. "His car's out front. It'll be there all night. Whatever chance I had of not being *that girl* in Comfort is long gone now, and its Grandpa Ernie's fault."

"Maybe everyone will think he's here for me," Belle giggled. The one beer seemed to have loosened her up a little. "But honestly, Tay, how old is that guy?"

"Oh, probably Clay's age. I don't know."

"Ah. I wondered." Belle pursed her lips and shook her head. "I thought his smile was kind of the same too." On that note, she took herself up to bed.

Taylor found a sleeping bag and a pillow for Graham. No point in making him too comfortable here. After all she hadn't invited him, right?

CHAPTER SEVENTEEN

*A*round midnight Taylor's phone vibrated on the nightstand, waking her up. She pulled it under the covers with her and checked the text. Though Graham was just downstairs, she hoped it was something from him. Maybe an invitation to join him....

But it was from Hudson. A picture, shirtless, his muscles perfectly shadowed in the soft light of his bedside lamp. Just a hint of his belly button in the shot and just a bit of his full mouth with its pouty lips. Too handsome to be real. "I'm awake," was the only message.

She stared at the picture and tried to remember what it was like when they'd first started dating. The infatuation had been there. The electric pleasure at his every touch or glance. The excitement of wondering what would come next, where this would lead.

It was only days ago she was in his bed, snuggled close, glad to have such a wonderful man in her life.

Why did infatuation have to have such a strong pull?

When you finally married someone did the risk of becoming

infatuated with others just disappear? Or did you have to constantly fight it?

And if you did have to constantly fight it, did that mean you weren't truly in love?

She wasn't truly in love with Hudson.

She was sure of it, because she hadn't really wanted to fight the infatuation. It was a silly thought, in its way. She was sure that some people were just wired to develop crushes. Her dad had been like that. She remembered clearly the way he'd tease her mom about movie stars, or waitresses. Harmless, sort of. He always followed those jokes up with how much better her mom had been. There had always been kisses and caresses after the little jokes.

But as her crush on Graham grew, she hadn't wanted to stifle it. She hadn't wanted to win the war in her mind. She hadn't wanted to caress Hudson and make sure he knew that of all the attractions in the world, she picked him.

But they'd been so intimate for so long. She opened her eyes and stared at his perfect body. She'd miss that. And his handsome face. But not enough to fight for it. At the first temptation, she'd been ready to jump.

She thought back to John Hancock and how jealous she'd been of his girlfriend Tatiana. He'd texted when Tatiana dumped him, and for a moment she'd considered it...considered meeting him at his brother's pub to spend the night consoling him over his loss. But they hadn't seen each other in a while, and that early infatuation had worn off.

Poor Hudson.

How many different men could she lay in bed dreaming about while staring at his shirtless selfie?

Another text came through. *Sleep well, love.*

She knew he could tell she'd seen the picture, but he was willing to pretend.

Her finger hovered over the screen ready to reply, ready to be honest with him.

She laid down the phone.

Graham was right here, right now.

She could go downstairs and glance at him in her dad's old hunting sleeping bag and see how the feeling compared. The last few days had been full of adrenaline and stress, after all. Maybe she didn't want to throw away a good relationship. Maybe she could grow to love Hudson the way he deserved.

Maybe this was an excuse to see if Graham was awake.

She was wearing heavy duty winter flannels—November nights got cold in the old house—the only way she could have been more modest was if she'd had footy jammies.

She padded her way quietly downstairs, just to see if he was up. Or if her heart would skip a beat at the sight of him.

But the couch was empty. The sleeping bag hadn't been unrolled, and his backpack and shoes weren't sitting by the front door where he'd left them.

She wandered the small room, double checking. Maybe his shoes were by the couch.

They weren't.

She listened to the sounds of the old house.

Maybe he was upstairs in the bathroom, but the floorboards didn't creak with footsteps.

She peered out the front window.

His car was gone.

She ran upstairs, pulled off her pajama pants and drew on her jeans. Then she texted him, *Where?* She pulled her winter coat on, grabbed her keys, and left. Comfort was a small area. She'd drive the whole thing till she found his car. It wouldn't take long.

Four minutes into her drive, she spotted his Prius parked along the back fence of the college. One side of the road was college property, the other was a cow field where happy animals usually grazed in the shade of ancient oak trees. Somewhere in the middle was a pond.

The night was clear. The dry, bitterly cold days had been free of the cloud cover that kept them in the dark so long in winter, and today's night sky was full of stars and a large moon. She pulled up behind his car and looked around both sides of the road. If he was investigating Erika, he might have tried to break into her classroom or her office. But there was no way of telling from here. Too many buildings stood between her and the offices.

She considered the field. Could someone have wanted to meet him privately in the middle of the night and used the field across from the school as a landmark?

In the far distance, under the moonlight, she thought she could make out some shadowy figures. She wished she'd brought the baseball bat, though now that she thought of it, she hadn't seen it in the living room either.

She sucked in a breath and slid as quietly out of her car as she could. If those distant shadows were people and not small trees or cows, then they had likely seen her headlights. Nonetheless, she slunk low and tried not to be seen.

The cow fence along the pasture was topped with barbed wire. Taylor slunk along it, looking for a low spot or a gate. The cold night air bit at her face. A sharp wind blew past, rustling the brittle grass. A shadow passed over, as when a cloud blows in front of the moon, but there were no clouds. She froze, then slowly turned her face, looking from side to side. The field. The ditch. The road. The grass rustled behind her now, without the wind.

She held her breath.

In the distance, somewhere behind her in the ditch, she heard slow, heavy footfall. One. Long pause. Two. Long pause.

Then they stopped.

The shadow had scared her like it would in a horror movie.

And if it were just the shadow and the rustling of the tall grass, she would have convinced herself all was fine, but the footsteps...she hadn't mistaken them. She gnawed on the inside of her cheek, a compulsive motion that she'd regret tomorrow but was the only thing keeping her from crying out in fear. She began to move along the fence again but listened for the footsteps that seemed to have been between her and the safety of her car.

A burst of frigid wind whistled through the field, carrying voices. She paused to see if she could make out what they were saying.

Moments later, though her cold, tense muscles felt as though she'd stood in place for hours, she heard the voices again.

She was sure the male voice was Graham. Her friend. Out looking for a story to make his career. She couldn't make out his words. She needed to get closer.

She crept along the fence, cautiously, wanting to reach them, though scared of drawing attention to herself. But the voices were getting farther away. She knew she needed to get over that fence with its old-fashioned twists of wire and it terrified her.

Surrounded, as she was, by sticks and dry branches and grass, there was no way she could follow the voices quietly. No way to disappear into the open field under the bright moon.

Like a child, she held her breath as she jumped over the fence. She landed with a loud thump on the frozen ground. They hadn't seemed to notice—that is, the group of shadows in the distance seemed to be keeping pace as they walked away from her, and every now and then the wind carried their voices, getting farther away. She thought she recognized one of the women, but had a hard time accepting that Sissy Dorney would meet Graham in the field at midnight.

She kept low, still scared of whoever had been behind her. It was hard to move fast with the razor-sharp blades of winter grass whipping her face as she moved. She had reached a small bunch of maple trees and stood, trying to blend in. She was close enough that she could see the figures distinctly. They had been walking away from her, but they turned, as though maybe they had just been moving to keep warm in the frigid night.

She hadn't been wrong. One of the group was Graham Dawson and another was clearly Sissy Dorney. There was no mistaking her, even in the distance, in the middle of the night. The third person was shorter and bundled in a coat, shaped like a woman's winter coat, but her back was to Taylor, and she couldn't place her.

Taylor leaned on the tree and considered just hollering out to them, but first, she tried to listen in. What had they needed the cover of night to discuss?

Rustling in the branches above her head stopped her heart for a moment. She wrenched her neck looking up and wrapped her arms around the slender trunk of the tree. Her friends were closer now, and she could hear them more clearly, if she concentrated.

"It's too dangerous." Graham's voice was steady, and she was almost sure that was what he said.

"Do you want the story or not?" Sissy pushed him, her voice was easy to hear as she faced Taylor.

"Not badly enough to die for. As much as I want to help the sheriff catch who killed these three people, I don't want to be number four."

"You can't just leave." The third voice was familiar, but who?

"You're not the only one in danger," Sissy snarled. She stepped closer to the other woman and put an arm around her.

Tansy? Was that Tansy?

"If Lorraine's snapped, none of us are safe," Sissy said.

"It wasn't her." Graham turned, now facing Taylor.

She longed for him to realize she was there, listening.

"She's too frail." Graham sounded tired. "No way she was strong enough."

"Then she was working with someone, but it was still her." Tansy's voice cracked.

"It's going to be okay, Kiddo." The motherliness had returned to Sissy's voice. She would nurture the whole town if she could. "They'll put her away somewhere safe, where she can't hurt anyone else."

"I didn't tell you that story to make you think she did it." Graham began to walk in circles again. They had gotten so close now, a stone's throw, but he didn't acknowledge her. "I just thought you should know before I left."

"You wanted us to know she'd killed before?" Tansy said between sobs.

"I wanted you to know that she'd been through serious trauma and needed your compassion. Listen, you called me. I came."

"And we told you what we know. What are you going to do with it?" Sissy demanded. Her voice carried so much better than either Tansy's or Graham's.

"File it. I'm not the cops. Call them if you have evidence that your mom is a murderer. I don't believe it."

"But all those notes about Gus. She knew too much about him." Tansy's voice trailed off.

At mention of Gus, Taylor felt sure she was needed. He was family, after all. She stepped away from the trees and headed to her three friends, ready to help them sort out their misunderstanding. She wasn't afraid. She was going to help.

She walked forward, repeating the words, "I'm not afraid. I'm going to help. I'm not afraid." She was within steps of them, almost close enough to touch Graham's shoulder when a shot rang out and everything went black.

CHAPTER EIGHTEEN

"*I* don't know where she is," Roxy said a little impatiently. Clay wasn't a lot younger than her, but sometimes having him around all day felt like having another child. It was a lot first thing in the morning.

"But she was supposed to be here to film. She never misses filming." Clay paced the sales floor of Flour Sax Quilt Shop.

"Why don't you get us some pastries from Cup o' Joe's." Roxy used one of the previous names of the coffee shop. She refused to keep up with the various brands that new owners had labeled it through the years.

"Comfy Cuppa doesn't sell pastries." Clay's voice had a whine to it that was going to send Roxy out the back door, if he wasn't careful.

"Seriously," Roxy said, "you need to get out and get a breath. Walk it off. Taylor will be here anytime, I'm sure."

"There have been three murders in less than a week, and Taylor is never late. Are you telling me that you aren't at least a little worried?"

Roxy narrowed her eyes and looked at her boyfriend. She had known what he was when she hooked up with him. She had known that this relationship couldn't possibly last forever, even if it was a good deal of fun at its best. And she had known that the real reason Clay lingered in this town was because it was where Taylor Quinn lived. But she decided this wasn't the time to confront him about it.

"All right. Forget walking it off. Forget getting pastries. Go find her."

Clay brightened like a dog who's heard "fetch!" "Are you sure you don't mind?"

"She's my friend too. Go find Taylor and make sure she's ok."

When Clay disappeared into the dark morning, Roxy looked around the shop. It was a little grim. They had done their best to keep things nice and welcoming, but certain maintenance issues were looming.

Roxy had to work hard not to nag Taylor about the condition of the store, but it bothered her that, while the leak in the apartment pipes had been fixed, the ceiling hadn't been repaired. There had been so much YouTube money so recently, but it seemed as though all that money had been lost on advertising campaigns. She took a seat on the stool and ran her hand through a tangle in her curly hair. It was comfortable there with the weight off of her hip. But she hated how often she got to relax at the store these days. She shouldn't have quite so much downtime.

It had to have been all the recent murders that killed their business. There'd just been so much death. She grabbed her phone and sent a text to Taylor. Clay was right. Taylor never just didn't show up. And those days she did skip, it was usually because she was caught up in something terribly dangerous.

She only waited a moment before she texted Belle, then Jonah. Maybe they'd be able to tell her that Taylor was safe at home. Maybe she really had just slept through her alarm.

Jonah replied about five minutes after the text. *Sleeping it off.*

Just as she thought. Roxy pocketed her phone. It was hours

before the shop opened, and if Taylor could lay around bed, so could she. She snuck to Clay's apartment and curled up on his little sofa for a rest. It was a pity they were letting the YouTube show slide this way, but she wasn't the boss.

TAYLOR'S SHOULDER ached and she was in a severe mental fog, but she was awake and aware of her surroundings, those being a hospital room.

But she wasn't inclined to sit up or look around just yet.

She had an IV in one arm, and a machine of monitors next to her. She stared at them for a few moments, unable to understand what she was looking at.

She closed her eyes again and was pretty sure she didn't sleep.

Something patted her gently on the arm that didn't ache.

She opened her eyes slowly, not excited about the bright lights in the room, and turned her head toward the patting person.

Grandma Quinny.

She made shushing sounds. "Sissy Dorney called me at midnight last night, young lady. What were you doing out on the Beckford farm?"

Taylor groaned.

"You're lucky Sissy was there."

Taylor tried to shake her head but didn't like it. She wasn't lucky Sissy had been there. If Sissy hadn't been there, Graham wouldn't have been there. And if Graham hadn't been there, she wouldn't have gotten shot. It seemed simple.

She opened her eyes and focused on the ceiling.

She'd been shot.

Someone behind her.

She remembered the noise and then passing out. And then

waking up in excruciating pain as Sissy pressed something on her shoulder to keep her from dying. Or so she'd said. At the moment, Taylor had thought death was not such a bad idea compared to the full weight of Sissy's intense pressure on the wound.

She'd passed out again pretty quickly.

Then she had been loaded into the ambulance—the local makeshift one since there hadn't been time for one from town. Sissy stayed with her.

Where had Graham and Tansy gone?

She started to ask but it came out in a groan.

"Shh. Rest child." Grandma Quinny patted her again. "I see they've overmedicated you. It can't hurt that bad." She stared at the drip, and clucked. "Don't they know the ravages opioids have in small towns like ours? Where's that nurse call button? We need the doctor." She rummaged around in the blankets that slightly hung off Taylor's bed till she found the button and summoned medical help.

"Grandpa Quinny is with Ernie. Belle wanted to stay at the hospital, but the girl's just so young. I thought it best to have an adult with you during this trying time." She leaned forward. "You know, darling, when I was younger and listening in on the police scanner and all of that, I never went out unarmed. You ought to consider it. I know it's not popular in the city, but this is why it matters." She patted her large purse. Apparently, it harbored some kind of self-defense weapon, though Taylor didn't think anything would have helped her not get shot in the back.

"Graham?" Taylor croaked.

"I'm sorry?" Grandma Quinny said in response. "What's that, dear?"

Taylor turned her head away. Grandma Quinny didn't know the journalist. She tried to remember where he had gone, but her mind drew a blank. First, the sound. Then the pain, so fast.

Then a blank. She'd probably passed out from shock. Then Sissy trying to staunch the bleeding. The pain had been so intense, it hadn't occurred to her to locate either Tansy or Graham.

The ambulance hadn't been much better, though by then she was aware the man was missing.

"Graham?" she said again.

The nurse entered, and Grandma Quinny ignored Taylor's request. "There you are." Grandma stood and went to the nurse, a woman with almost as much force of presence as Grandma Quinny, herself. If Sissy had been in the room as well, it wouldn't have been able to contain the sheer power of the women. "Lower her pain medicine, will you? She's loopy as anything and there's nothing wrong with her."

"She did get shot, Ma'am," the nurse said.

"That doesn't mean she needs to drown in morphine."

"The doctor will be in shortly." The nurse approached Taylor. She looked her up and down, waved a single finger in front of her drowsy eyes, then clucked, rather like Grandma Quinny had. "Her dose might be a little high." She left without making any changes.

Taylor cleared her throat, but it did nothing to clear her head. "Where did they go?"

"Doctors are busy people, dear."

"No...my friends. Where?"

"Sissy went home. She was completely worn down. She wanted to stay with you, but could you imagine? How anyone could rest with a woman like that around. Her daughter went with her."

"And Graham?"

"Oh, is that a person? I thought you meant me. I don't know, dear. No one tells old ladies anything. I'm sure this Graham is fine."

Taylor swallowed. Despite the medicine, her shoulder ached. It shouldn't have. It was unfair.

"Darling, you should try to sleep. I'll call Hudson. I doubt Sissy thought of it. Poor boy."

Grandma Quinny sat in the guest chair again and dialed.

Taylor closed her eyes and hoped she'd sleep.

"WELL! YOU'RE AWAKE FINALLY."

It felt like she had just closed her eyes, but Grandma Quinny's rousing tone made it clear it had been a while. "Do you need to tell me something about this Graham character?" She stared down her granddaughter.

Taylor's head was clearer, and her pain was more acute. "Did the doctor....?"

"Yes, he did. There was no reason for you to be that loopy. The bullet went right through your muscle. They didn't have to dig around to get it out or anything. If you hadn't kept passing out, you probably could have gone home, but you've never been good with pain. Now, I called Hudson several times, but didn't leave a message, this isn't the kind of thing one says to a machine. But I just got off the phone with his *mother*." The implication in her tone was clear. "And she doesn't think he'd want to come by the hospital to see you. Please don't tell me that you've been unfaithful. This is not how Quinns behave."

Taylor closed her eyes and turned her head.

"Don't try that with me. You're not high right now. Sit that bed up so you can look at me."

Taylor obeyed, adjusting her hospital bed to more of a sitting position.

"Have you been having an affair? Because if you have, I don't know what to say to you right now."

"No." Taylor looked at her left hand, which lay limp on her lap. She tested a finger and it moved with ease, though her shoulder hollered at her about it. Maybe that was just psychosomatic. Shoulder muscles surely didn't operate fingers.

"Taylor." Her name was a reproach in Grandma Quinny's mouth.

"No. I haven't cheated on Hudson." She wrapped her fingers in the blanket, rubbing them back and forth for comfort, like she had as a child. "But Grandma, I don't think he's the one."

"After all this time?" She sighed heavily. "You've been dating for years,"

"Not quite. Not really. Just…it's not been that long."

"Your mother passed three years ago this coming spring and you've been together the whole time. We all thought you'd be married by now."

"I think he was the person I needed to date for a while to get over Clay."

"Oh, Clay. What a waste!" Grandma Quinny's voice reverberated in the little room. "I prayed you'd break up for years. Never was so happy when you finally did, but he's still here haunting you."

Taylor adjusted her bed again, slowly lying back down.

"You owe that nice young man an apology."

"Why?" Taylor's voice was a whisper. "What did I do wrong, exactly?"

Grandma Quinny stared her down, her mouth a tight circle of disapproval. "Only you know the answer to that."

"I love him. But I'm afraid I'm not…*in* love with him."

"Children. That's what all of you are. In love, my foot. Well, I had hoped better for all of my grandkids than this, but between your relationships and Reid's divorce, I have to wash my hands of the lot of you."

Taylor wished her grandmother would go away or that the doctor would come back and up her meds again.

Her wish came true, moments later, and Grandma Quinny had to settle down while the doctor explained what the emergency room x-rays had revealed and what it meant for the long-term health of her left shoulder.

CHAPTER NINETEEN

"*N*o surgery. That's the good news." Sissy had taken over for Grandma Quinny, but only because of a minor crisis in Grandma Quinny's current charity case, her great niece Coco.

"Yes." The bullet wound through Taylor's deltoid had been cleaned and stitched up, and the arm was taped tightly across her chest. She'd fractured her clavicle in the fall, and only isolation, ice, and rest were needed to heal it.

"But why you fell on the shoulder you were shot in, I don't get." Sissy shook her head. "You'd think your instincts would have prevented that."

Taylor was tired of getting the blame for being shot, but she dearly wanted information from Sissy. "What happened? Who did this?"

"Not, The Cutter, that's for sure," Sissy snorted. "No scissors here."

"Is Tansy okay?"

"You mean is Graham okay, and he's fine as far as I know. We heard the shot, saw you fall, and he took off."

"Oh." Taylor dropped her head back onto the pillow. This

thing she had for him…it was just her brain telling her to set Hudson free. It had to be. You can't fall in love in a week. Graham certainly hadn't.

"Don't get your feelings hurt about that. He chased down the shooter. We heard another couple of shots, but I think whoever had the gun was an idiot. Graham was ready to knock the guy to the ground. Tackle him and kill him with his bare hands, probably. You do have a way of inspiring men. But instead of shooting Graham, the guy ran. I think he tried to shoot over his shoulder, don't know. I'm going to see if Breadyn wants to go out with her metal detector to find the bullets. Could be fun."

The amount of words overwhelmed Taylor. She didn't know what to do with them all. She wasn't as fuzzy as she had been on the IV drip, and she was dressed and ready to go home, just reclining on the bed now, waiting for her discharge, but she still felt that distinct separation between herself and reality.

"Your grandma told me to take you to her house, but I won't if you don't want me to. Though I'd say Belle has enough on her hands with Ernie."

"It's okay." Taylor didn't know which house she was agreeing to, but it felt like the polite answer.

"Knock, Knock." Hudson stood in the doorway. His face was ashen, and his hands were in his pockets. He looked like he needed the bed more than she did.

"Now's not a good time for whatever you two have to figure out." Sissy stood and crossed her arms.

"I heard you got shot," Hudson's voice was quiet.

"Yeah." Taylor patted her left elbow. "They've got me all taped up under my sweater."

Sissy interrupted with an overly dramatic sigh. "I was just telling her that they didn't catch the guy who did it. Graham tried, and the police scoured the place, but he had a motorcycle parked by the fence and was long gone by the time the sheriff got there.

Motorcycle.

Sheriff.

These felt like things Taylor should remember.

"I won't stay. I just had to see you with my own eyes. See that you were okay."

"Thanks."

"Taylor..."

"I said this was not the time, Hudson East, go home. She'll be much better in a couple of days and then you two can have whatever heart-felt, cry-it-out you need. Since she's not having sex with anyone any time soon, this will be good for both of you. No hormones to get in the way."

Hudson ignored the lecture from Sissy. He couldn't pull his eyes from Taylor, but though his mouth was turned down in sadness, those eyes looked suspicious.

"You don't have to go." Taylor sounded as unsure as she felt.

"Later. I'll see you later." He stepped out of the room as quietly as he had arrived.

"He could have stayed," Taylor said.

"No, he couldn't. You're in no place to speak to him. You should have heard the things you were saying while you were dozing off all those drugs. If I didn't know what you felt about Graham before, and anyone could tell, then I do know."

"Drugged dreams don't count." She looked up at Sissy, forcing a smile on her face, begging her to agree.

"Sure, if they come out of nowhere. But this didn't. Everyone knows his car was at your house last night, and you can't hardly go to Reuben's anymore without seeing the two of you, eyes locked, having some kind of secret thing. It's shameful, honestly. Hudson is the best man in Comfort, and who even is this Graham character?"

It hurt to shrug, so she didn't.

"I'll take you to your grandmother's. I'd rather just take you to my place, but Cooper and Dayton are holed up there still.

Those two are enough to drive anyone bananas, much less someone recovering from a serious injury."

"He's going to be okay, you know." Taylor was still staring at the door Hudson had disappeared through.

"Maybe, maybe not. They don't get over their first loves, you know." There was a bitter note to Sissy's words.

Taylor turned to her. Sissy was her husband's second wife. "Has it been hard?"

"Yup. I'm the opposite of his first wife, in every single way, and he loves it. But that means when he thinks of what he loves about me, he's always a little bit thinking about her." Sissy took her seat in the extra chair. "I wouldn't trade him in just so I could be someone else's first wife. I love the old guy too much. But that doesn't mean it's been easy."

After a few moments passed, Taylor swung her feet over the edge of the bed and stood. She took a few careful steps. "Hudson is the complete opposite of Clay. I never stopped thinking about that."

Sissy nodded. "And so it goes."

JONAH, Belle, Grandpa Ernie, Grandma and Grandpa Quinny, and young Coco were all at the Quinn family strawberry farm waiting for Taylor. She had no idea what time it was when she arrived, but there were balloons, scones, strawberry freezer jam, whipped cream, pigs in blankets, those sweet and sour meatballs her mom used to make in a crock pot, a three bean salad, and a folding table covered just in two liter bottles of soda.

"Your grandfather is responsible for this mess." Grandma Quinny laughed. "But he did his best."

Grandpa Quinny gave Taylor a very careful side hug. "Baby girl, I don't know what we would have done if we'd lost you."

His voice cracked on the word lost and he kissed the side of her head.

Outside, the rain Yamhill county had been longing for had finally come, in heavy bucketfuls.

Grandpa Quinny led her to a chair at the dining room table next to Grandpa Ernie.

Grandpa Ernie had his portable oxygen in, but still looked irritated. "Thought I taught all you girls better than that. Three girls I've had to raise—your mother, you, and that one there." He nodded toward Belle. "You're the only one of you who ever had any sense and look what you go and do." He looked to Grandpa Quinny. "What kind of girl runs after strange men in the night? No granddaughter of mine."

"I'll take the blame. Quinn women always run a little wild."

Though she wasn't a Quinn by any stretch of the word, young Coco blushed.

Taylor watched the girl as she carefully filled a pink Fiestaware plate with the hodge-podge feast. What kind of trouble had Grandpa Ernie's erstwhile sitter gotten herself into?

The doors at the Quinn's faux farmhouse never creaked or squeaked so no one noticed Clay till he stood in the dining room, dripping with rain. "I've been looking all day, and I can't find her anywhere. Someone's got to know where..." His words broke off when he spotted Taylor.

"Hi." She stared at him. He was as wet and attractive as Toby McGuire playing Spiderman. Was this who her heart saw when she looked at Graham Dawson? Maybe so. But her heart didn't beat with any kind of excitement as she looked at Clay.

"Fix yourself a plate." Grandpa Quinny passed one of the vibrantly mismatched dishes to Clay. "She got shot and spent last night in the hospital, but she'll recover."

Clay stared. "Shot?"

Grandpa Quinny chuckled in a hearty manner, but it was clear to everyone looking that his eyes were full of unshed tears.

"She's letting us take care of her for a few nights. But please, join us. We've got plenty. It's late for lunch but we felt like celebrating.

Clay set the plate back on the table. "I can't stay, sorry. I um, God. I'm glad you're okay. Why did no one call?" he asked Jonah, not Taylor.

"Sorry. I told Mom." He put a whole meatball in his mouth at once.

"Oh, sorry. I don't know why she didn't tell me. Okay." Clay took his phone out looking for a text or a message, then shook his head. "I'll get back to the shop. Um, but, yeah, Taylor, Roxy was supposed to have tomorrow off...." The room went silent.

"It's okay," Belle said, to all of them. "She deserves it. I'll work with you. Don't worry. Merely a flesh wound, as they say. She'll be fine." Her words were fast and high pitched, clearly nervous, but it cleared the tension.

"You are a good girl." Grandma Quinny sounded surprised. "Thank you, dear."

"She's my sister." Belle's voice broke on her last word.

Clay left, but the impromptu celebration went on in those starts and stops, no one feeling entirely sure what they should say or do.

"Motorcycle," Taylor savored the word. "You guys, he rode a motorcycle, and Lorraine, she probably killed the guy in the biker gang. It is all related."

Grandma Quinny reached over and felt Taylor's head. "You need to lie down, dear. I think you might have a fever."

WHEN TAYLOR finally woke up from her enforced nap, she resented her grandma's interference in the pain medicine. Her shoulder ached beyond her ability to bear. She lay on her right side and bit her pillow, willing herself not to cry. When she opened her eyes again, she saw a little bell on the bedside table. If Grandma Quinny was going to deny her even Codeine laced Tylenol from their last trip to Canada, then Taylor was absolutely going to make use of the good old-fashioned sick-person-bell.

Taylor slowly but surely shifted up and rang for her grandma.

Instead of Grandma Quinny, Jonah Lang came up. "Hey, Tay." He leaned against the door jam. "Belle's downstairs, but I wanted to check in on you."

Taylor squeezed her eyes shut, sort of hoping when she opened them again, he'd be gone.

"Head hurting?" he asked.

She opened her eyes. "No, just the shoulder. I'd love some Tylenol. I think I get some now."

"Sure. Anything else? Coke? Coffee?"

"I don't know what time it is."

"Probably too late for coffee," Jonah offered. "Dinner? We're having fried chicken. Your Grandpa Quinn is hilarious. He has Belle in stitches down there. She told me she didn't really know the Quinns, but you wouldn't know it listening to the two of them."

"Where's Grandpa Ernie?" Taylor pressed her right hand to her forehead. Maybe she did have an incipient headache.

"He's here too. Grandma Quinny invited us all for dinner. He's snoozing in the TV room. But he ate first, scouts honor."

"Good."

"You want fried chicken and maybe a Sprite?"

Taylor shook her head.

"It must be killing you not to know what happened to the shooter."

"Any news?"

"Nope. Haven't seen Graham, either," Jonah added.

"Ah."

"You might be stuck in bed a few days, depending on how that shoulder heals. I hear it's the break that hurts worse than the bullet hole."

"Who knows. The whole thing feels like it's on fire." She grimaced. Talking hurt. Sitting up hurt. Lying down hurt. She just wanted to make the pain go away.

"I wanted to offer the Juvies to you while you're laid up. Is there anything they could hunt down online? Just to keep you from going crazy with worry?"

"Did they ever look up Graham, speaking of?"

"Sure. He's a journalist in Portland. Works for *Oregonlive.com* just like he said. Graduated with a degree in digital journalism from Penn State. Never married. Originally from Hutchinson, Kansas," Jonah rattled off Graham Dawson's CV.

Taylor never thought of Jonah as being particularly smart, but she wondered if maybe he had one of those photographic memories like Belle.

"Kansas?"

"Yup."

"How'd he end up out here?"

"I assume because we were hiring." Jonah glanced over his shoulder as though something more interesting was happening in the hall.

"Interesting. No skeletons in his online closet?"

"None my girls could find."

"Thanks for checking."

"I like him," Jonah said.

"He's an awful lot like Clay." Taylor stared out the window. Why she admitted that to Jonah, she didn't know. Maybe just to test the waters with the idea.

"Nah," Jonah said. "Clay's insinuating and insincere. Graham's genuine."

"Hmmm," Taylor wondered. "About that Tylenol."

"Sure, I'll be right back. And just so you know, I know where the good stuff is. Belle showed me. And it's not out of date yet."

"The Canadian stuff?"

"Yup."

"Hey, before you go. How good are the Juvies?"

"They constantly surprise me with their ability to dig into the darkest corners of the internet between their middle school classes," Jonah said with a chuckle.

"Think they could find out who the troll on Shawna and Tansy's website was? I suspect the troll is also the person she met online. And if so...."

"Got it. Can do." He left, a little too sprightly, as though this was a kind of seal of approval from Taylor.

It wasn't.

Or was it?

If he delivered on the codeine-laced meds it might well be.

CHAPTER TWENTY

*G*randma Quinny foiled Jonah on the meds. The regular old Tylenol barely took the edge off and Taylor found herself in bed for another full day. But the next morning Grandma Quinny woke her bright and early. "You have company." She pulled the curtains open to let in the insipid winter sun.

"What time is it?"

"What day, more like it. Did Jonah slip you something?" Grandma Quinny crossed her arms and looked at her granddaughter with a surprising amount of love in her eyes.

"I wish." Taylor sat up and stretched with one arm. "It's bad still, but I guess I'll live."

"Good girl. Now, get dressed. It's after ten, and I said you'd be down quickly."

"Who is it? Taylor swung her legs over the side of the bed gingerly, as though it was her hips that had been hurt.

"Jonah and some girl with red hair, like a crayon. I don't know her." Grandma Quinny reminded Taylor of the infamous gif of Mariah Carey saying she didn't know Jennifer Lopez. But Taylor couldn't place a girl with crayon-red hair either.

Downstairs Jonah, Belle, and a cherry-red head Taylor would have recognized anywhere, were sitting around the island eating scones and drinking coffee. "Valerie Ritz!"

"They really did shoot you!" Valerie was one of Jonah's more grown up fans. They'd met when she'd come to Comfort for the Cascadia Quilt Expo. "Here, let me help you." She took Taylor by her good arm and led her to a stool.

"Thanks, my feet are fine though." Taylor picked up a scone and slathered Grandma Quinny's famous strawberry freezer jam on it. "Aren't these the church scones?"

"Generous of her, right?" Belle smiled broadly and took a bite of a jam laden scone.

"Thanks for coming to see me." Though the pain in Taylor's shoulder had made a whole lot of hours disappear, it did strike her as odd that the quilter and TikTok fan had come. They hadn't so much as retweeted each other since the tragic death about a month ago.

"Jonah put out a plea yesterday for some info about a regular on Shawna Cross's blog." Valerie broke a small bit from her scone and ate it. "We got to the bottom of it pretty quick, and I couldn't help but come by to chat in person."

"She means she wanted in on the content house," Belle said.

"True. I definitely want in on that." Valerie's face was as bright as her hair. So cheerful this morning. "But about your murder. Amongst the Juvies there was a disagreement, but the majority have pinned the identity of the main troll as Yves St Michel, a thirteen-year-old from Quebec. It seems unlikely he's your murderer. However, there was another troll—not so regular a poster, but meaner. Much meaner. Again, the Juvies aren't in complete agreement on the identity, but the posts are coming from Northern California, right near the border, and all evidence points to it being her new online boyfriend, a forty-seven-year-old man named David Smith."

Taylor sipped her coffee and considered the information.

Northern California. You could get there in a day. You could even get there and back if you didn't stay long and didn't go very far from the border. "What odds are the Juvies laying that David Smith is a real person?"

"There's no way on earth he's real. He's really sending messages from Northern California though, probably not far from Eureka. But who he actually is? Not sure. I have a friend running some samples of his messages, both the dating app messages and the comments, through some data bases. There's always a chance his unique writing style could match up with something that reveals his real identity. It's a long shot but we're giving it a go."

"I don't think it's a long shot." Taylor shifted on the stool. Having her left arm snugly bound to her chest was bad for her balance. "Maybe the deep dive into writing styles is a long shot, but someone who would write such vicious things on a fairly innocuous blog and then take the time to set up a fake dating profile just to hurt her more must hate her. That can't have come from nowhere."

"Sure, it can," Belle interjected. "It's been a while since the psych class I took in high school, but some of these mental disturbances can fixate on a target for reasons that seem completely out of proportion to the rest of us."

"Sure...." Taylor sipped her coffee but dribbled a little. She set her mug down and scowled at it.

Belle passed her a cloth napkin. "You'll get the hang of this eventually."

"Thanks. I would think that kind of criminal psychopathy," Taylor hoped Belle was impressed with her vocabulary, "would be rare. Not that it's not possible but looking at people who knew her well seems like a more reasonable place to start."

"Maybe." Belle didn't look convinced.

Taylor stared at the three young people. All at least ten years her junior. Worry groaned in her heart. How could she protect them when she couldn't even protect herself? The constant deep ache in her shoulder was all the evidence she needed that this job was too big for her. "It's really great to see you, Valerie," Taylor said. "But this isn't safe. I've been shot and two journalists were murdered. I can assume anyone else in this town caught looking for clues is also at risk."

"I won't get caught." Valerie had the confidence that comes from both youth and wealth. "And besides, there's no way I was going to miss the big event."

"Sounds exhausting." Taylor slipped off the stool. I think I need to go lay down again."

"Try the recliner," Jonah suggested. "I loved it when I broke my arm in third grade."

"Thanks." Taylor shuffled off to her grandpa's TV room.

To be rich, young, not injured, and headed off to who knows what kind of big event sounded exhausting. Right now, living like Grandpa Ernie from one recliner to the next, sounded perfect.

She paused at said recliner.

Big event?

In Comfort?

She scuttled back to the kitchen. Her shoulder cried out for her to recline, and maybe find an audiobook, and definitely fall asleep, but her curiosity demanded to know what kind of big event was planned for the murder-riddled town of two-thousand.

Three heads were bent together over the scones, whispering, when Taylor got back into the kitchen. "What big event?"

"Just Black Friday." Valerie's face exuded innocence.

Taylor didn't buy it.

"The guild backed off Black Friday. Last year's numbers didn't impress us much, so we spent our various ad funds on the expo instead. There's not going to be a big event."

"Oh, sure," Valerie nodded. "Not a store-planned event. Not

like that. But it should be fun." She looked at her phone.
"Speaking of, I want to get back to my Airbnb—I'm outside of
town. See you all later." Valerie sauntered out of the sprawling
house like it was her own.

"What's she talking about?" Taylor leaned her hip against the
island.

"Not sure," Belle said. "I'm afraid it's some kind of fan-
planned event, and I don't like it."

Jonah shook his head in denial. "I didn't plan anything, but I
can't help it if they organize on their own."

"Why not ask them?"

"Oh, I have." He held out his phone. "But so far no one's
breaking rank."

"Black Friday is the day after Thanksgiving. Wouldn't
Valerie want to be with her family?"

"She said places to stay were filling up too fast. I guess she's
going to fly to LA for Thursday and come right back. Ritz
money is easy to spend."

"She ought to fund the content house." Taylor groaned
quietly.

Her shoulder.

It hurt so bad.

"Why?" Belle countered. "She doesn't need to make more
money, we do. A million dollars isn't what it used to be."

"Fine. I'll just have to believe Jonah's fans are planning to
descend on our town for Black Friday. Why not? Weirder things
have happened." She turned again, headed for the recliner that
was calling her name, but planned to call the sheriff when she
got comfortable. It seemed wise to let someone with power
know that there were going to be a whole lot of vulnerable
young people running around a town with a murderer on the
loose.

Once she had her feet up, she dug around in her purse for
her phone to make the call. She hadn't looked at her phone in

ages and was surprised to see dozens of messages. Roxy had sent several in the few days that had passed since they'd seen each other. Hudson had sent a couple, including another shirtless shot.

She stared at it. He was hot, Hudson. No other word really worked as well. And yet that need to send pictures was so juvenile. She'd been sure the whole time they were dating that four years was hardly any difference at their age, but as she looked at his firm, fit abdomen it felt like a hundred. Then again, maybe he wasn't immature. Maybe he would always be the kind of man to send pictures, or at least if he always looked that good.

There were also three messages from Graham.

Just three.

Though Jonah had hunted down his background, she hadn't asked how old he was. For all she knew he was a solid ten, fifteen years her senior. Some men looked younger than they really were. If so, she was the immature one. The one who flirted even though she had a boyfriend. The one who'd hunted him down in the middle of the night and gotten shot.

She opened his messages trying not to hope for too much.

Back in PDX. He used the airport code for Portland, like all Portlanders do. *Not sure how long.* That was the most recent message, and very ungratifying.

The one earlier wasn't too much better: *Heading to Amity on a lead. I know what questions I'm going to ask.* But she smiled as she read it, that call back to his advice to her felt warm and personal, there at the end of an otherwise throw-away message.

The earliest text though…. it was good.

She read it several times.

You got shot coming after me. I got his motorcycle license #. Gave it to the police. Here's what I was doing out in that field, if you didn't know. I was following an anonymous lead on a story I no longer believed in. A serial killer in this charming little town? Nope. I was convinced it was the vivid imagination of a fevered mind, and that the anonymous tip was from Lorraine. I wasn't going to leave her in that field for God knows what to happen to her. But, you ask, because you have your questions prepared in advance now, if not a serial killer sprung from the past to gain his fame, who killed Gus and Ramona, the most innocent victims in this mess? He's a serial killer now, that's who. Whoever killed Shawna got wind of the rumors of The Cutter and decided to make use of the coincidence of the murder weapon to draw attention away from himself. What I'm saying is: Ignore the past and find out who wanted Shawna dead. That's the only motive that matters. I'm glad you're tough because amateur sleuthing is a tough business and I'd hate to see someone so good at it give up because of a little thing like a bullet wound. I wanted to see you at the hospital but thought better of it. You have actual family and friends who deserved to have you all to themselves. I may have to run back to Portland soon. If I do, I'll come back. We're not done with this story yet.

She read it several times, then took screen shots to save it.

When he said they weren't done with this story, did he mean the murder or something more personal? And was he sincere when he said he wanted her to keep detecting? Because Clay had said that earlier, but she hadn't thought he meant it. He'd just wanted her out of his hair. And Hudson really wanted her to stay out of trouble.

And how did one respond? It had been a lot of days and she was just seeing these now. He must have thought he meant nothing to her.

She took a deep breath and held it till her chest burned. What did she want to say to him?

Been laid up. Just seeing texts. Things might get crazy soon. I will prepare my questions in advance. I always follow up on a good lead. She hit send.

It almost meant nothing, that selection of phrases. Almost. But, if he wanted it to mean something, it could.

His reply was immediate. *I'm back in town. Can I see you?*

She sent the address to her Grandparent's home.

I'll be there in five minutes.

The thumping of her heart distracted her from the pain in her shoulder. Just a little, but she'd take it.

"THAT LOOKS LIKE IT HURTS," Graham's sincere voice warmed the large, French country inspired TV room. "Can I get that for you?"

Taylor had been reaching for an icepack that had fallen from her shoulder when she jumped at the sound of his voice.

He reached between the recliner and the side table to collect it, then settled it back on her arm.

"Thanks." She tipped her face up to his and bit her lip.

He smiled slowly then stepped away and looked around.

Taylor lowered the footrest of the recliner, awkward with her one-armed motions. "Can I get you something? Coffee maybe?"

"I'm good." He settled into a light green plaid wingback chair.

"I didn't see your messages earlier. I was kind of knocked out."

"Pain meds." He nodded and his eyes were big and sad.

"I wish. Grandma Quinny wouldn't let me have any."

"Sorry." He scratched his chin, then he stood, again, and walked a circle around the room as though taking notes for a future story. "Despite the different weapon, I think you were shot by our killer."

"The motorcycle...." The icepack fell from her shoulder again. She set it on the table.

"You sound like Lorraine."

"Graham, what did Gus know? He promised he could show me what all of the earlier deaths had in common with each other, and to Shawna. But he was killed before we could talk. Did he ever tell you?"

"No, but I went to his office, with permission from the sheriff and the college, and dug through his papers." Graham sat in the same chair again, but on its edge. He leaned forward with his elbows resting on his knees.

Her pulse raced like crazy. She'd have given anything to dig into Gus's years and years of research.

"Was just there yesterday," Graham continued. "I knew I owed you one. A big one. But here's the thing: conspiracy theories often have logic without sense, and his was no different. Logic is only as useful as the premises it's based on."

"You didn't take pictures, did you?"

"Sure." He got up again and moved to her side, crouching by the chair so she could see the screen of his phone. "He kept a lot of hand-written notes, and those are hard to read on this small screen, but here are some good ones. This is a timeline he'd created." He scrolled through a timeline that reminded Taylor of history class notes. "The important part is how early it starts. It begins with Erika Wainwright, roommate of the supposed suicide. Three years before the events in question, she was arrested for assault on her schoolteacher."

"It couldn't be...."

He nodded. "The same school-teacher who died in a car crash."

"With injuries that couldn't have been caused in the crash." Taylor stared at the timeline wishing she could see the whole thing spread out on a wall.

"Exactly. Erika was a freshman and new to Comfort. The teacher in the car accident moved here right after she'd been assaulted by Erika."

"Did Gus know anything about the assault?"

"Nothing. Juvenile records are sealed. He only got this much from an interview with the family of the schoolteacher. A brother who couldn't remember the why's of it, only that a student attacked her after school one day."

"She wouldn't have happened to attack her with scissors?" Taylor didn't dare get her hope up.

"Fists."

"Did the teacher's brother drive a motorcycle?"

"No, but when I asked, he lit up, saying he'd always wanted to," Graham chuckled.

"So not a biker gang member back in the day, and also not suspicious of why we'd have asked that."

"Exactly. Moving on from the timeline, we've got this article from the 1975 Comfort High School newspaper about the girl who left town. A goodbye article." He swiped to the next picture.

"That's some find!"

"I was impressed." Graham zoomed in so the text was readable. "Here's the important part. She was leaving school to join her parents on a tour of Europe. Her French class threw her a party."

"Must not have been a memorable party. No one we've questioned has mentioned it."

"Sounds like it was just cupcakes in class. News for the school paper, but not much else." He was already swiping to the next picture.

"Gus wasn't able to track her down again, was he?"

"Sadly, her name was Jennifer Anderson, one of the most common names in Oregon in the 1970s. Gus had notes on literally two-hundred Jennifer Andersons, but none seemed to get him anywhere."

"There wasn't any evidence of this Jennifer Anderson dying or being whisked away to have a baby or anything, was there?"

"None. For all we know, she really did go to France."

Taylor shifted. Leaning over to stare at the phone was killing her collar bone. "He swore he could tie them all together."

"The best I could do to connect the missing girl with the others is that the schoolteacher's sister-in-law's last name was Anderson. If you're a conspiracy theorist, that's enough. The brother and the Anderson lady were married in 1978, so it was conceivable they were dating that infamous fall and winter of 1975. But her name is Tina. There were no Tina Andersons in Comfort High School in 1975, so she wasn't Jennifer's sister. Maybe a cousin, but he doesn't say."

"These are all little facts," Taylor exhaled, trying to control the pain, but not wanting him to notice. "Where's the logic you promised?"

"There were a few other facts, such as Lorraine, Erika, and Erika's roommate all having fake IDs so possibly all being regulars at the same bar. It can't be proven, but it's good enough for conspiracy theorists. Here's what he does with all of this though." Graham cleared his throat. "Premise 1: Erika had a record and history of violence. Premise 2: Erika had a connection to all of the victims, note, I find the connection to our travelling teen Jennifer to be specious at best. Premise 3: Erika studied the fiber arts so was likely to have access to sewing sheers. The next is one I hadn't mentioned yet. Deep in the files Gus had notes on the Love family. Deep notes. He seemed in awe of the local gentry and thought that Lorraine was a lovely, misunderstood girl. Poor little rich girl, even. So, Premise 4: Lorraine Love was meant to be the scape goat. Premise 5 is pretty sexist, so please remember it's Gus's and not mine. Gus is from a different generation." He smiled apologetically with charming crinkles around his eyes.

Taylor waved it away. "Continue, please."

"Premise 5: Women can be twisted by jealousy."

Taylor didn't argue. She herself hadn't been twisted to murder by feelings of jealousy, but that had been the primary motive for the murder of her own mother. "Ergo?" Taylor prompted.

"Thank you, yes. Gus would say ergo: Erika was jealous of her teacher, her roommate, a random teen who was going to go to Europe, and a wild young rich girl in her small town, so she murdered them all with sewing sheers."

Taylor exhaled slowly. "Sure, why not? But you could find another random person connected to all of those ladies and make the same kind of argument. It's not hard, in a town this size, we're all connected."

"Would that random person have the hinge pin of a history of violence and access to the murder weapons?" Graham pressed.

"I don't like this. Erika stopped by my house the other night, just, came over, walked in, chatted like we were old friends, and invited me and Grandpa Ernie back to the scene of Shawna's murder."

"That brings us to Gus's theory and how Shawna ties in. Are you ready for this?" He lifted an eyebrow but couldn't hide the concern.

She nodded and put a smile back on her face. She'd push through the conversation and then get some Tylenol. She'd be okay.

"The Cutter, possibly Erika, has laid low all these years. But she's getting closer to retirement age and has left no significant impact on her field. No big awards, no popular books. Just a tenured position at a small, though respected, college. Gus suspected she found the old quilt in storage at the school, made up a history for it, and set it up as an abandoned quilt she could discover and make waves with. But the expo crashed and burned. The quilt wasn't given to her to study, like it should have been if the expo hadn't been a disaster. Instead, it was given to your quilt shop owners guild. And Shawna, who was just some random kid without even an education, was already outing it as a fraud. Cherry on top? Shawna was going to get famous for it."

Taylor closed her eyes. The pain was beginning to make her head spin, but she wasn't ready to give up.

"Gus had to die because he'd figured it out. And Ramona as well," Graham concluded.

"You say that the case has logic but isn't believable. And yet, after laying it out for me, I believe it. Can't we bring this to the police?" Her voice was breathy and dramatic, but only because of the pain. She bit her tongue. She wasn't going to fall apart now.

Graham reached his hand toward her, like he was going to feel her forehead, but stopped, then rested it on her hand. "That's the trouble with conspiracies, Taylor. The logic makes you believe. Never forget that logic is just a system of arranging things so they make sense. It has nothing to do with reality."

She couldn't respond, and found her eyes were closing again.

"There's not one shred of evidence that the high school student Jennifer Anderson was murdered. Maybe she went to France like the school paper said. Maybe she went to Portland to have a baby the way everyone believes. As for the attack on Lorraine, didn't we already decide that was a fight with her boyfriend gone wrong? What happens to all of the evidence of the motorcycle crash and her trip to the hospital if we buy this story instead?" Though he continued their conversation his voice was quieter, gentler.

"You're right, aren't you? We came up with them based on facts, but you told me Gus's theories with a straight face, and I just…followed the logic and bought the story."

"Don't trust logic on its own. Finding bad logic is great if you want to disprove something. But good logic is only as good as the facts it's based on. Whatever else you do in life, don't forget that." This time he did touch her forehead with his hand. "Where do you keep your pain pills?"

Taylor groaned softly.

"Give me a minute, I'll find them," Graham left quietly.

It was a relief. She couldn't have taken anymore of the conversation, eye-opening as it was.

The back door swung open, letting in a cold wind that refreshed Taylor. She breathed in deeply and willed herself to relax.

"Woah, what's going on?" The voice, that deep, sexy voice, that had become so dear to Taylor over the last few years came from behind her.

She didn't open her eyes. She couldn't face Hudson, not with Graham wandering around the house.

"Babe, Taylor, are you okay?" Hudson was kneeling next to her now, the familiar scent of his regular old soap overwhelming her senses. A good man. Such a good man. So strong and capable of taking care of her.

"We should get you to the hospital." His hand was on her forehead. "You're burning up."

She liked his hand there. So familiar.

CHAPTER TWENTY-ONE

*W*hen she woke up, she was bumping through the country road in the minivan that was their local ambulance. She was alone except for the volunteer paramedic, one of her Grandma Quinny's good friends.

Taylor was painfully awake through the poking and prodding at the ER. Her shoulder was infected, and a course of antibiotics was written for her. She described the pain and the ER doctor prescribed the appropriate medication. Just enough for three days, but no grandparents were around to tell her she couldn't have them, so she was able, after the inspection of the bullet wound had been completed, to relax in hope that the pain would die down sooner rather than later.

Hudson had called 911, gotten her in the ambulance and swept her away to get help. He was good at that, taking care of her. Being responsible, mature, trustworthy.

She didn't know if he'd bothered to find Grandma and Grandpa Quinny before whisking her away, or if he'd discovered Graham in the house. As was his way, he'd thought of her needs, and how he could meet them.

He stared at her now, in fact, from the spare chair in the tiny, curtained ER cubicle. "I should have been there for you that night. If I'd been at your place, or you'd been at mine…"

"But we couldn't. Not anymore." Taylor was surprised by the sound of her own voice. She'd expected it to come out in wispy clouds, like the thoughts she was barely able to hold on to.

"But why? Because I started a business without talking to you about it? I've never been sorrier about a lapse in communication in my life. I regret it. I should have talked to you about the Bible Creek Care Home Hotel thing because you are the love of my life. It's always been you Taylor."

She tried to close her eyes but couldn't. Where was that sleep she'd been longing for? She needed to escape his deeply held feelings.

He sat there, shaking, his five o'clock shadow aging him. He didn't seem like a young man, not even twenty-seven yet.

"It's not just that," again, her voice sounded absurdly sure of itself.

"Graham. So what? You met a guy who was interesting and attractive? I've met interesting girls over the last few years. The world is full of attractive people who might catch our eye for a minute. That can't be a reason to throw away something as good as we have."

"You're so good." Taylor thought her words would come out in a sweet murmur and buy her some time, but again, it came out in that firm, strong voice.

"We're so good. Imagine this…." He lowered his voice, both volume and tenor, and wove her a dream. "A big, blue sky overhead, white topped mountains in the distance. The smell of hay being mowed. A cabin like mine, but bigger, with room for kids, or Grandpa Ernie. Light filling it from windows on all four sides. Somewhere in the distance is town with your shop. But you only go in on days you want to, and the kids help too."

She cringed, but not at the word kids. "What?"

"Montana, Taylor. Let's get away from all of this. From the

pain and the bad memories. From the cramped spaces and town crowded with people who tell you what medicine you can and can't take. I'll finish up the Bible Creek Care Home project, sell my shares, and we'll head to the mountains where we can be free to be us. I've already got a partner to build a project just like Bible Creek. Only this time it's in some place better than Oregon, someplace sunnier and snowier and more epic in every direction. Mom asked if she could stay in my place while I'm gone. She's already packing up her big house and ready for a change."

Taylor's mouth seemed to curl into a curve of disgust against her will. While the picture he painted was literally beautiful, it wasn't her dream.

Comfort might be small, rain-soaked, and shadowed by the Coast Range that stood between them and the ocean. It might be full of people who wanted to interfere in her medical care, and her house might be crowded with stuff. But it was her stuff. And her people. And the mountains might not be as epic as Montana's mountains, but they were hers. Comfort was her home, and she didn't want to move. She wanted to explain it to him, but she couldn't bear to hear her own cold, firm voice again.

She just watched him until a voice said, "Knock, knock," at the curtain as it rattled its way open.

"Press pass got me in."

Graham.

A bit disheveled and looking like he'd gotten caught committing a crime.

Hudson stood, but there was hardly room for his tall, broad-shouldered frame in the space. "What do you want?"

"Just a quote for the paper." He held out his phone like an old-fashioned reporter's tape recorder. "Taylor Quinn?"

She shook her head, but she knew she was smiling.

"About a kidnapping case. A sick young women disappeared

from her grandparent's home not two hours ago while her guest was running to the store to get some medicine." He kept his tone light, but his face was ashen.

"Knock it off," Hudson's voice was a deep and dangerous growl.

"Care to make a comment?" Graham moved toward Taylor, not disguising his actual concern anymore.

"How dare you? It's your fault she's here." Hudson's fists flexed.

"Ho ho ho!" Another face popped around Graham's shoulder. "Sissy Dorney said I'd find you here, though why my business partner was at the ER in McMinnville I couldn't guess."

Taylor's old friend, the well-dressed banker John Hancock, took up the last of the breathing room in her curtained space. "You must be the chump who got Taylor shot." He looked Graham up and down. "Anyway, before you get yourself arrested for assault, will you give me five minutes?" this he said to Hudson. "We have some papers to sign for the hotel."

Hudson stared at the man who had been one of his early rivals for Taylor's affection with pure disgust on his face.

Then he turned to the journalist, cocked his powerful arm, and smashed Graham's face in.

It took about an hour for the hubbub to die down.

Somewhere in the hospital Graham was getting his face x-rayed.

Hudson had been sent home with a stern warning.

Reg, the deputy Taylor used to date, would have liked to do more, so he said, but Graham refused to press charges.

The ER wasn't overcrowded at the time, and the hospital staff, while annoyed there had been so many people with Taylor, weren't going to bother to charge Hudson with anything either.

Reg sat on the arm of the visitor's chair. "So."

She tried to decide if he looked more tired or annoyed. "I didn't invite any of them in here."

"That's what they all said. Especially John Hancock who wanted completely out of all of this."

"He came for Hudson, some business thing." Taylor found the low dose of Vicodin had taken the edge off her pain.

"Sure. Makes sense. I'm not really concerned about John or Hudson."

"But Graham didn't do anything."

"He didn't, but I'm not sure I like the company you've been keeping."

"He's just a journalist." She frowned at the handsome face of her old suitor. He was a deputy. A lawman. She'd always respected his wits and bravery. But she didn't like that tone—too condescending and controlling.

"You can't always trust those guys, you know. They don't want what's best for the rest of us."

"It must be the pain medicine...." Taylor glanced around the little cubicle wishing Grandma Quinny would energetically fling herself into the room and end this awkward conversation.

Reg stood and shook his pants leg down. "You need to rest. But be careful, will you? Guy's like him will twist your words for their own agenda. They hate our small-town way of life."

She stared him down, daring him to say one more nasty thing about her friend.

"We all care about you, Taylor. Just remember who your friends are." Reg patted the rail on the side of her bed and left.

UNFORTUNATELY FOR TAYLOR, Thanksgiving did not come and go in a haze of heavy medicine. Her arm was in a regular sling now, which meant she sometimes moved it in ways that hurt so bad she wished she could...well... she didn't wish she was dead, but she sure wished she was knocked out on heavy drugs.

She hated that she wouldn't be at Flour Sax the next day. The last ten Fridays-after-Thanksgiving had almost all been spent in one store or another, and though she would never admit it to her old retail buddies in the city, this year she missed it. After all, Flour Sax was her very own store.

A good third of her multifarious aunts, uncles, and cousins had come to the Quinn family strawberry farm for the holiday. Reid, the newly divorced, was a glaring absence because his ex-wife Hollis had come with their two-year-old.

The house bubbled over with chatter and love, and everyone graciously left the two large comfortable recliners in the TV room for Taylor and her Grandpa Ernie. Hollis joined her after dinner. "You haven't seen Reedsy, have you?"

Taylor wasn't sure if Reedsy was a nick name or the full name of her cousin Reid's two-year-old daughter, but she kind of liked it. "I think she's off with Grandpa Quinny feeding the chickens. He took a little posse of kids with him."

"Good, I'm glad. You won't believe where your rotten cousin is today."

"You're probably right. Reid and I were never that close." She remembered her somewhat younger cousin as being a computer snob—the kind who knew he was smart and resented the rest of the world for being stupid.

"You wouldn't think a guy like him would be overly aware of influencer culture, but something about your brother-in-law is driving him nuts."

"He's in good company." Taylor reclined her chair just a little more and closed her eyes.

"He didn't come with me to *his* grandparents' house where we promised to bring the baby, even though we've already filed the papers, because *he* wants to out Jonah as a cheater."

"How do you cheat at TikTok?"

"Not at TikTok, at marriage. Ironic, no? Reid and his girl-friend, in fact, are holed up in some Airbnb eating microwave meals and waiting for Jonah to slip up this weekend. Reid doesn't think Jonah's got just one girlfriend, and he thinks Jonah invited all those girls to Comfort so he could party with them. I mean, why else would he be planning a content house of his own?"

"It sounds like you agree with Reid." Taylor prickled with defensiveness. Jonah was not her favorite, but he adored Belle, and would never hurt her.

"I mean, he's kind of a fame-hungry teenager, it seems to fit. But I wouldn't make outing him my life's mission or anything." Hollis had that millennial vocal fray that Taylor found so forced.

"Belle and Jonah are at Jonah's mom's place for Thanksgiv-ing, and anyway, he didn't invite a bunch of young girls to come here."

"Sure." She pursed her lips. "But Clay did. Your Clay, and everyone knows he did it for Jonah. If Clay is Jonah's role model, well!"

"You're nuts. Jonah hates Clay, and besides, Clay wasn't a cheater." Taylor's shoulder hurt, but her jaw hurt worse from clenching it. She wished this girl would go find her toddler and hang out with the other young parents.

"Whatever. She's your sister, not mine. I just think Reid's an idiot for wasting time on it instead of being here."

"I'm sure he's enjoying the little getaway with his new girl-friend." Taylor felt bilious. The idea that people thought Clay had cheated on her stung. She'd broken up with him, not the other way around. And she'd also broken up with Hudson, for that matter. She turned her head away. She'd wanted to hurt this girl by mentioning the new girlfriend, but that was the nasty kind of thing she hated, and she wished she hadn't said it.

Hollis left without further comment.

Taylor wondered what the girl's parents thought about her

spending the holiday with people she wasn't even related to anymore. Familial politics are hard enough without divorce and small children. But this move, coming here with the child, was definitely political. What could Hollis gain from it? Taylor let the idea sift around in her tired, turkey-drugged brain as she lay in the comfortable chair.

Hollis could make the Quinns like her better than Reid. The Quinns were a popular family. All the strawberries you could want every spring. An unending source of shoestring relations to babysit.

She couldn't remember what Hollis's maiden name was. Maybe never knew it. Hollis and Reid had met online during college. She'd moved out here to get married. Maybe it was nicer here. Where had she been from? Somewhere hot and dry maybe?

If she wasn't from here, she'd need all the family support she could get. Might not have had anywhere else to go for the holiday. Just her and the baby alone, otherwise.

Spreading mean stories about Reid so they'd like her better.

Like a troll that way.

Like Shawna's vicious troll from somewhere in Northern California. Why had he hated her so much? Maybe he was friends with her ex, and they'd come up with this scheme together.

Maybe he was her ex.

But Owen wouldn't have had any reason to kill the journalists.

She wondered if Graham was stuck in a tiny rental somewhere eating a microwave dinner and then overwhelmed by the loneliness of that picture, texted him. *Our previous conversation was interrupted. Care to continue?*

Anytime. His response was prompt, if not effusive.

Taylor dictated her text, since it was hard to hold a phone and type: *If we dismiss the attack on Lorraine and the girl who went to France, we're left with Erika who'd attacked the teacher once already and lived with a girl who committed an improbable suicide. Erika had access to the quilt which may have been the motive and sewing scissors.*

He responded immediately: *True. But how likely is someone to kill for one last hurrah at academic publishing?*

Taylor countered: *If she had a history of instability and violence, it might not be absurd.*

Graham had another question for her: *How does her motive compare to others you've come up with?*

She left him on read for a moment and considered it as she lay back in the new recliner with the automatic buttons that made it so easy to use. She'd have to go home someday, but she was glad she hadn't just yet.

Erika had a professional motive, access to the weapons, and the quilt.

Lorraine had a similar motive but would have had to luck into the quilt. A less planned murder.

Maybe Owen would have killed Shawna for breaking up with him. But would he have trolled her blog and catfished her? And why would he have killed the others?

Taylor needed the Juvies to tell her more about both Owen and the troll. What was his or their problem?

She replied: *Someone has a better motive. I'm just not sure who."*

Graham had another immediate reply: *Then keep asking questions.*

Her finger hovered over the little heart emoji, but instead she sent a thumbs up.

CHAPTER TWENTY-TWO

$\mathcal{T}$aylor woke up early on the morning after Thanksgiving. Around 4:00 am, to be precise. Long years in retail had left their mark on her. She hurt just as bad as she had the day before and tried not to be impatient with herself. Breaks heal slowly, and gunshot wounds, well. She assumed they did too. The infection had been causing most or all of the pain, and the antibiotics were sure to knock it out soon.

Grandma Quinny was an early riser, so Taylor dressed quietly and snuck out the back door only to realize she hadn't driven herself to the family farm.

She sat on the Adirondack chair by the back door. The frigid November air nipped through her winter coat. It was almost a relief, that cold air, like an icepack for a wounded spirit. She didn't just want to go to her store. She needed to. She had no idea what her lousy ex and those Juvies had drummed up, but she didn't like it. Trust Clay to have a steamy affair with an older woman while inviting hundreds of eighteen to twenty-year olds to come on down to the quilt shop. It disgusted her, but she had to be there. She needed to turn these fans into shoppers, if nothing else. And if it was all a little too much, Grandpa Ernie's recliner was right there, waiting for her.

She texted Belle begging for an escape from the loving family nest, and twenty minutes later, just before 5:00 am, her darling baby sister arrived to take her to work. The light had flicked on in the window to Grandma Quinny's bedroom. They had left just in time.

Bible Creek Quilt and Gift had its lights on at 5:00 am, as did Dutch Hex. Comfort Cozies didn't seem to be opening yet, though the yarn shop next door to it was. The quilt guild agreement to not push Black Friday wasn't necessarily being honored. As Belle pulled into the back alley to park, Taylor wondered if the other shops had run ads without telling her.

But why would they? After all of the years they'd spent trying to build a community around quilting, they knew that rising tides lifted all boats.

"Relax." Belle opened the car door for Taylor. "Those shop owners are good folks. They just wanted to be here early, like you did. If there had been some great big advertising scheme going on, you'd have heard of it."

"It was that obvious?" Taylor tried to sling her purse over her good shoulder with one hand, but only managed to twist it around her elbow.

"Grim face, stiff shoulders. Anxious energy. Plus you begged me to drive past all the shops." Belle smiled softly at her sister. "You wear your anxiety on your sling."

"What are the Juvies going to do today?" Taylor unlocked the back door and opened it wide for her sister to go first.

"I wish I knew. I keep thinking this weird era of internet fame is going to pass soon, but Jonah just got invited to Ellen."

"Excuse me?"

"That's what I said too. The Ellen Show likes to nab flash-in-the-pan internet people, and I guess she just discovered quilting

TikTok. I don't know. He's supposed to fly down next week to film."

"But you're not thrilled with this?"

"I liked things better before." Belle chewed her lip, looking younger than she had a year or two ago.

They went straight to the classroom space with the snack bar and made themselves cups of coffee in the Keurig. "Before you were married?"

"Marriage is fine, honestly. I like that he's mine, but I liked us better before he got famous, when we were just like, working on the Flour Sax show together, and falling in love. Right after I broke up with Levi."

"Was Levi your first love?" Taylor had only met the young genius a couple of times.

"Not love, no. I love Jonah to death and it's so different. But Levi was my first serious boyfriend and that was kind of special too." She settled into Grandpa Ernie's well-worn recliner. "Sucks that your first love was Clay."

His heavy footsteps in the apartment above punctuated that remark, and Taylor laughed. "Maybe he wasn't my first love. I don't know. Maybe I haven't ever been in love the way you and Jonah are."

"Maybe this kind of love is rare. I hope not. If something happened to Jonah, I'd like to think I could feel this way again."

"That's pretty macabre." At the same time, Belle had grown up with a widow who never looked at another man after the death of her first husband, so it was an understandable mindset. Belle had married young, like her mom. It seemed reasonable she'd fear a future without Jonah.

Taylor left her sister in the comfortable chair and gave herself a little tour of the shop. Christmas sewing projects had been heavily marketed for the Cascadia Quilt Expo crowd, but since murder had soured sales, there were plenty left for today. Roxy and Clay had done an impressive job creating vignettes with sample projects, vintage winter décor, and heaps of things that Taylor recognized as stuff she'd tucked into corners and cupboards of the store over the last couple of years. If people did come to town for a little after-the-holiday shopping spree, they wouldn't be disappointed with what they found.

Around 7:00 am Clay joined her. "I've got a surprise for you today." His goofy little half smile filled her heart, just for a moment. Memories of hoping that surprise would be a diamond for left-hand ring finger bubbled up.

She squashed those old feelings though. "An onslaught of Jonah's fans?"

He gave her a look of mock horror. "Who squealed?"

"Valerie Ritz."

"Ah well, you'd have found out in an hour anyway."

"You decided we'd open at 8:00 am?"

"Yup. I did coordinate with the other stores though. I'm not out here trying to disrupt your community."

"What exactly is going to happen?"

"The crowds of beautiful young women will descend on Flour Sax in about an hour to try to woo Jonah away from your sister." He accidentally let his motive slip, but Taylor didn't take him seriously. "Jonah will be here for photos and autographs. Then they'll do the Main Street loop with Jonah leading the tour. The Yarnery is ready for anyone and anything, though they know this is a quilty crowd. At Comfort Cozies, June is offering mimosas to anyone with proper ID. Then they cross the street and hopefully give lots of business to Comfy Cuppa, before strolling on down to the antique mall to buy lots of cool midcentury modern stuff for too much money. They'll cross again to visit Bible Creek Quilt and Gift, but Carly never did tell me what she was going to do for the girls. They'll end at Dutch Hex where Shara has a display about the murder the Juvie's helped solve."

"And Jonah is cool with leading an all-day tour of the Juvies around town?"

"Can you blame him?" Clay laughed. "I wish I could get in on the action."

Jonah arrived ten minutes later with glittering eyes and a bounce in his step. He kissed his wife good morning. Belle gave him a quick hug, then headed to the back door.

"Give Grandpa Ernie my love," Taylor called out after her.

"Always." Belle waved behind her as she left.

Jonah looked absolutely giddy, and Belle had looked determined not to mind. Taylor felt bad for both of them. If they really had fallen into some kind of fairy-tale romance version of "love" that Taylor herself had never experienced, then they were probably headed for a similarly fairy-tale level conflict before all was said and done.

For the first time since she'd heard the news of her sister's elopement, she hoped the marriage wouldn't end in divorce.

At 8:00 am, Clay unlocked the door.

Taylor had lived through ten years or more of Black Fridays.

She'd seen crafters throw themselves on the shelf for the last of the 75 % off fat quarter packs. She'd seen shelves of scrapbook paper empty in seconds. She'd seen a woman wrestle a full sewing machine out of another woman's arms. Just the once, but it had left an impression.

But she'd never seen anything like this.

Jonah waited on the stool at the cutting table wearing a Santa hat. The shelves behind him had been turned into a Christmas village of vintage porcelain houses, Christmas wall hangings, and three-dimensional quilted Christmas trees.

A flood of women in their thirties poured into the room, lost in a flurry of tweens. Eleven-, twelve-, thirteen-year-old girls in their Christmas-best with pink lip gloss, big earrings, and absurdly dark eyebrows poured through the space in their rush to get to Jonah.

Taylor was pushed back against a wall of gingham, her aching arm and shoulder nudged, butted against, knocked, and even elbowed by a remarkably tall dad with three rangy girls in tow. She needed to make her way over to the register but couldn't find a path through the people.

The clammer of high-pitched voices was Hitchcockian in its ability to cause terror in Taylor's heart.

She scanned the room over and over, trying to catch customers with their hands in the bins of smalls. Again and again consumer habit studies had shown that white moms in their thirties with two kids were the most likely of all customers to shop lift, but no one was looking at the merchandise. The crowd pushed and pressed against each other, parents as bad as children, trying to get to the young man behind the table.

Taylor tipped up on her toes to catch his face in action.

He was beaming.

In seventh heaven.

Clay stood at one side of the table, letting kids around it one or two at a time to take photos.

Jonah grinned and mugged and made peace signs for phones of all sizes, then nudged the kids out the other side.

It was slick, their operation, but the crowd was restless.

Her phone buzzed in her pocket, and she just barely managed to pull it out, though her own elbow knocked the glasses off a girl who couldn't have been older than ten.

"Sorry! So Sorry!" Taylor tried to bend over to pick them up but managed to butt into a mom who turned and smacked her bottom. "Hey!" Taylor hollered.

"Sorry!" The mom laughed but didn't even blush. "Mistook you for one of mine."

The child managed to save her glasses from the floor, and Taylor managed to check her messages.

Good luck with the big event today. It's newsworthy, so I'll be around if you need me. If her adrenaline hadn't already been high enough to give her tremors, this text from Graham would have sent her over the edge. She hadn't seen him since the incident at the hospital and hadn't been sure he was up for a second round. He'd stand out, not only because he was tall, but because the men in this horde were few and far between. Just Clay, Jonah, a couple of dads, and a man in a black leather jacket who looked completely lost.

IT WAS ALMOST 11:00 am before the crowd followed Jonah down the block, and Taylor's cash register was overflowing, metaphorically. They had sold out of the quilted three-dimensional tree kits, the last of the left-over Row by Row kits, and all of the Christmas themed pot-holders and apron sets—projects almost guaranteed to be easy enough for a crowd of middle schoolers who desperately wanted something to remember the day they'd met their hero.

This was the power of the internet.

This was the power of social media marketing.

This was exhausting.

The shop had been quiet for a few moments when the bells over the door jingled and Valerie Ritz strode in. "Color me surprised." She had a paper cup of coffee from Comfy Cuppa. "Those were children, all of them."

"My cousin Reid is going to be disappointed." Taylor leaned on her counter with her good arm. Now that the room had emptied, she had time to really feel how badly her shoulder ached.

"So many of the Juvies at the expo last month had been girls my age. I hadn't realized that online they really were juveniles, actual children. Boy though, those kids are internet savvy. I was talking to a twelve-year-old with a nose ring who told me she was the one who confirmed Shawna's troll was also her online boyfriend. How do these kids get that good?"

Taylor shook her head. "Makes one a little scared to be a parent."

"Seriously. But I wanted to give you a little warning. Since Jonah's audience is so very young, he'd better be extra careful with these fan selfies and stuff." The way she lifted her eyebrow made her meaning clear.

"The internet is full of vigilantes, isn't it? People out looking for crime." Taylor swept invisible crumbs off the counter.

"These kids are evidence of it."

"Makes me wish I hadn't asked them for help."

The door opened again, and her cousin Reid sauntered in. He joined Valerie at the counter and leaned in to lay a kiss on her pale white neck.

Taylor's eyes flew wide and she shook her head in surprise. The hotel heiress was Reid's other woman?

"This is why Jonah will die young." Valerie's vocal fray added a little gravitas to the sentence, as though it were a threat.

"Excuse me?" Taylor tried to pull herself back to the conversation.

Valerie waved it away. "Figure of speech. He's stressed to death about keeping these kids safe."

"Then why did he invite them all to a town being stalked by a murderer?" Taylor shifted, but no position seemed to relieve the pain.

Reid stood quietly next to Valerie, one hand playing with her cherry-colored hair. The other holding his phone so he could read it.

"He didn't. Clay did. There are three SUV's marked Yamhill Co. Sheriff parked on Main Street, so you're probably safe. Glad they were tipped off. I'm out. Don't think I'll be able to get near Jonah again before the day's over. Tell him congrats if you see him first."

"Valerie, I need your help," Taylor stopped her. "We know

Shawna's troll also catfished her. But I need to know if that troll was actually her ex-boyfriend, Owen."

Valerie looked Taylor up and down as she considered the question, then narrowed her eyes. "Sure. Reid, get on it. Find out who that Owen guy is online."

Reid disentangled his fingers from her hair and got to work.

"You know, when I met Reid last year, I didn't know he was married. And no one had even heard of Jonah back then." Valerie gazed at Taylor's bookish cousin while she mused.

Taylor cringed, but tried to play it off like her shoulder was bothering her, which it was.

"We were friends all year before I told him how I felt. But I still didn't know he was married, much less had a child. He was just an online friend, and I'd fallen in love. When he told me about his family, I should have backed away. I know that. My parents divorced when I was an infant. I know how much it sucks."

Reid flinched at the words and took his phone to the back of the store. Taylor had her doubts he could harness the magic of hacking from just an iPhone, but she was glad he seemed up to the challenge.

"When you're in the heat of passion, it can be sort of hard to think of others first. Especially if you've never even seen the little one whose life you're upending. I wish I hadn't broken up their family, but I am in love. You know, as much as I wanted to meet Jonah, I only came to the expo to be with Reid for a while. We had a room together."

"Life happens, I guess." Taylor didn't try to come up with anything clever to help Valerie feel better. One naturally wants distance from the-other-woman.

"I figured you'd understand." Valerie had a sort of smirk to her face. "I heard about you and your boyfriend breaking up. A little family gossip at Reid's parents' house over breakfast."

"These things happen." Taylor didn't think it was the same at all. No commitments. No kids. And yet, she hadn't had any a commitment or kids with Clay, but the pain of that breakup had stuck with her for ages, even though she'd left him.

The two women looked away from each other. Valerie may have been hoping to find an ally in her boyfriend's family, but it wasn't going to be easy.

"You think the ex-boyfriend may have killed Shawna?" Valerie turned the subject.

Taylor sighed in relief and shifted the position of her sling ever so slightly. She was glad the sordid details of her cousin's life were at an end. "Call it a hunch."

The bells over the door jingled again, and Valerie skimmed to the back of the store to be with Reid.

CHAPTER TWENTY-THREE

*T*he return of the crowds was sudden, like a flash flood, and the buzz of voices was electric. Young, high pitched, excited, and loud. The store filled with young children, girls in their late childhood, early teens, and tired moms.

It was the same crowd, surely, and yet Taylor didn't recognize anyone. Graham had slipped in at the back of the crowd. His right eye was black, and his nose covered in a white plaster bandage. He stared at her with false shock, eyes wide, but laughing. "I knew there was a story in this."

Taylor shifted her way back to the cash register. She needed Roxy or Belle at the cutting counter, or at least Clay here at the register. Why hadn't he thought to hire Willa for his big event?

Roxy was about the height of the kids, so it took a moment for her to elbow her way through the crowd. "I meant to be here earlier." Her face was flushed, and despite the cold outside, she had little beads of sweat on her forehead. "I can't believe that daft Clay followed through with this."

Taylor glanced at the clock. It was just after noon. "Thanks for coming in."

"I was in the back by the door earlier, but you probably

couldn't see me. I decided to follow the Juvies for crowd control. I'll say this, some of the guild isn't going to be happy. They didn't even make it all the way to Bible Creek Quilt and Gift. These kids aren't interested in porcelain statuettes or themed gift books."

"They aren't actually into quilting either. Where's Jonah?"

"He's stuck in the back of Comfy Cuppa. This is the second wave. Clay didn't expect a second wave. I'll go to the cutting counter, just in case." She eased her way slowly through the crowd, but she couldn't make it to the work side of the work-table, as it was crowded with shoving kids taking selfies in front of the Christmas display.

From across the room Graham waved and mouthed, "I'll come back." He ducked out and she stared after him.

"If he doesn't get here soon, I'm leaving!" A dad whose silver cashmere sweater matched both his silver hair and silver eyes with dark bags under them, hollered at Taylor. "Did you hear me?"

Taylor mouthed, "I hear you!"

"When do you expect him? The invite said he'd be here." The dad held out his phone and pointed at the screen.

Taylor maintained her smiling, nodding face and held up her phone as though to indicate she'd find out.

He stared at her with eyes narrowed. A slim, tall girl with a sheet of icy blonde hair stood next to him, her chin up in defiance.

Taylor didn't text Jonah. Instead, she sent a text to her cousin. *Any movement on the troll's ID?*

She held out her phone, hoping he'd think she was waiting for an answer.

Reid said he'd come to town to prove Jonah was a playboy. He probably just wanted to find someone as bad as he was to justify his own behavior. And maybe he was jealous too. After all, the woman he'd left his wife and child for was a huge fan of Jonah's.

Instead, Reid had found a town full of well-chaperoned kids. Or at least Taylor hoped they were well-chaperoned, because Valerie was right, this event could destroy Jonah if something even looked like it was inappropriate.

"Well?" The dad with the matching hair and sweater pushed his way to the register. "Is he coming or not?"

"The agenda says he should be at Bible Creek Quilt and Gift at two. Might be best to head him off. There's already quite a crowd." Taylor's professional smile was locked in place, like a face guard.

The dad grabbed his daughter's arm and dragged her out of the store. The daughter's platinum hair flying behind her. Taylor had a good idea who the Juvie was in that family.

A young woman in an oversized college sweatshirt noticed him leave and followed. The floodgates broke, and the rest of the people crowded the door, moving like syrup that's been in the fridge.

Valerie flowed slowly with the crowd, right at the tail. "It's him. Took Reid no time at all. The catfish was Owen, and the troll was the catfish."

"He killed her." Taylor mouthed the words but couldn't hear herself over the din in the room.

There seemed to be a log jam at the door. The people who'd been trying to leave were moving backwards now, past Taylor again, but still trying to go forward. A small boy, no more than ten and wearing a spiderman costume, rammed both his elbows into a teenager in front of him. She turned and smacked his face, then grabbed his hand and dragged him forward, but there was no room to go. They smashed up against a woman who had three round faced girls with her. One of the girls twisted around. When she saw who had bumped her, all four girls jumped, and hugged, but they knocked over a display of quilted Christmas balls.

"All right, everyone freeze!"

Taylor spun around, Roxy stood on their worktable, arms over her head, waving, and hollering.

"We can unstick this crowd if we just take turns!"

The hubbub barely dimmed in response.

"One at a time, the door is big enough for two-way traffic!" Roxy's voice held its laughter—that quality of hers that made her so wonderful to be around. "You, in the pink sweater, step to the right! Think of it like an escalator! One way up and one way down!"

Taylor turned her attention back to the door. A girl in a pink rain jacket tried to step to the right but got shoved back by someone coming in that side.

"All right! You've got this gang! We can use doors like grownups!" Roxy laughed, but her laugh stopped abruptly.

Taylor swung around to see what had happened, but Roxy wasn't on the table anymore. Taylor picked up her shop's landline phone and set it to loudspeaker. "We're in violation of the fire code. Everyone back away from the door, so I don't have to call the deputies to sort this out."

Something in the back crashed. "The back door is available for exit only."

Someone in the back screamed.

"Clay Seldon, please attend the back door," Taylor announced. She scanned the crowd for a familiar face. She would have given up several vacation weeks for a glimpse of Sissy Dorney and her commanding presence. Just on the other side of the glass front door she spotted Graham. She couldn't think of anything that would make the crowds part for his entrance, so she hung up. Leading with her good shoulder, she shifted out the far side of her register counter, pushed through a group of young teens, and ducked under the stairs where her desk was. The crowd in the back was mostly parents trying to rest their feet. One mom was blocking the path with a preschooler in a zebra print umbrella stroller. "Excuse me!" Taylor waved to nab the woman's attention.

The woman looked up and around, but she had thick glasses on and the distant look of someone whose vision can't be fully corrected.

"I'm sorry! Did you hear where that scream came from?"

"Oh! Yes, up there!" The woman pointed in the general direction of the stairs.

Crap.

If some pervert had dragged a child up there, she'd murder them.

Taylor bolted up the stairs, but hooked her sling on the handrail, and fell. At least she landed on her uninjured arm. She shook as she stood but attempted to dial 911 with one hand as she stumbled up the stairs to the apartment.

She kicked open the door, but the room was dark.

"Ambulance, Sheriff, or Fire?" The soothing voice on the other end of the phone responded.

"Sheriff. Flour Sax Quilt Shop." Taylor flicked on the overhead light as she gave the address. She slid the phone into her sling to keep it safe but didn't listen to the rest of the call. She knew the drill. Stay calm. Stay on the line. Etc.

The room was empty, but the apartment had a bathroom and two bedrooms. She listened with her eyes closed, focusing in on noise from this floor only. Something was shifting in the second bedroom—the one she used for shop storage. She didn't want to alarm the perp and make him do something stupid, so she sort of slid across the floor instead of taking steps, careful of the creaky wood under her feet.

She rested her hand on the doorknob and listened.

"They'll think Taylor did it." The whispering voice carried

well. "Her shop, her apartment. Her quilt. All of it will come back to her."

The response was muffled but accompanied by the sounds of feet kicking cardboard boxes.

Taylor pushed the door in and flicked on the light. "Why me?" She only had the one hand to work with, so she kicked a box too. It held a large stack of smaller boxes full of company polo shirts. The stack only wobbled, so she kicked it harder.

They fell with a crash, landing on Roxy and Owen. Roxy kept kicking, and the boxes on top of her legs shifted like a road in an earthquake, but Owen kept the pair of sewing sheers tight up against her rib cage.

Taylor froze. The scissors were shut, and Roxy was wearing a jean jacket with decorative studs. Owen could never shove the rounded ends of those scissors through her—at least not from the angle he was at now, pinned down by both Roxy and the boxes.

But it would be the work of a second to open them, shift his angle and slice Roxy's abdomen.

The sound of distant sirens wasn't a comfort—Owen's eyes narrowed when he heard them. He pushed against the boxes, grappling with Roxy to get to his feet again.

"Taylor Quinn, murder fiend, attention whore, desperate to keep her name in the lights, killed her rivals and then anyone else who got in the way. Capped it off with the murder of the girl who stole her man." Owen's face was maniacal. "The perfect cover. No one would ever suspect heartbroken Owen, who desperately wanted his one true love back."

"Everyone always expects the wronged lover," Taylor corrected. And again, her voice surprised her. That same, strong, confident tone from the hospital. The one that had told the handsomest and best man in all of Oregon that she didn't want him anymore. "Insecure, jealous, violent. That's why you guys were so on and off. A troll online and in real life." She pushed a mirrored cathedral window frame between herself and Owen, but it did nothing to get Roxy out of his grasp.

Taylor grabbed a box of printed pencils with one hand and flung the contents at him, but they just hit the mirror and spilled on the small bit of floor in front of her. She cursed herself for not overbuying something useful in a crisis, like pepper spray.

But Owen was distracted and fumbling with the scissors. They slipped from his fingers as he tried to open them. Roxy squirmed in his grip, not allowing any one part of her body to stay still for any length of time.

"You had to kill her. You always knew you would. You hated her," Taylor said. "You hated her because you couldn't control her anymore. But when did you first learn about Lorraine's conspiracy theory? How did you learn about her imaginary serial killer?"

"How lucky was I when I heard that crazy woman say someone else had murdered women with sewing scissors, just like me? I'm not an idiot. I knew they would look at the ex first. But not now, huh? Now they'll look at you." His eyes were bloodshot, his face red. He looked like one wrong move would give him a heart attack.

Taylor threw herself at him, knocking Roxy to one side as she did.

With Roxy out of the way, he rolled onto his knees and plunged the open scissors deep into Taylor's thigh. But she jumped on him, knocking him on his back then rammed her knee into his stomach.

Roxy wrapped her small hands around his throat.

His eyes rolled back in his head.

Roxy released him, and rocked back onto her heels, staring at the man on the ground.

Taylor's leg was limp and her shoulder on fire. It was only after she saw for sure that Roxy was safe that she realized she'd thrown her injured side at Owen. She lay on top of him now, panting in pain. He was breathing hard too.

She'd never been so glad someone evil was still breathing.

"Hands up," the calm, secure voice of Deputy Maria spoke from the other side of the door.

Roxy scrambled to her feet with her hands over her head. "Taylor Quinn is injured. She's been stabbed. The guy is in here too."

Maria stepped into the room with her gun drawn. The space was never big to begin with and seemed to close in around Taylor.

"Can you help her up?" Maria held her gun away from where Taylor and Owen lay.

Roxy bent to help Taylor, but her hip gave out, and she crumpled.

"You okay?" Maria asked, her voice as ever, unflappable.

"No." Roxy's voice was small.

"Reg, in here."

Reg lifted Roxy and led her to the couch while Maria held Owen in place with her well-aimed pistol.

When Reg came back for Taylor, Maria got Owen to his feet and cuffed him.

"Oof." Maria stared at the scissors in Taylor's leg.

"Please don't make me go to the ER again." The one blade of the scissors went deep in her thigh, but there was no blood to be seen.

"You're dreaming," Maria laughed.

Taylor flinched.

"Sorry." Maria cleared her throat and used her radio to call for an ambulance. "It's already on the way. Apparently your 911 call is still live. Also, the operator heard the whole confession. Get that guy down to the Jeep."

"Yes'm." Reg followed with due deference.

"But the crowd downstairs...." Taylor frowned at the scissors in her leg. The shock was definitely wearing off.

"We cleared them. You're looking a little green. Why don't you put your head between your knees?" Maria said.

Taylor looked from her shoulder in the sling to the scissors sticking straight up from the top of her leg. Instead, she laid her head back on the couch and prayed she'd be in and out fast this time.

CHAPTER TWENTY-FOUR

*T*aylor had not been in and out of the hospital fast that time. She'd crushed her already broken shoulder bone and needed surgery to pin it back together. The surgery had only taken an hour, but it had been surrounded by several hours of waiting.

She had also been surrounded, like Rabbit from Winnie the Pooh, by her many friends and relations. But she'd slept through as much of the loving care and concern as she could.

After the surgery, she'd gone back to her own home. The Quinn family farm was a shelter, and she had been very grateful for it, but she had a terrible feeling she'd stay forever if she went back this time.

Three nights after the blackest of Black Fridays, she slunk off to Reuben's to enjoy a piece of pie and a little quiet to think.

Earlier in the day, her counselor had asked her to list two-hundred and fifty things she'd survived in her life.

It felt like an impossible number, and Taylor didn't know where to begin, but if she ever wanted to sleep at night, she'd have to do it.

Less than three years ago she'd had a show down with the

woman who'd killed her mom. She'd survived that, and it was on the list. But that had left her with trauma and a lot of anxiety and fear. She'd thought she'd dealt with that, and was doing great, but it turns out, she wasn't. Or, she had been, so long as she had a strong young man around to make her feel protected.

She'd hated to admit it but breaking up with Hudson seemed to have contributed at least as much to the new nights of panic as getting shot *and* stabbed had. As she lay in her bed trying to sleep, it hadn't been the threat of what was outside her walls that filled her with terror, but the idea that she'd have to face it alone.

Two-hundred and fifty individual moments of survival, things that at the time felt like they would destroy her but didn't. The length of the list alone was supposed to give her a sense of security. If she could survive all of that...!

"Pecan pie today?" Graham slid into the booth. The bandage was off his nose, and the bruising on his face was headed from purple to green. But he looked good to her.

She passed him the plate. "Help yourself."

He did.

"Would you say I survived the onslaught of tweens or not? I did end up in the hospital, but eventually they let me out."

"It depends on how much blame the kids get for it." He cut a healthy bite of pie with the edge of his fork.

She held out her one good hand and pretended to count off on her fingers. "I think I should lay the blame on my ex. It's got to be his fault." She pictured Clay's dismay as he saw his failure to draw the right kind of bait for Jonah.

Graham lifted a finger to his now crooked nose and gave a crooked smile. "I barely survived him."

She blushed. He was obviously thinking of Hudson. "Sorry."

"How's his hand?"

She gave a one-shouldered shrug. "I haven't spoken with him."

"I see." He pushed the plate back to Taylor. "I'm headed back to Portland this afternoon, but I'm hoping to write a killer conclusion to my story on the Amateur Detective of Comfort, Oregon."

Taylor swallowed. That wasn't exactly what she'd wanted to hear. "You're not really doing that, are you?"

"You did it, my friend. You took a bullet. You wrestled the killer to the ground."

"I threw pencils at him." She laughed.

"That's the kind of thing I'm talking about. No one else has access to those details. I'm going to make you famous."

"Please don't. That's what Owen claimed I wanted."

"Did he ever say why he shot you that night in the field?"

She shook her head. "Rumor is he was going to kill you but freaked out when he saw the crowd. Shot me to distract you all. That's what I hear from Sissy who heard from Tansy who talked to Reg. Apparently after he heard who he shot, he realized I was the one he wanted to pin the murders on. That's why he came up with his plan to kill Roxy on Black Friday."

"It's all a bit twisted." Graham reached across the table for more pie.

"Murder is like that."

"Since you're the victim here, I can keep your name out of the article. But it will mention the town and the story and internet darling Jonah Lang. I'm sorry. I know that won't be great for business."

"It won't. But it might get me some more viewers. YouTube money spends as well as anything." She felt bound by her sling and shifted in her seat.

"Any news on the mystery quilt? I could file an article following up on that." He didn't seem put off by her refusal of his fifteen minutes of murder-fame. "How about we head to the museum and see what they have to say? Bring your grandpa. I've got some more questions for him too."

CLAY HADN'T BEEN sure he could still fit every single thing he owned in the back of his Rabbit, but he did. He shut the hatchback with a satisfying click, ready to put Comfort behind him for a little while. He took a long, deep breath of the cold November—almost December—air. It was a good, clean, honest smell and he might miss it after a while.

The back door of Flour Sax opened, and Roxy stepped into the alley where the dumpsters were kept and where Clay was planning his getaway. She rested on a cane. Her old hip injury had taken a hit in the fight with Owen. "I still think you're overreacting."

"I think Shara of Dutch Hex put a curse on me."

Roxy laughed. "She'd never."

"The Juvies never even made it to her shop." He leaned on the back of his car and looked at his pretty little girlfriend. He'd miss her. "Jonah didn't even flirt with anyone."

"Right? My nineteen-year-old son didn't flirt with a single tween or their almost forty-year old parents. Shocking." She looked so pretty in the bright, crisp air.

"There's two seats in the old Rabbit, Roxy. It's not a long drive to Canada."

"You're a crazy kid, Clay."

"I owe my grandparents a visit. All this time with that family of Taylor's has convinced me. Just a visit. I'll be back."

She smirked, like she didn't believe him.

"I will. I couldn't leave a girl like you behind. It's just for Christmas."

"Christmas is a whole month away."

"Just till New Years. And Willa wanted the extra hours to buy things for her grandkids. There was no way Taylor could afford the both of us. And you were wanting me out of the apartment above the store, anyway, because it costs her too much."

"So true."

"And despite the offer, you know you didn't really want me to move in."

"Maybe not permanently." She stretched one arm over her head and her little sweater lifted just enough to show those firm flat abs that let out her secret as a fitness junky. One never expected it because of her limp, but Clay had learned that Roxy's years of physical therapy had led to a life-long passion for fitness. "But if you come back to town, you're welcome to stay."

"When, Roxy, not if. I promise I'm coming back." His feelings were starting to get hurt. It's like people in this town had forgotten that Taylor was the one who'd broken his heart. And the next girl he'd just started to date had moved away too. He'd always been one of the monogamous types. He liked a little structure in his life. But the quilt guild was ready to string him up. The calls he'd been fielding from June at Comfort Cozies who'd gotten a citation for underaged drinking when the children had gotten into their mother's mimosas, Carly at Bible Creek who had found explicit scribbles on gift pictures of Jesus, and Shara from Dutch Hex who'd been prepared for a flood of fans, but had been skipped entirely, were enough to make any man run and hide. He was hated in Comfort at the moment and was more than happy to flee to the safety of his grandparents who lived over the border.

"Then stay with me when you come home," Roxy said, agreeably. "It's so quiet at my place now that Jonah's gone."

"Any movement on that mansion-of-teens he's planning?"

"They liked the old Magary place, but it sold already. They're so young. I don't think they'll do anything yet, but it would be nice if they'd get out of Taylor's hair and start their life together."

"Tell them they can have the apartment. They can pay for utilities with their internet millions."

A motorcycle pulled into the ally. The rider nodded at Clay. "Is Taylor Quinn around?"

"Not sure. It's her day off." Last Clay had heard she was nestled safely in her little house on Love Street, but he wasn't going to tell a stranger that.

"No prob." He revved the bike and rode away.

"Competition for that journalist already." Roxy rolled her eyes.

"I don't trust that guy." Clay frowned. "She should have stayed with Hudson. He was a good man."

"I think we all agree about that."

"Graham is going to hurt her, just wait."

"You sound like you're glad." Roxy narrowed her eyes at him.

"Sorry. Didn't mean to. I'm the last one that wants to see her get hurt, but man. She can be cold-hearted sometimes."

Roxy chuckled. "Now that you're packed, come have a goodbye lunch with me. Willa and Belle are working the store. I'll buy if you drive."

He held out his hand for her, happy to have a free lunch on his way out of town.

IT TOOK a few minutes for Taylor to convince Grandpa Ernie to go to the museum with them, but by the time everyone was buckled into the old family Audi, he was in pretty good spirits. "I told that Jonah he had to get out of our house." His eyes glittered as he made this pronouncement. "Enough dithering. A married man needs to provide a home for his family."

"Wise words," Graham said from the back.

"No one asked you," Grandpa Ernie's tone took a turn for the worse.

Graham had the sense to be silent.

"Did Jonah say he'd move?" Taylor asked.

"He yammered on again about that content castle he's planning."

"It's a castle now?" The trip to the museum was short, and she hated to pull in. She never knew when Grandpa Ernie was going to lose his comfortable grip on the moment.

"Whatever it is. He talked on and on about it until Belle piped up and said she wasn't going to let me bully him." He paused, then said, "Your mom never did spank her, did she?"

"Oh, Grandpa. They'll get it figured out. I like having them around." She laughed because she knew she was lying. Sharing a house with Jonah was a pain. "We're here. I'm hoping we can give Lorraine more information about that blanket for her exhibit."

"How much they paying to show off that blanket?"

"It's a loan, Grandpa." Taylor winced as she parked the car. Some motions hurt her leg more than others. The doctors didn't think she would have any permanent damage, but the thick blade of the scissors had left a serious wound. Graham had offered to drive, but Taylor couldn't bring herself to let him be in control.

They found Lorraine at the front desk of the museum chatting with Erika.

"Ernie!" Erika reached out with both hands, more animated than Taylor had ever seen her before. "I'm so thankful to see you. Isn't it a relief that that horrible man has been arrested?"

Grandpa Ernie huffed into his mustache, but his eyes sparkled. He was always pleased with attention from ladies, apparently even when he suspected them of murder. "Town's getting too big, is what it is."

Lorraine nodded. "I feel horrible that he was recreating those evil deaths from years ago and wonder if my telling the stories might not have contributed."

Taylor stared at Lorraine, wishing she could speak her mind, but unwilling to do anything that cruel. If Lorraine had kept her mouth shut, Gus and Ramona would still be alive.

"Now, now, Lorraine." Erika patted her shoulder awkwardly. "We've spoken about this again and again. You've done your best for your friends, and seeking justice is always right. You can't hold yourself responsible for what someone else has done."

"Can you elaborate?" Graham's tone and posture were so casual. He could have put the most defensive interviewee at ease. "Which of the six victims were you friends with?" He included all of the people Lorraine claimed were victims in his count.

"I know when we spoke earlier, I was inebriated," Lorraine said. "Alcohol has always been a weakness of mine, but Erika is my sponsor, and I'm all right."

"That's good news," Graham encouraged.

Taylor led Grandpa Ernie to a visitor bench, not sure when, if ever, they'd get to the matter of the quilt.

"Lorraine had been school friends with the first victim," Erika stated matter of factly. "I knew Lorraine from our association with the same group of..." she hesitated, "older men."

"They were a criminal biker gang." Lorraine held her chin up high. "And I, at least, was a child. A victim of them."

"She was a young teen," Erika agreed. "My college roommate and I were both purchasing drugs from them. Our taste ran to hallucinogenics, which are what I think caused my roommate to commit such an atrocious suicide."

Or, Taylor thought, had caused you to commit such an atrocious murder, but again, she kept her thoughts to herself.

"Lorraine didn't know the teacher who died in the car accident, but I had known her back home. When I was still in high school, she had given me my first taste of LSD. She said it was to help me relax and do better in school. But when I took it, she tried to kiss me. I had to fight her off. She was fired but imagine my horror when I met her in this tiny town. I was sure she'd come after me, but I think that was the paranoia speaking. The drugs we had access to back then weren't very safe."

"Do you think drugs had something to do with her accident?" Graham asked.

"I do," Erika stated. "She had self-inflicted wounds up and down her arms."

"I do not believe they were self-inflicted," Loraine stated.

"Lorraine was very young, and I have read that drugs in that category leave lasting damage, paranoia being just one possible effect."

"I believe this is a subject we may never agree on." Lorraine pressed her thin lips together. Though she was likely five years younger than Erika, she looked much older.

"Unless we find Jennifer Anderson," Graham casually offered.

Lorraine's face lit up. "I've been trying to remember her name for years. It's terrible the things that slip away. But my dear, she has been found. She was found that very winter and left unclaimed."

Erika shook her head at Graham, and he nodded, understanding. If Lorraine suffered from the Love family psychosis, exacerbated by LSD, Taylor was glad they were dropping the subject of The Cutter.

But that didn't mean she trusted Erika.

"I hear we have a conclusion for the story of the mystery quilt," Graham said.

"Indeed." Erika didn't wear mascara, and her graying hair was pulled severely from her face, yet she seemed to glow. "I would hate for you to quote me on this, but I should have known what I was looking at. Lorraine and I were so pleased to have something unique in our little town, something that might have had great historical significance, that I missed the very obvious nature of the appliqué work."

"Indeed," Lorraine said, "we were both seduced by the idea that the blanket was as old as the information tag said it was, and we missed what was truly remarkable about it. Though Erika would like us to believe that she ought to have recognized the wool, you will recall it had been heavily embroidered and the actual quality of the fabric hidden because of it."

"That's kind of you to say, Lorraine, but this is my specialty, and students will tease me about this until I retire, I'm sure." Erika gave a rueful half-smile. "Your sister visited not long ago," she said to Taylor. "And told us all about how this beautifully appliquéd quilt came to be."

"Button blanket," Grandpa Ernie corrected.

"Yes, in this case we could call the quilt a blanket, and no one should be bothered." Erika had nothing but kind words for Grandpa Ernie.

"But Erika," Taylor asked, "how did the quilt end up in the show, and mislabeled at that?"

Erika flushed, a little. "I believe this was my fault. I invited the freshmen to volunteer at the event. As you remember, we hosted the expo during our two week fall gallery break, but most underclassmen don't have shows to work on. I thought this would be a good experience for them."

"But what does that have to do with Grandpa Ernie's button blanket?"

"I spoke with every single one of my volunteers and found a small group who had accessed the fiber arts storage. We have dozens of donated textiles. They found several and entered them into the show."

"Without proper labels?" Taylor asked.

"Most of the textiles in our storage have full documentation. The little group of ladies didn't remember which one of them was responsible for the button blanket. They really did think they had dated it correctly, based on the type of field fabric and the similarity of the appliqué to *Broderie Perse*. Students often get ahead of themselves, but they mean well."

"But we've been hunting for the responsible party for weeks. Why didn't they bring forward their information?" Taylor wasn't going to let it go. It was too coincidental, and it nagged at her that Erika was ultimately responsible for this mystery. And though Owen was in prison, the quilt and the murders were linked to her now.

"I felt the same way when I spoke to them, but I promise it's as innocent as could be. When the group of ladies, all seventeen and eighteen-year-olds mind you, saw our appeals for information, they believed that they were merely the first ones to find the mystery quilt. They didn't think of themselves as the one's responsible for the mystery."

It was plausible but rang hallow.

"Graham, I'd be happy to connect you with the students. They'd be thrilled to be a part of the news story," Erika said.

"Perfect." Graham made a note in an old fashioned, long, skinny reporter's spiral notebook. "That's just the hook I needed."

"Can we show you the exhibit we've been putting together?" Erika directed her question to Taylor.

Taylor nodded her assent. Erika had all of the answers now, and was willing to put them up for inspection, it seemed. She'd try and trust that the professor wasn't also a secret killer.

The group followed Lorraine into the high-ceilinged mill room that doubled as exhibit space.

Dead center in the room an eight-foot trifold had been erected, with the blanket in the middle panel. The blanket was framed with strings of mother-of-pearl buttons. "Belle strung the buttons and brought them to us. She said it kept her hands busy while you were in surgery."

The left panel of the trifold displayed enlarged black and white photos of Grandpa Ernie's grandparents. They weren't framed yet. It looked as though Lorraine was still building the exhibit. The largest photo was a proper Victorian wedding portrait, mouths in firm lines, the groom black-suited, and the bride in a high collared dress with layers of lace trim, a few shades too dark to be white. A best dress to be worn throughout the years.

Under that was a brilliant photo of the same man. His mouth was a straight line, but his eyes shone as did his mother-of-pearl button covered suit. Grandpa Ernie stared at the vision. "Where'd you find that nonsense?" his gruff voice broke, but out of pleasure.

"We contacted the Pearlies themselves and asked if they had anything in their files they could share. They emailed us files from their digital library immediately. They were terribly pleased such a far flung museum was interested in their work. Much of the information on the other panel is from their website, with permission."

The third side of the trifold did tell the history of the Pearlies and their work for the poor of London, but it also had a darling portrait of Grandpa Ernie and Grandma Delma in their wedding clothes. Two fine suits Grandpa had made himself, his of dove gray and Grandma's of ivory, though Taylor only knew that from having seen them in person, not from the black and white photo. But the story under that portrait told of decades of charitable giving from the Baker family. From quietly paying school lunches to offering anonymous scholarships to fiber arts students at the college, Ernie and Delma had given back to Comfort the bulk of the profit from their two businesses.

"Oh, Grandpa Ernie...." Taylor whispered, tears in her eyes.

Erika also had tears in her eyes. "I didn't learn the source of my scholarship until I was made staff several years ago. Dear, dear sir. I could never thank you enough for what your gift did for me. The tutelage of your lovely wife helped direct me away from the bad choices I had been making and set me on a path that has blessed me through the years."

"Rubbish." He tapped his cane on the concrete floor, but when Erika leaned over to kiss his cheek, he blushed a charming pink.

"I have a new idea for a story," Graham whispered in Taylor's ear. She hadn't realized he'd moved behind her. "But it means I'll have to come back to town for more interviews. Shucks."

Her heart was full to overflowing already. The promise of seeing Graham again so soon sent shivers of pleasure up her spine.

They all seemed to float back to the car. Such a good and wholesome thing after so many dark days in a row. No words seemed necessary.

After Grandpa Ernie was safely settled at home, Taylor lingered on the front porch with Graham. He'd left his car on Main Street but didn't mind the walk of two blocks back to it.

Alone on the porch, she thought it would be the perfect time for him to take her into his arms, kiss her, declare his love for her, anything along those lines.

But he didn't.

He looked into the distance. "If you're up for it," he said, "I'll come back in a couple of weeks to write up the story of your grandparents. It's a good story or I wouldn't do it, but I think it might help undo the damage the string of murders has done to this town. Good press is always good."

"I thought no press was bad press." Taylor's cheeks burned in the cold. The November evening was already dark and frigid.

"You know better than that." He turned to face her. His eyes were worried and his smile seemed weak. "You going to be okay?"

She patted her elbow, still not up to patting her damaged shoulder. "Eventually."

"Good. Take care, all right?" He stepped away.

"Belle and I might go up to Portland to shop for Christmas. We have, um, some family there."

"Sure. Text me anytime you come to town." He looked down, then up, catching her eye and holding her gaze. "I want to see you." He took a step off the porch.

"Graham…" She followed him, but her steps were weak and she leaned heavily on the rail.

He exhaled. "It's been a wild ride, Taylor. I'm glad we met. Very glad." His eye went from her damaged arm to her leg, then back to her face.

"But…?"

He gritted his teeth. "Let's not do anything stupid, okay? You've been banged up pretty bad this week. That's probably enough."

"I don't think I understand." She wished her eyes weren't smarting with tears.

He shoved his hands in his pockets. "I'm not exactly sure where you and your boyfriend stood before I showed up."

She couldn't speak. Things, before Graham had showed up, had been lovely between her and Hudson. Or at least as lovely as she'd come to expect. Nothing in life is perfect after all.

"Let's see how we feel next time I'm in town, when things aren't so dramatic. How's that?"

She nodded. "I'll have my questions ready."

"Perfect." He turned again and left, strolling away in the cold night.

Had she really just thrown away a good relationship for someone who didn't really want her?

She gripped the wooden rail till her good hand hurt. Why would she do a thing like that? Had it all been because of that familiar smile? Was Clay still controlling her romantic decisions?

The loud engine of a motorcycle cut into her thoughts as it turned down Love Street and then into her driveway.

The driver got off with swagger and removed his helmet. "Look what I got!" John Hancock beamed. There was nothing crooked about his friendly smile. He wore tight jeans, a tight cashmere sweater, and a black leather jacket. His face, usually clean shaven, had just a hint of stubble, and his bright, clear eyes shone under the streetlight.

"Did you get a deal on it after the owner was arrested?" Taylor was still in shock from Graham's departure and didn't register what she was saying.

He laughed. "A nasty coincidence. I needed to shake things up after Tatiana left me. What do you think? Want to go for a ride?"

She looked from the bike to her bandaged arm.

"Oof. Sorry. I forgot. Can I take you out for a drink anyway? I'm tired of spending all my nights alone, and I hear Hudson isn't in the picture anymore." He lifted an eyebrow in hope.

"Jonah and Belle are home...."

"Grandpa Ernie is safe, then. What do you think? For old time's sake? I can leave the bike here and drive your car."

She hesitated for a moment, but then, why not? John Hancock was a good friend, and she needed all of those she could get in this terribly dangerous world.

FRUIT BASKET UPSET

SHE's ready to reap the rewards of her hard work, but this harvest is a killer.

THOUGH SHE'S STILL HEALING from serious injuries, Taylor Quinn's heart is ripe with happiness. Business at Flour Sax

Quilt Shop has blossomed in the early spring sun, and with it hope for the future of Comfort, Oregon. But the promise of the season is poisoned when she discovers a dead body.

MURDER at the family strawberry farm uncovers a scandal she'd do anything to bury. But when her messy romantic life sullies both her investigation and her alibi, she's going to have to dig deep to catch the killer.

CAN Taylor pick the rotten fruit from this crop of suspects before she gets bagged for the crime?

FRUIT BASKET UPSET is the sixth cozy in the heart-felt Taylor Quinn Quilt Shop Mystery Series. If you like witty dialogue, charming settings, and stitching together the truth, then you'll love Tess Rothery's page-turning whodunit.

BUY **Fruit Basket Upset to taste sweet justice today!**

LOOKING FOR THE QUILT BLOCK?

SIGN **up for Tess Rothery's newsletter at tessrothery.com and get the Emperor's New Quilt Block Pattern delivered to your email.**

ABOUT THE AUTHOR

Tess Rothery is an avid quilter, knitter, writer and publishing teacher. She lives with her cozy little family in Washington State where the rainy days are best spent with a dog by her side, a mug of hot coffee, and something mysterious to read.

Sign up for her newsletter at TessRothery.com so you won't miss the next book in the Taylor Quinn Quilt Shop Mystery Series.

digistore24
helpdesk@digistore24.com
800 356-7947

Made in United States
Troutdale, OR
01/05/2025

27628067R00181